He led her into the warren of narrow and twisting lanes that were the old original Montmartre. She went along willingly, pleased to be with the one stranger who had responded to her singing.

There was a dark doorway with a broken stone step – he pushed her into the corner of it and stood close. He had long eyelashes like a girl, Suzette noted, and full lips. But there was nothing girlish about the way he kissed her, with his hands over her breasts.

His touch made her tingle with desire and sway just a little. He held her face and tilted her head back while he kissed her throat. Then his hand was under her skirt, up between her legs.

'Mademoiselle . . .' he murmured, '*je t'aime.*'

Amour Amour

Marie-Claire Villefranche

HEADLINE

First published in 1993
by HEADLINE BOOK PUBLISHING PLC

10 9 8 7 6 5 4 3 2 1

ISBN 0 7472 4053 1

Typeset by Avon Dataset Ltd, Bidford-on-Avon

Printed and bound in Great Britain by
HarperCollins Manufacturing, Glasgow

HEADLINE BOOK PUBLISHING PLC
Headline House
79 Great Titchfield Street
London W1P 7FN

Amour Amour

INTRODUCTION

Marie-Claire Villefranche is a daughter of the very well-known writer, Anne-Marie Villefranche, whose stories about Paris have been published in sixteen languages around the world. Daughter and mother were on the best of terms, although no secret was ever made of the fact that neither of Anne-Marie's husbands had the honour to be Marie-Claire's father.

Marie-Claire's story is set in the Paris of her youth, in the mid-1950s. It is as outrageous, as amusing, and as scandalous, as her celebrated mother's tales of improper love-affairs.

It concerns Suzette Bernard, a show-girl at the Folies Bergère. She is one of a dozen lovelies on stage wearing a spray of ostrich plumes and nothing else. They provide a living backdrop for the big singing stars. All that is required for the job is perfect body.

Suzette wants to appear on stage one day with her clothes on. Her ambition is to become a singer herself, though her voice is not outstanding.

Her friends, lovers, colleagues and rivals are extraordinary — dancers, acrobats, jugglers, illusionists, costume designers, businessmen, poets, musicians, frauds. Their love affairs with each other are as preposterous as their personalities.

SUZETTE IN THE MORNING

The bedroom windows were so well curtained and close-shuttered that even at ten in the morning the room was still in darkness. It was Robert who was first to wake – he rolled over on to his back to stretch his arms and legs without disturbing Suzette.

She lay on her side, facing away from him, breathing gently, having slipped from his embrace while they were both sleeping. Her knees were drawn up a little and her warm bare bottom just touched Robert's hip.

As he came fully awake he was aware of her perfume. It was so elegantly sensual and exquisitely costly, it seemed to fill the close air of the room. *Soir Fol* it was called, a gift from him to her, one of his many gifts in the few months they had known each other. He sat up with care, so as not to disturb her, and rested his arm along the wooden bedhead so he could lean over and see her face.

In the dimness of the bedroom her hair looked impossibly dark against the pillow, a pool of blackness like the bottomless pit itself. By daylight its shining raven-wing colour seemed to be so strikingly black that he wondered at times, was it entirely due to Nature or did an expert hairdresser assist?

She wore her hair short, pinned up sleekly at the back, with a fringe over her forehead. Unpinned, it spread over the white lace-edged pillow and made her look younger than her twenty-two years. Fashion had nothing to do with this short style she chose – the

3

sole reason was to show off her long and elegant neck.

Her face was indistinct in the darkness, but no matter — the classical beauty of it was deeply imprinted on Robert's heart and mind. If he had any skill with a pencil, he could have drawn a portrait of her from memory better than an artist in a Left Bank studio could draw in several sittings.

The thing about Suzette was that she was extraordinarily beautiful in face and body. To be beautiful was her profession, so to speak. At the Folies Bergère, she appeared on stage every evening with that marvellous body of hers naked, drawing quiet sighs of admiration from all the men present and setting their fantasies running.

Naked, that is to say, except for a gold-spangled *cache-sexe* no bigger than the palm of a man's right hand and a head-dress of white ostrich plumes a metre high, set with glittering glass jewels.

She didn't appear on stage alone, of course. She was one of a dozen very beautiful young women who stood in seductive poses together, on turning carousels, and under cascades of flashing coloured lights, and in front of sumptuously designed cardboard arches and domes like Old Baghdad or other romantic locations. The twelve of them formed a fascinating living back-drop, young and delectable, nine-tenths of their bodies exposed to the gaze of the appreciative audience — and it was against this the Big-Name stars of the Folies Bergère performed.

But to say 'a dozen like Suzette' was not really accurate, and does her a great injustice. All twelve were beautiful, or they would never have got the job in the first place. To succeed on stage plain women, Edith Piaf for example, needed to be talented to the point of genius — in her case she had the voice of an angel from the gutter, singing of heart-break.

Ugly women, though it would be cruel to mention one by name, had to be even more exceptionally talented to succeed on a stage. But beauty was a talent in its own right and required no other support.

For men it was different, needless to say. A man on the stage could be almost as odd-looking as a Notre-Dame gargoyle, but as long as he could sing a little and dance a little and put on a veneer of charm, he could become a great success — as so many have. As ever, men have the best of it.

That aside, though the other eleven lovelies with Suzette in the Folies' line-up were almost exactly the same height as she and had breasts and bodies almost as perfect, with entrancing little dimples of belly buttons, long well-shaped legs, elegant arms and hands — in spite of all this and much more there was a certain something in the way Suzette's individual perfections were assembled that made her exceptional.

That, at least, was the opinion of Robert Dorville. He leaned over further to kiss her uncovered shoulder and smiled to hear her sigh a little in her sleep. Her skin was warm to his mouth and very smooth. He drew down the sheet further to uncover more of her, screwing up his eyes to discern the shadowy outline of a round and enchanting breast. But all this perfection was lost in the darkness, the rose-pink of the pert little tip merely a sombre blur against the pale gleam of her skin.

With infinite patience he reached down over her bare shoulder until he could cup her warm breast in the palm of his hand. The pleasures of touch are not affected by light or dark, sunshine or shade, neither augmented nor diminished. Very slowly, so as not to disturb her, Robert lay down beside her again, close to her long naked back. From her breast he let his hand glide down to her soft belly, the feel of her body delighting him. And then further down still . . .

But she had drawn up her knees as she slept and her thighs were together, one on top of the other. Robert was unable to reach the prize he was aiming for. With any luck, he told himself, by caressing between her thighs he could wake her gently, excited and ready. She would roll over on her back for him to slide on top, as her legs opened for him.

His male part was stiff against the warm flesh of her bottom, quivering in eagerness. Very delicately he massaged her belly with his palm, hoping to impose his desire on her dormant will, so that her legs would straighten out and let him feel a little lower down.

She stirred and murmured something unintelligible, perhaps to herself. Robert suspended his caress, aware that the pleasure of his hand smoothing over her belly was causing his impatient part to twitch strongly and seem to prod her.

At this nervous little movement against her skin she stirred again, and began to turn on to her back. Her legs straightened out, Robert's hand slid downwards to where he wanted to put it.

A tender fingertip on the right spot and very soon she would be sighing and shaking, her hands clutching at him to pull him close, eager for him to slide into her!

But Robert's elation was illusory, her legs remained together — and even in the dark he saw her eyes were open and staring up at him.

'*Bonjour chérie*,' he said softly and he kissed her, his hand still trying to prise her legs apart.

'*Robert, chéri*!' she said.

She sat up in bed, nullifying his attempt to feel

between her thighs. 'Is it early or late?'

He looked at the luminous dial of the gold
wristwatch he was wearing. Suzette thought it
uncivilised to wear a watch in bed but it was a very
expensive one, more a piece of jewellery than a time-
piece. He took it off only in the bath.

'A little after ten,' he answered, 'but what of it?
Lie down again and let me hold you in my arms.'

He had an elbow on the pillow and was propped on
it, staring at her in the dimness, his mind's eye filling
in the details of her beautiful oval face that he could
not make out in the dark. She reached down and
briefly grasped his stiffness in her hand, to give it a
friendly squeeze.

'Tell me you love me,' she said.

'I adore you, Suzette,' he said at once, his
headstrong part bounding in her hand.

'You only say that because you want me to lie
down while you molest me,' she announced. 'After
last night I wonder you have the energy left to even
think about it!'

'When I am with you I can think of nothing else,
chérie,' he replied, his hand on her belly trying still to
insinuate itself between her closed thighs.

His fingertip had advanced to where the curls
begin on most women's bodies, so that only a few
centimetres lay between them and their goal.

There were no curls between Suzette's thighs, as he
well knew. In her nightly appearances on stage she
wore interesting varieties of the tiny *cache-sexe*
required by decency. For some of the scenes these
were of black leather with rhinestones, for others
they were of gold lamé or black lace even, sometimes
no more than wisps of white plumage. It was a
question of what caprice came into the costume
designer's mind.

7

In consequence, more for the sake of appearance than modesty, Suzette removed her own natural little black fur coat entirely. Her skin was smooth and bare and gleaming from belly button to – well, all the way down between her legs.

'Are you a man or are you a steam-engine?' she demanded, and she squeezed Robert's hardness once more. 'Do you never stop?'

'But you adore me when I molest you,' he retaliated and his longest finger was now within a centimetre of the soft lips he sought.

'That's true,' she agreed, 'but not before breakfast. I must have my coffee.'

Before he could prevent her, she twisted from beneath his arm and slid her legs over the side of the bed. He lay crestfallen while she went on bare feet to the window and threw open both curtains and shutters.

The brightness of the light dazzled him for a moment, then he heard the traffic going past on the rue de Rome and the rattle of trains at the Gare St Lazare.

As soon as his eyes adjusted themselves to the light he had a superb view of Suzette's bare bottom as she leaned out over the bright red geraniums on the window-sill to take in the morning scene below.

It was a very pretty bottom, to be sure, and Robert felt the urge to leap out of bed and kiss the two taut round cheeks that confronted him. And then to bite them, holding her by the hips, until she squirmed prettily in his grasp and said, *Non, non!*

Between those superb cheeks, visible because her thighs were no longer pressed together and because she was leaning forward over the window-sill, there was possibly just a glimpse of the long and smoothly bare pink lips that had been the goal of his frustrated attentions.

Adorable! he sighed to himself. After he nibbled her bottom, he decided, he would grasp her thighs from behind, on his knees on the floor, to force them further apart so he could flick the tip of his tongue into that delicious flesh . . .

Naturally, since she was naked, everyone in the rue de Rome — and in mid-morning it was a busy street — who stared up to the second floor would be rewarded by the view of Suzette's tousled head sticking out of the window. And, even more interesting, her marvellous breasts, which must also be fully visible from down there!

This thought flashed into Robert's head while he admired from his position in the bed the firm cheeks of her beautiful bare bottom. Fierce pangs of most unreasonable jealousy struck him like knives, how dare these idiotic passers-by feast their eyes on Suzette's breasts!

The emotion was unreasonable not only because he had no claim on her — they were not married, he was not her fiancé, not even her first lover, and they had never given serious consideration to the possibility of a lengthy *affaire*. It was unreasonable also because hundreds of strangers every night stared at her breasts on stage at the Folies Bergère.

But when were intimate relations between men and women ever a subject for reason and logic? Robert's impulse was to get out of bed, put his arms round Suzette and clap his hands over her beautiful breasts to conceal them from prying eyes outside. The pleasure of feeling them while he shielded her modesty would be purely incidental.

And necessarily, he would be standing close to her,

his stiff part pressed against her bottom! Trapped, one might say with a sigh of pleasure, between his belly and her warm cheeks!

That would, in all probability, lead on to acts of increasing affection. If he turned her away from the window and the voyeurs in the rue de Rome, it would be possible to remove one hand from a breast and slide it down her belly to where he really wanted it to be — between her legs.

Then a gentle caress would put her in a mood to return to bed and let him get on with his not-yet-abandoned plan to make love to her. Last night was superb, but last night was last night — this was an entirely new day. A day of renewed promise and hope — a Wednesday to be greeted properly.

All this happened in Robert's mind, and nowhere else. Suzette pulled her head in and turned away from the window. She stood a second or two, arms stretched above her head, long back arched, as she flexed her body and yawned.

Robert found the sight enchanting — beautiful Suzette on show fully naked. He was infatuated with her, of course, but any man lying there on the bed would have been equally affected to see her breasts rising to the upward stretch of her arms. His flesh would have risen stiff as Robert's to observe her belly pushed forward by the arching of her back. Above all, to sigh in open admiration at the long pink lips between her thighs, perfectly displayed by the way she stood, her feet apart and most of her weight on one leg.

The sight was so very arousing to Robert that under the sheet his eager part twitched furiously. To restrain its movements he was compelled to take it in his hand.

'Come back to bed,' he begged her, 'I adore you!'

Robert was a sensualist, he lived for these charming moments in women's bedrooms, he worshipped their bodies, he kissed them and caressed them, he gave them delicious sensations, thrills of ecstasy, breath-taking climaxes, being adept in all the arts of lovemaking. But alas for him, he was also a romantic, prone to confuse sexual pleasure with deep and lasting emotion. This was regrettable and sometimes made him very unhappy.

'Coffee,' said Suzette, picking up a short kimono of turquoise and scarlet from where it lay across a chair.

To Robert's intense chagrin she put the kimono on, tying the belt around her narrow waist, covering up all her charms except her well-shaped calves and slim ankles.

Before he could say another word, she opened the bedroom door and was gone. He slumped back in the bed, clutching his sad and disappointed part to stop its throbbing, and in a little while he heard two voices in conversation outside the bedroom.

The apartment was shared between Suzette and a friend – Gaby Demaine – a dancer in a troupe appearing twice-nightly at the Cabaret-Mouchard. Gaby was the same age as Suzette, a tall and long-legged charmer, with the supple body of one who kicks her legs up on stage for a living.

In contrast to Suzette's raven-black hair, Gaby was a blonde, so very blonde in fact that she was silvery blonde – almost too blonde, if anyone were to ask Robert's opinion on the subject. It goes without saying no one ever did ask and Gaby remained as blonde as she wished.

On those evenings when Robert waited for Suzette

at the end of the show and took her out, he would have preferred to return with her eventually to his own apartment for a continuation of their pleasures. It was off the Boulevard de la Madeleine in a well-kept building, spacious and comfortable, furnished in good modern style. But though Suzette had accompanied him there two or three times, she was happier in her own apartment, far less pleasant or convenient though it was. And despite the presence of Gaby.

Robert found this preference for the rue de Rome contrary, to say the least, but then everyone knows women are contrary by nature. From the heavily scented bedroom he made his way to the tiny cramped bathroom, then put on shirt and trousers and found Suzette and Gaby standing and gossiping while they drank coffee in the kitchen. Gaby was not in a kimono like Suzette or even a taffeta dressing-gown. She was more or less dressed, she had been out already to buy fresh croissants from the baker.

She had not yet troubled with make-up, not even on her mouth, but her long blonde hair was combed and she was wearing a pink striped pullover over a pleated grey skirt. No stockings, Robert noted as they said *bonjour* to each other, evidently she had got out of bed and pulled on skirt and pullover without the bother of underwear.

This he knew because the pullover clung close to her breasts and showed she wore no brassiere. And the shapely curves of her dancer's bottom were outlined by her thin skirt, with not a suggestion of knickers.

All in all, if Robert had not been as immensely devoted as he was to darling Suzette, he would most certainly have taken up with Gaby. She knew that, because pretty women always know what men are thinking about them, especially if the question is one of wanting to remove their underwear — even if the woman is not wearing any.

Gaby had never given Robert the least sign of encouragement, not the slightest. To her way of thinking, men come and men go, without all that much to choose between them. She regarded her friendship with Suzette as far more important.

A note of formality crept into the proceedings now that Robert was out of bed. Places were set at the table and croissants for him put on a plate with a little butter and some sweet apricot preserve that he liked. The women sat with him, nibbling small fragments of croissant and drinking their *café-au-lait*.

Gaby's breasts were as good as on display, thanks to the thin pullover, and Suzette's kimono was open at the top to exhibit most of hers. Altogether it was a breakfast scene appealing to Robert.

'Dear Gaby, did you get a newspaper?' he asked.

'What for?' she said, and her little shrug made her breasts quiver delightfully inside the pullover. 'It is too depressing to read every day of rapes and swindles and murders and whether or not the government has fallen.'

'Has it?' Robert demanded anxiously.

'How do I know?' she replied. 'Turn the radio on if you want bad news. Governments never last more than six months before their scandals are found out. This one is overdue for collapse. This idiocy is because General de Gaulle was allowed to resign after he liberated France. To let him go was stupid, even for politicians. Ever since that day the crooks and pimps have been running things.'

'And you, Suzette, do you agree with Gaby?' Robert enquired, his voice suggestive of outrage at what he had heard.

'I take no interest in politics, you know that,' said she in a cool voice.

Her perfect lips pouted deliciously to indicate her disdain. Robert wanted to kiss her, to thrust his hands into the top of her kimono and feel those marvellous breasts. Ah, if only she'd gone with him to his apartment last night instead of her own! With no Gaby about, he would have made love to her twice since waking up, in bed and on the breakfast table!

In the circumstances, Robert thought it best to let this talk of politics drop. It occurred to him as he finished his second croissant that it was unlikely he could persuade Suzette to return to bed with him. But it was worth trying now she had drunk her coffee and presumably was fully awake at last.

He reached for her hand across the table and pressed the back of it to his cheek. He smiled and told her at some length how very beautiful she was in the early morning, when she first got up. He went so far as to describe her as 'dewy-eyed', which made Gaby giggle.

To call the day early at half past ten is an assertion only those who sleep late are likely to make. It is not necessary to say that Suzette liked to be told she was beautiful, every woman likes to be told that. On the other hand, so many men had said it to her since she turned fourteen that she had come to regard compliments as a prologue to wanting to make love to her.

Not that she had any objection to that. To make love was what she preferred most in the world, except for appearing on stage. But it was well to keep in mind that men harbouring a certain stiffness in their trousers were capable of saying anything and promising everything. Even the plainest woman was told she was beautiful at times like that, and penniless cadgers would offer hypothetical diamonds and rubies to get their hand in a woman's knickers.

Gaby also knew the signs well. She winked at Suzette, grinned and reminded her they were going to the Boulevard Haussmann, to look for underwear in the Galeries Lafayette.

'Yes, of course,' said Suzette, getting up from her chair to the chagrin of Robert. 'I'd better get ready — I won't be long. Robert, *chéri*, do you want to come with us? You could take us to lunch afterwards.'

Her pretty silk kimono of turquoise and scarlet, another gift from Robert, had become disarranged while she sat at the table, with her legs crossed. She pulled it a little closer, covering her legs, and retied the belt round her waist. For an instant, scarcely more than the blink of an eye, Robert had a glimpse of smooth thigh.

It was enough for his active fantasy, which at once conjured up a mental image of two long and lovely thighs fully bared for him with bare pink lips between — thighs parted gracefully for his pleasure, thighs ready to rise from the bed and twine round his waist, thighs to grapple him to her superb belly!

But it was in vain. The kimono was decently tied and arranged and Suzette evidently had no intention of letting him see more. Would she let him help her take her bath if he offered to wash her back? he wondered, his male part trembling in his trousers with turgid desire.

He adored getting in the bath with her. It was easy enough to progress from washing the back with expensive scented suds — a present from him — to washing the breasts and handling them so very tenderly that soaping became almost the same as caressing, if anyone wished to make a distinction. And from then it became progressively easier to slip the palm down the warm belly . . .

'It won't take me twenty minutes to bath and dress,' Suzette assured Gaby. 'Can you lend me a pair of stockings – I laddered my last pair yesterday.'

Robert decided ruefully that there was nothing doing. Bed was out of the question. He might as well leave.

'I'd adore shopping with you but I can't today,' he said with a shake of his head meant to indicate serious business. 'I've a lunch meeting with someone.'

'What a pity,' said Gaby, looking at him under long eyelashes as he stood up. Her tone was faintly ironic.

By way of *au revoir* he kissed Gaby on the cheek and pressed her shoulder. Her flesh was warm and very desirable through the thin pullover. Suzette took him to the door, where he put his arms round her and kissed her properly, squeezing her bottom as he did so.

After he'd gone, Suzette sat down again, there was no great rush to get to the Boulevard Haussmann. She and Gaby chatted of nothing very much for a quarter of an hour. Then in a few words she surprised her friend by remarking that she was beginning to have doubts about Robert.

'But why?' said Gaby, shaking her blonde head in disbelief. 'He's good-looking and he treats you well.'

'Should I be grateful? I'm good-looking too and I treat him well.'

'Well,' said Gaby, raising her eyebrows, 'as a lover

he rates five star, if the squealing I hear through the bedroom wall is any guide. He's crazy about you and he's got plenty of the ready.'

She illustrated her comment by twirling thumb and forefinger together in the common gesture for cash.

'I know all that,' said Suzette with a sigh. 'It's not what I want, though.'

'*Bon Dieu*! If that's not enough for you, what *do* you want? A foreign millionaire with a yacht and an airplane and a suite at the Ritz? You don't pick them up at the stores like a pair of stockings, you know! You'll never find a better sort than Robert, he's worth hanging on to. If you spit in luck's eye now you may live to regret it.'

'The thing is,' said Suzette, 'he's not sympathetic toward my ambition. He pretends to be, but at heart he thinks I'm just a pretty face on a pretty body. A big doll to play with − that's what he thinks of me.'

'Ambition is a very fine thing,' said Gaby, 'everyone should have ambition. Mine is to dance at the Lido and then go on tour with the troupe to Monte Carlo and New York and London. And get a fantastic contract from the film people in Hollywood − they need me there now Betty Grable is almost forty, not to mention the fact I'm a better dancer than she ever was. And then I want to marry a Duke or a Count with a big house and servants to wait on me in the Avenue Foch and a chateau by the Loire.'

'That's changed a bit,' said Suzette with a grin. 'Last week you wanted a Brazilian landowner who played polo and owned a gold mine and had the biggest apartment in the best part of Rio de Janeiro.'

'I've decided I wouldn't be happy anywhere but France,' Gaby said, twitching her perfect nose, 'I am no longer looking for a rich foreigner.'

'So much the worse for the Brazilians,' said

Suzette. 'But I still want to be a singer, and that's *never* going to change. In a year, two years, I could be right at the top. All I need is a chance and a little encouragement.'

'Does Robert pay for your singing lessons?'

'Certainly not! I'm not going to have it said someone else made my ambition come true. I pay for my own lessons. Robert doesn't approve — he thinks I am wasting my time, though he never actually comes right out and says so.'

'Half the girls born in the rue de Belleville want to become singers,' Gaby said, shrugging one slender shoulder, 'the rest want to be whores. Guess which half realise their ambition.'

GABY FINDS A NEW FRIEND

It was after midday when Suzette and Gaby reached the Galeries Lafayette. It was one of their favourite places – they enjoyed the stylish Belle Epoque ambience of the department store, the gilt and glass, curlicues and swirls. They liked to be part of a bustle of shoppers looking at the displays in the glass showcases. They were amused by customers demanding the assistants show them this and that, finding fault where no one else could, particularly middle-aged women with small pet dogs.

They particularly adored watching the vagaries of brightly chattering young women with older boyfriends in tow. And they were amused by lone males giving the staff endless trouble as they tried to choose a gift for someone special. Men seemed to have so little imagination they chose underwear or perfume nearly every time, and sometimes both.

The lingerie department, to which Suzette and Gaby made their way, had an elegant display of nightdresses. The mode then was for long lace-trimmed confections in satin, or less expensively in nylon, high-waisted to emphasise the breasts. And scooped at the neckline to show enough to interest a man. Gaby gave the display a curious stare before announcing that she had no idea what sort of women wore these garments in bed – it must be the plain types who slept alone and needed to cheer themselves up! Or perhaps it was women long married, trying to rekindle a husband's interest by putting a new

19

wrapper around goods he knew all too well.

For herself, she said, she considered it not worth putting a nightdress on, only for it to be taken off three minutes later by a panting man. It was easier to get naked into bed.

Suzette disagreed and claimed Gaby was of so remarkably dense an opinion only because she did not have to spend her evenings naked at the Folies Bergère being stared at by panting men. If she ever did, she would think less of nudity and understand the pleasure of wearing something pretty on her body.

And besides, there was a thrill in having it taken off.

'What! You expect me to believe you put a fancy nightdress on when you bring Robert back to the apartment!' exclaimed her friend. 'Don't tell me fairy tales. He throws you on the bed and has your clothes off the second the door's closed.'

'You watch through the keyhole, do you?'

'No need to, that's how men behave when they get you into the bedroom − it's what Claude does to me. And I love it when a man dominates me in bed.'

'Have you seen Claude recently?' Suzette enquired, trying to sound casual about it.

'No,' Gaby confessed with a shrug of irritation. 'His wife is pregnant and he's gone back to her. I always thought he was too good to be true, that one.'

'He may be generous with his money, this missing lawyer, but that doesn't make him too good for you,' Suzette said firmly, 'and as for domination, each to her own taste. It's when you let them tie you up and whip you that your head should be examined.'

'*Oh la la*!' said Gaby. 'What do you take me for, Bluebeard's girlfriend? I didn't mean that sort of domination. But I love it when a man holds me so tight I can hardly breathe and runs his hands over my body — that's when I wish he had eight hands and could feel every part of me at the same time.'

'You are in love with a giant octopus!'

'Don't pretend you don't know what I'm talking about. There's nothing better than to be flat on your back with a handsome man kissing you, a hand feeling each breast and a hand between your legs, two hands on your bottom, one gripping each cheek, a hand stroking your belly and another rubbing your back!'

Suzette grinned and her eyebrows arched upwards.

'Just thinking about it makes me excited!' said Gaby. 'To be held tight and suffocated with love, with such thrills running through you that you know you'll explode like a bomb in another ten seconds!'

Suzette had been keeping count.

'That's only seven hands so far. What do you want him to do with the eighth?'

'Why, to grab the nape of my neck and hold me helpless and in his power, as if I were a rabbit in the jaws of a hunting dog.'

'But that's being a victim!'

'No, it's not,' Gaby said firmly, 'I'll never let a man tell me how to manage my life, however much I like him. In bed it's different, I want the man to be masterful. Don't you?'

'I refuse to be a doll to be played with,' Suzette declared. 'It's the mistake Robert makes.'

Gaby shrugged and they strolled on to examine other garments, which it must be said were of a type likely to appeal to men as much as to themselves. Of particular interest was a display of silk chemises in pastel colours, with a chiffon trim at top and hem, fastening between the legs with a pair of small mother-of-pearl buttons.

They stood comparing colours and discussing the

advantages of primrose over crocus, if any, and the reverse, when they became aware they were being watched. He was standing by a display of black lace brassieres on blank-looking dummies, attempting to appear as unconcerned as the dummies themselves — a dark-haired man in a bright blue suit.

'He's watching us,' said Gaby 'is he the store detective, do you think? He can't think we look like criminals!'

Both women were dressed prettily for the shopping outing and both were so beautiful that not even the most flint-hearted and cynical detective in all Paris could have harboured suspicious and hostile feelings toward them.

'He's too good-looking to be a store detective,' said Suzette with a little frown. 'Look at his suit, it cost money and it's new. Store detectives aren't paid enough to afford clothes like that, not even with a staff discount.'

'Well then, in that case we know what his interest is!' said Gaby. 'He's trying to pick us up. Perhaps he'll offer to buy us an expensive bra each if we let him watch us try them on. Let's string him along and see if he's good for a laugh.'

'His type is not very amusing,' said Suzette, shrugging.

'What type is that?'

'The type who steal knickers from washing-lines. You know what they do to them behind locked doors.'

'I've never met one of those,' said Gaby and she giggled.

She directed a dazzling smile and the tiniest twitch of a hip toward the display of brassieres. If the lurker in a blue suit included himself in the general radiance of Gaby's smile that was his own choice, it was not launched specifically at him.

A moment later he was beside them, raising his hat to reveal the glossy waves in his dark-brown hair. Without the least sign of nervousness or hesitation he introduced himself and said how sure he was that he had seen both of them before, though precisely where had slipped his memory at the moment.

It was hardly an original or interesting approach but he *was* good-looking, this Lucien Cluny, with a certain charm he took to be reason enough for Suzette and Gaby to allow his approach in a public place.

His interest had become clear, it was the usual and he was open about it. While the three of them chatted casually, Lucien picked up one of the silk chemises the assistant had brought for them to look at — the one in a crocus-yellow shade. He held it out at body height by the ribbon shoulder-straps, staring at it thoughtfully and then at Gaby.

She and Suzette knew beyond a shadow of doubt what was in his mind. He was using his imagination to undress Gaby — to remove her frock of bold tangerine with the swirling skirt and scooped neckline. He was visualising her in the silk chemise. His eyes were shining, he was wondering how her flesh tints would show through the silk. He was contemplating the pleasure of undoing the two little pearl buttons between her thighs.

He spoke not a word while he stared at the crocus chemise but his thoughts were so brazen it was impossible not to laugh. And both women did so. This put them in the best of humours.

'It's the wrong colour for you, mademoiselle,' he informed Gaby, returning the chemise to the patient shop-assistant. 'It would suit your friend perfectly but for your beautiful blonde hair you should choose the orchid pink or perhaps the cerise. As you know well, for the colour of your dress is excellent for you and chosen with style.'

'Monsieur is an expert on women's underwear?' Suzette asked with an upward twitch of her perfectly drawn eyebrows and Gaby laughed again.

'Not an expert, mademoiselle, an admirer.'

'Of underwear? Are you a fetishist?'

He disarmed her with a smile, took her arm and Gaby's gently and by sheer charm he led them away from the counter, through the store and out into the street.

'But . . .' said Suzette when they stood on the pavement.

'But . . .' said Gaby in a sort of puzzled echo.

He took them to a restaurant close by, not a grand place with a gourmet choice of food, a temperamental chef de cuisine and a Michelin star, where fat men wrapped napkins round their necks. It proved to be a smaller establishment in a side street, where they cooked superb pancakes and served a very drinkable wine of no easily identifiable vintage.

Lucien was a fluent talker. He chatted on almost without a break, a light and easy flow of conversation about nothing of any consequence but altogether charming. Nor did he ever quite sit still – his hands were constantly moving, gesturing in time with his words, touching, mesmerising.

He shrugged, he smiled, he wrinkled his nose, he nodded – the impression he gave was of a wind-up toy that would go on and on until the spring ran down. To some extent this comic aspect of him was reinforced by his height, that is, by the lack of it.

Lucien was not a tall man. He was shorter than Suzette but show-girls were selected for height as much as for their other bodily charms, men of average height found themselves four or five centimetres shorter than Suzette. But Lucien was not even of average height, not quite. Although dancers are not selected for height, he was a few centimetres shorter than Gaby.

And it was on Gaby that his heart was set, that was obvious, though he spread his charm equally between the two women while they ate the pancakes and drank the wine he ordered. Her blonde hair had captivated him, most likely.

Gaby thought him amusing, which he undoubtedly was. The plan to get a laugh out of his hot-eyed pursuit had changed, he was suddenly too amusing a person to laugh at. Gaby responded in a friendly manner to him. She asked him if he'd ever been to the Cabaret-Mouchard. When he said he had, she gave him a smile.

'Then you have seen me before,' she told him. 'I'm one of the exotic dancers — the second from the left of the line.'

'I knew I'd seen you — I remember now!' Lucien exclaimed, an expression of delight on his face. His words were most probably untrue but what of it? They pleased Gaby, every woman likes to think she is unforgettable.

Whether Gaby believed him is another matter. She was no fool where men were concerned, she had been a cabaret dancer ever since she left school after all.

'But when you dance your hair is put up and almost covered by a sort of black Spanish hat with a flat brim,' he said.

At least he had seen the troupe, if he knew that.

'The memory I have of you,' he continued, one of his restless hands lightly touching the back of her hand for an instant, 'is of long and marvellous legs.'

'I never met a man yet who didn't look at a girl's

legs first before he looked at her face,' said Suzette, intervening in the conversation.

'Ah, legs are not much on show since the New Look arrived and every Parisienne lengthened her skirts almost right down to the ankles,' Lucien replied.

There was a tinge of regret in his tone at the thought of the small pleasures Christian Dior had denied to men in the name of high fashion.

'Superb legs like Gaby's are very attractive,' he addressed Suzette. 'Legs in silk stockings are the most beautiful of all. I am sure yours are perfect, are you a dancer too?'

She shook her head and decided not to tell him she appeared on stage at the Folies Bergère stark naked but for a feather or two. Not that she was ashamed of what she did, because in fact she was proud to have been chosen out of thousands. But Lucien seemed a little too excitable.

The way he stared wide-eyed at the silk chemise in the store, then at Gaby, with an obvious bulge in his trousers to betray his condition, this caused her to decide against inflaming his active imagination by mention of nakedness. She was sure he had seen her before, on stage with no clothes on. Probably most of the men in Paris had seen her at the Folies Bergère, but it was not her face they remembered.

In any case, Gaby was not pleased at having the conversation switched away from herself and her gorgeous dancer's legs.

'Perhaps you were surprised,' she said to Lucien, 'to see us high-kicking in our act. The South American dancing you see in cabarets is mostly Spanish Flamenco in rumba rhythm, with foot-stamping and hand-clapping, castanets and guitars, long skirts to swish about.'

'Very lively,' Lucien agreed, sounding as if he liked it.

'But the management were not too happy with that,' said Gaby. 'They decided the types who frequent the Cabaret-Mouchard would be bored by old-fashioned routines. So we wear skirts split up to the belly button and we do high kicks to show our thighs.'

'Enchanting,' said Lucien with enthusiasm, 'it is like a sort of Spanish Can-Can. But how do you keep those flat hats on when you dance so energetically?'

'You are a comedian, Lucien. I talk about artistic integrity and the idiocy of gangsters who run show business, you are more interested in how I keep my hat on my head!'

'You are very beautiful when your emotions are engaged,' said Lucien. 'Your eyes sparkle like stars in the sky.'

Gaby and Suzette looked at each other, shook their heads, and laughed. Banality on the scale Lucien was demonstrating had an eerie charm of its own. He was probably the sort who kept his socks on in bed.

When they had finished their meal and emptied the wine bottle there was a little pause indicating a certain indecision on his part. He was not sure how to separate Gaby from Suzette without offending either. Suzette made it easy, she announced she had a singing lesson at three o'clock and she must leave them.

In truth, the lesson was not till five but it seemed to her a friendly thing to do, to push off and give Gaby a clear field.

Lucien sprang to his feet with a thousand expressions of his regret that Suzette must leave so soon. He kissed her hand with style and hoped he would have the good fortune to see her again before long. And so on. When she had gone, he sat down and told the waiter to bring two glasses of his finest cognac.

He lived in the Boulevard de Magenta, Gaby discovered when he took her there in a taxi. She didn't know what to expect of his living arrangements — he evidently had money but he preferred to remain discreetly vague about how he made it. When she asked him what he did for a living, he said he had business interests and was an investor. Naturally, she didn't believe him, but if he was a crook then he was such a charming one that it didn't matter, just so long as he didn't involve her in what he did.

The apartment was large and furnished with no style at all, a curiously anonymous place, much like a furniture shop display. He kissed Gaby hotly the moment they were inside the door, his arms tight around her, hugging her to him, his leg between hers to press his thigh against the tender parts for which he was so ardent. Gaby surrendered, intrigued by this masterful approach now he had stopped being amusing in favour of direct action.

Though she was a few centimetres the taller, height ceased to be of any importance when they were lying down — and they very soon were. It took about thirty seconds to progress from inside the apartment door into the bedroom and another thirty seconds to get her tangerine frock off.

He undressed her with a skill and subtlety that pleased her, he lingered as he slipped her knickers down her long legs. They were of white silk *crêpe* trimmed with hand-made lace — and Gaby wondered for a moment when she observed the look on his face, so intent, so eager, if perhaps Suzette had been right to call him a fetishist.

She was standing by the bed while he paid these attentions to her and he was down on his knees to take her knickers off. She heard his surprised sigh when he saw what he had uncovered. His hot palms lay on her thighs, then his fingers probed gently in between them and he touched the soft petals there. After a moment or two his hand moved up to the little patch of silver blonde curls.

Like her friend Suzette, Gaby wore scanty theatrical costumes for her work, though dancers were not required to display their breasts. Gaby's troupe were billed as South American dancers and for their act they wore little bolero jackets in gold lamé, cut short enough to expose their bellies, with ankle-length skirts split to the waist in front.

To avoid showing more than the audience had paid for when she kicked her legs up nose-high, Gaby too removed her natural fur with a safety razor — but not as completely as Suzette did. She left a charming little tuft at the top and bleached these remaining curls to the same pale blonde as her hair. The effect was entrancing.

Lucien had his hands flat on the cheeks of her bottom and was holding her still while he pressed his lips to the denuded lips beneath her blonde tuft. She was quite used to this response to the sight of her treasure, she took a considerable pride in her ability to make men kneel to kiss her between the thighs.

It was true homage to her beauty. She not merely expected it, she insisted on it! If a new boyfriend proved to be brutally insensitive, if he was not sufficiently devastated by her blonde charms to get down on his knees and press a kiss to her pretty peach, he got no second chance!

Lucien passed the test magnificently, kneading the cheeks of her bottom with clever hands while he kissed her again, and yet again. He flicked with the tip of his tongue until he made the tender lips open a little as if to return his kiss. She stroked his hair, her long fingers gliding over the glossy waves and from them rose a burnt-orange scent of expensive hair tonic.

He timed his moment to perfection to conclude his kissing and rise to his feet. He urged her to the bed and laid her on it. His sharp blue suit was off in a flash, shirt, shoes, underwear — and his socks!

Gaby noted with interest his socks were silk, so was his shirt — evidently Lucien was well-off. He was on the bed beside her, his hands feeling her breasts. She saw with approval his body was well-made and strong, a matting of dark hair on his chest. In the curls there nestled a small gold cross, hanging from a thin chain round his neck.

Lucien hadn't struck her as a religious sort of man and what he was now doing to her, delicious as it was, seem unlikely to get a blessing from his parish priest. But what of that? Men were such sentimental creatures that the little gold cross probably was a confirmation present from his mother. Or a keepsake from his first girlfriend.

Down below he sported a thicket of equally dark hair and out of it there jutted upwards as useful a part as Gaby had seen on a man. It was not too long but it was thick and it had a good and sturdy look about it. In brief, it had the robustness she preferred.

She was on her back and Lucien's restless hands were roaming all over her — they traced the shape of her shoulders, then the tautness of her breasts, the smooth-shaven hollows beneath her arms. From there he slid his hands down her sides to her narrow waist, gliding inward with the curve and out again over her hips.

He slithered half on top of her and began to kiss her very thoroughly. He commenced with her eyelids and worked his slow way down to her mouth, her chin, her throat, and the rose-pink tips of her breasts.

Gaby was proud of her breasts — they were perfectly round and set high, not as large as Suzette's but that was all to the good. It is inconvenient if a vivacious dancer has too much to swing about up top in the faster rhythms. The effect of that is not aesthetic, indeed, it can be comic. Breasts that were firm, beautifully shaped and of moderate proportions, in Gaby's view that was the ideal.

None of which was of any importance at that moment. The parts which moved were not her breasts but Lucien's lips on the firm buds. Gaby gave little sighs, her limbs were trembling to the pleasure his touch was giving her. He changed his position on the bed and his kisses continued — down to her belly, lingering there, then to her thighs, which parted slowly as his mouth advanced, until at last he was pressing kisses to the soft bare flesh between them.

Gaby became so exquisitely aroused by all he was doing to her that she was hardly aware of the exact moment when that sturdy-looking part of his slid inside. Her entire body was awash with desire — the sensations that were acute before now soared to a pitch of intensity that was almost unbearable. And Lucien, too, was almost at the peak of sensitivity. He thrust hard and fast, panting in delight.

Those dancer's legs of hers were strong and supple, and they were twined round him, holding him tightly to her belly. Lucien could hear her gasping breath, her curiously regular moans, the thump of her heels against his bare bottom. He had no knowledge of her insistence to Suzette that she adored being dominated by a man in bed. And if he had been told he wouldn't

31

for a moment have believed it — the truth was that now they had reached this delicious stage together, it was Gaby who was dominating!

She was doing it from beneath, of course, and his male pride had the satisfaction of lying on top, as if the initiative were his. But if honesty played any part at all in lovemaking, which it never does for that would be to put an end to romance, then Lucien would have been compelled to admit that his role now was to do what Gaby wanted.

Whether this entered his thoughts at so charmingly fraught a moment, who can say? After all, the most intense sensations of pleasure were tearing through him, this kept at bay any strange consideration of being the means to Gaby's ecstasy and not the usual arrangement. It goes without saying that Gaby would never accept she had reversed the psychological position.

It was hardly surprising Gaby reached the critical moments first. Her back arched, her legs gripped Lucien so tightly the breath was almost driven from his body. She gave a loud sob — a thrilling little explosion of female sound and exquisite sensations overwhelmed her.

This unconstrained response to his lovemaking flattered Lucien and raised his excitement to the final limit. His wailing cry matched her pleasurable sob and he spurted his desire into her shaking belly.

Afterwards they lay propped up against the bedhead while they drank a glass of champagne together. Lucien brought it from the kitchen, it was colder than need be. Evidently it had been in his refrigerator for a little too long, but for all that it was refreshing.

His bedroom was not very interesting. It had a broad bed and a dressing-table with a mirror, a wardrobe, a couple of chairs, all in nondescript shades of pale brown wood. There was a beige carpet on the floor, it seemed to have no identifiable pattern, and a boring picture on one wall — a reproduction of a nude by Modigliani.

Gaby knew who the artist was because every amateur dauber in Paris tried to copy him. They displayed dud copies of his work for sale on the cobbles of the Place du Tertre, hoping to fool tourists into parting with cash. Perhaps they bought them as souvenirs of Paris, though it was not easy to understand why.

The Modigliani on Lucien's bedroom wall was of a naked woman lying on a dark red divan, a turquoise-blue cushion under her head.

Gaby compared her own assets with the figure in the picture — the model had short dark hair, a narrow face, pointed chin, big round breasts, over-heavy hips. Gaby decided she herself was far the better-looking. If this Modigliani dauber hadn't drunk himself to death before he was thirty, he might have tired of the Italian-looking women he painted.

If that was Lucien's taste, what was Gaby doing on his bed? But the picture, like the furnishings, gave the impression that Lucien had walked into a furniture store one day with pockets full of cash and pointed round without bothering to look. *That, that, and that — and deliver by this evening*!

Gaby giggled when he dipped a finger into his glass and drew lines on her bare belly — it was some time before she realised he was writing his initials in champagne — LC around her belly button, LC over her pert round breasts, LC between her thighs.

'Why do you lurk at women's underwear counters, Lucien? Is it your hobby?' she asked.

Now that he had been put through his paces and

shown what he could do, she wanted to know more
about him before deciding to say yes or no when he
asked her to meet again. Not for a moment did she
doubt he *would* ask her — every man who had ever
had the inestimable pleasure of making love to her
had been anxious to meet her again and again.

And rightly so, in her private opinion! She was,
after all, a beautiful young woman with a superb
body and an enthusiasm to match any man's for
sexual pleasure. It was the duty of men to ask her and
it was her right to choose which man she wanted — to
say *oui* or *non* as the mood took her.

This Lucien was satisfactory enough but he
mustn't get above himself because she had opened
her legs once for him to try him out. Scrawling his
initials on her belly in champagne was not a game
that engaged her sympathies — it was too much like a
claim to ownership!

'I wasn't lurking about,' he said.

His pleasant smile and all his charming gestures
were again on show now it was a question of talking
and persuading, 'I was passing through the store and
by chance I saw you and your friend. The moment I
laid eyes on you I felt as if I'd been struck by
lightning. I was dumbfounded, my feet were stuck to
the floor. I had to speak to you, it was as simple as
that.'

'Does that happen to you very often, Lucien, being
struck by lightning at the underwear counter? My
friend thinks you are a sex maniac.'

'Mademoiselle Suzette is very charming,' he said
with a shrug of his shoulders, 'but how can she know
anything about me?'

Gaby did not trouble him with the explanation that
there was no need to know about him individually
once you had met his type, that would have deflated

his pride in the cruellest way. Instead, she rolled over on the tangled sheet and reached down for her knickers – they lay on the carpet where Lucien had dropped them when he had had so much fun undressing her.

This manoeuvre put her face down on the bed, the round cheeks of her pretty bottom exposed. Lucien took advantage at once of her position to plant a smacking kiss on her behind.

His hand was between her thighs when he sank his teeth gently into the cheeks he fondled. Gaby shrieked and laughed, rolling back toward him, pushing him away from her. She had him on his back then and he was laughing. Her bent knee was on his chest to pin him down and she loomed over him, her smile just a little malicious.

On one finger she swung round in a circle her silk knickers with the lace trim, making them brush over Lucien's face.

'Oh!' he said, his tone very thoughtful, his hand sliding up the inside of her thigh.

'Fetishist!' exclaimed Gaby.

She ground her knee ruthlessly into his chest to keep him in his place and changed her target with the circling knickers – now at each revolution they flicked the slack part lying on his belly.

It did not remain limp for long – six or seven flicks of the silk *crêpe* underwear brought about a rapid change. Gaby stared in fascination as it grew straight and thicker, then longer and harder. It pointed up at her belly like a revolver cocked ready to fire.

'Ah, ah, ah . . .' she heard Lucien moaning softly, almost under his breath.

A glance at his face showed how flushed he was, how his eyes stared. It required no vast experience of

35

men and their bodily response to see Lucien was approaching a decisive moment. A few more flicks of her knickers across the uncovered purple head of his shaking part, that was all he needed, and his passion would come squirting out uncontrollably.

'I don't believe it!' said Gaby. 'You prefer my underwear to me, do you? You'll be sorry!'

She spun the knickers faster on her stiff forefinger, making them brush over his throbbing part with each turn. He gasped in consternation to realise what was about to happen. But then, on second thoughts, it might well not be consternation, Gaby said to herself, Lucien had surely played games with knickers before and loved the result. No, not consternation, anticipation.

'Gaby!' he said in a hoarse voice.

Her knee pressed hard down to prevent any escape, not that he had the slightest intention of sliding away from what Gaby was doing to him but he appeared to enjoy this little illusion of being at her mercy. His hand on the inside of her thigh jerked upwards and clasped at the blonde-tufted lips at the very moment his loins rose from the bed and his desire gushed out.

It spurted in a long arc, it would have reached his throat if Gaby's perfectly shaped leg had not been in between. Evidently Suzette had been right about him, Gaby said to herself, he was a rampant fetishist. But what of it? Most men behaved strangely in bed, those who didn't were so predictable that they quickly became boring.

'Pervert!' she said, grinning as he spattered her thigh. 'You will regret this!'

But he didn't regret it, not at all. The truth was he enjoyed this unusual diversion. He smiled up at Gaby with lazy eyes and pushed away her knee, he took her hips in both hands and pulled her down to lie on top of him.

She felt his stiffness, wet and hot against her belly, and at the thought of it she giggled. His restless hands were gliding across her back, stroking her shoulder blades, his busy fingers trailing over her flesh, dipping into the hollow of her back, clasping the cheeks of her bottom, never being still for even an instant.

He lifted his head up from the pillow to kiss her mouth with a warmth of affection that was in its way impressive.

'Gaby, you are adorable, *chérie*, truly adorable,' he said, 'I love you to distraction.'

His dark brown eyes were staring deeply into hers, gazing in a devoted and soulful manner, amusing in its intensity, Gaby thought. A galloping fetishist he surely was, on the other hand he was charming. Her casual acceptance of his capricious nature was interrupted by his next words, surprising her by taking her totally for granted:

'Now you're my girlfriend you can have anything want, you've only to ask me – anything at all.'

SUZETTE HAS A
SINGING LESSON

The man who was teaching Suzette to sing — so she could become an overnight star at the Casino de Paris or the Folies Bergère, perhaps both, and sing on the radio as well, earning millions of francs from grovelling theatre impresarios while keeping all her clothes on — was called Jacques-Charles Delise.

He was a tall skinny man in his mid-thirties, thin-faced and with luminous brown eyes. He had a vaguely distinguished look, almost intellectual, which was the result of his hair receding at the front, doubling the size of his forehead.

He claimed he was a student of the Paris Conservatoire in his youth, which might even have been true. But doubts grew thicker and darker after a few glasses of pastis or cognac in any bar, the dingier the better, where Monsieur Delise would maintain he had been the best student of his year. A certain winner of the Prix de Rome gold medal and cash, he declared. To cap this, he insisted he had been a pupil of the celebrated Francis Poulenc himself.

In two words, the destiny of Jacques-Charles Delise was to be a concert pianist of international reputation.

What, then, had gone wrong? Instead of adding to the musical glory of France by hammering out the melodies of Claude-Achille Debussy and such-like in the best concert halls of the world's capitals, why was he heard only in the cheap bars of Pigalle? And not every night at that.

39

How was it possible to reconcile his impressive claims with a shabby reality — thumping away at the nicotine-stained keys of cigarette-scarred pianos, a Gauloise dangling from his lip?

Alas, this was a question impossible to answer. Whoever had the cheek to ask it received a confusing reply. Usually Jacques-Charles ascribed his cancelled career to the War. Naturally, it had all been the fault of the damned Germans.

Indeed, at the start of hostilities Jacques-Charles had been despatched with his regiment to reinforce the Maginot Line and to man its concrete fortresses and gun-emplacements. He and his *copains* would have held back the onslaught of Hitler's frenzied Nazi horde if the madman attempted to invade France.

But, as all the world knows, the perfidious Fuhrer completely bypassed Monsieur Maginot's impregnable fortification — he went round the side and invaded France through Belgium.

Without the opportunity to fire a shot, in 1940 Jacques-Charles found himself a prisoner and for the next three years his home was a scruffy POW camp. For this reason his important studies to become an international celebrity were interrupted, as were many other careers at the time. Some forever, alas. But it did not explain why he failed to return to the Conservatoire after the Liberation.

Perhaps it was a case of *ars longa, vita brevis* — music was all very well but life was too short and precious to waste most of every day practising at the keyboard. Not when the streets were full of pretty girls and a few francs would buy a drink and a meal. The bohemian life had its advantages and pleasures, there were always friends only too pleased to talk for hours about everything under the sun, while there was still something in the bottle.

Whatever the reason, Jacques-Charles Delise made his choice and to his credit it must be said that he never fell into self-pity or maudlin rambling about *what might have been*, not even on the nights he was so drunk he fell off the piano stool.

He lived very simply, in a single room situated in a dank and crumbling building in Montmartre, and sustained his modest way of life by playing in grisly bars and down-at-heel cafés.

For a pianist he had a surprisingly good voice — the result of training to sing in the choir of the Sacre Coeur when he was a boy, according to him. He added a few francs to his miserable income by giving piano lessons, and singing lessons. Though it must be stated that at the time of these events, his only pupil for singing was Mademoiselle Suzette Bernard.

A little in advance of five o'clock that afternoon Suzette tackled the slope of the rue Lepic, uphill from the Boulevard Clichy. The greengrocers' and poultrymongers' shops along both sides of the street were less well-stocked this late in the day and only a few people sat talking at little tables outside the cafes — and they were obviously foreign tourists out to see the colourful life of the quarter, as they thought of it.

The market barrows standing end to end along the gutters were nearly sold out, the sharp-tongued housewives weighed down with shopping bags were long gone, but the stall-traders were not ready to pack up before the last *sou* had been pocketed and the last bunch of wilting flowers palmed off.

In all, it was a pleasant enough day for a walk. Fortunately Jacques-Charles Delise didn't live too far up the hill to make the walk a struggle on high heels. An alley to the left led the way to the building he lived in, but there was more climbing to be done

41

inside, up flights of steep stone steps to his room on the top floor.

She knocked twice and pushed open the creaking door and went in, not waiting for an invitation. Sometimes he was fast asleep in the afternoons − if he had put in a long stint the previous night at some dismal late-hours joint or if he had been drunk at lunchtime with his cronies in the zinc-topped bar down the road. But today he was awake and sober, his face shaved and his white shirt clean and newly ironed.

The familiar smells of his room greeted her as she entered. A mingling of pungent cigarette smoke with the aniseed sweetness of Pernod. He had few possessions, a battered old black upright piano against the wall, a divan bed over which he had thrown a threadbare red-and-blue patchwork spread, a small square table with one leg shorter than the others, two wooden kitchen chairs − and the suit he wore when he played in bars. It was clean and once smart and it hung on a wire hanger behind the door.

He told different stories about the piano, which was kept in perfect tune for the reason that he tuned it himself. It was a good make though, like its owner, it had seen better days.

In one mood, he would claim it was given to him by a great lady, the Marquise de Saint-Chapelle. He had been hired to play at her daughter's twelfth birthday party, he said.

In another mood, he said he had paid fifty francs for it in the Flea Market and pushed it home all the way from Clignancourt. But it was very obvious to anyone visiting his lair he had not humped the piano up the stone steps, neither alone nor with help − it was impossible to get it round the corners. His room looked out over the courtyard a long way down below and the piano had clearly been hoisted up on a rope and in through the window.

Naturally, he was always delighted to see Suzette Bernard, as which man in his right mind wouldn't be? To have so beautiful a woman come to visit was a privilege that millionaires in big apartments on the Avenue Foch would have fought each other for. And when it was a question not of a superb apartment with many servants and paintings on the walls worth a fortune, but a dark and dreary little room in a broken-down old tenement, well, the privilege was so much the greater.

When they exchanged greetings Jacques-Charles kissed her hand and told her she was looking very beautiful. As indeed she was, she had dressed and given her face and hair particular care for her shopping expedition with Gaby.

The lesson began at once — this was the tedious part where he wanted to hear her sing scales. And he kept her doing so until he was certain she was getting the notes right — or as right as she would ever get them.

The truth must be told — Suzette's singing voice was not all that outstanding. She had no formal voice training and couldn't read music. Her singing was light and pleasant and she brought to it a confidence that was half the battle — a calm confidence developed by standing before large audiences night after night dressed in only a feather or two.

Suzette had listened to all the good singers, including the old stagers from before the war who were still belting it out in their sixties: the great Mistinguett and Jean Gabin and Maurice Chevalier. And she listened very carefully to the newcomers, Charles Aznavour and Edith Piaf and Yves Montand. When any of them appeared at the Folies

Bergère, she had a close-up view.

Others she went to hear at the Olympia music hall or at the ABC, or wherever they were on. When she was at home in the rue de Rome she played their records on the gramophone, listening hard, until the discs were scratched and crackly.

At the Folies Bergère, when it was a question of a male star, Chevalier for example, the naked show-girls were placed at the back of the stage, to add a little glamour. On the other hand, female stars insisted on being alone on stage, having no desire to risk a cruel comparison with the bare-breasted lovelies.

At the piano Jacques-Charles rippled his agile fingers across the yellowing keys for a moment or two, while Suzette breathed in and out a few times to prepare herself. He started to play an old heart-breaker – *'Plaisir d'amour'* – to give Suzette's voice a run-through on holding high notes without quavering.

Suzette put her heart into it: *'Plaisir d'amour ne dure qu'un moment'* she sang, aiming to show what she could do.

'Good, good,' said Jacques-Charles at the end and he played the first two bars of another song, equally slow but in a very different mood – *'La vie en rose'*. He praised the way she sang it and then asked for that other tear-jerker *'J'attendrai'*.

Suzette warbled to the melancholy tune: 'I will wait for you, night and day. I will wait for you forever'. It was in her mind that only a complete fool of a woman would let herself become so dependent on a man to utter such words sincerely.

With only the shortest of pauses, Jacques-Charles switched to a song forever associated with the divine Mistinguett – 'Like a flower'. Suzette sang it meticulously – and two more after it. When he stopped playing at last, she spoke her mind.

'You know I cannot sing these songs well,' she said, 'this is not my style, Jacques-Charles.'

'You must be able to sing any song well,' he replied with a shrug as he spilled grey cigarette ash on to the piano keys.

'As an exercise,' she conceded, 'but before I become a star I must find someone who can write songs that suit my personality. You promised to look around among the deplorables in the dives you go to. There must be broken-down poets propped up on bars who can string a few lines together.'

'Ah, if life was so simple!' said Jacques-Charles, tinkling away at the keyboard. 'Be patient – I am still looking, and I shall find you someone eventually.'

'I hope so. I shall never get anywhere with these back-street tear-jerkers. There are enough people bawling out songs of the gutter. That might have been all very well years ago, but this is the new France. I want to sing songs with a touch of glamour and high-life about them. No more of this "whore with a heart of gold" trash and "I love my man even though he beats me senseless" idiocy.'

'Ah well,' said Jacques-Charles, raising his hands from the keys in a gesture of resignation. He had heard all this before from her.

'I do not intend to become an idol for toothless old hags of fifty and their permanently out-of-work men in the Belleville slums. That's not for me, never, never! I mean to sing for the people with fashionable clothes and the smart cars and de luxe apartments, people who drink champagne for breakfast everyday, the Place Vendome and Champs-Elysees people.'

'But of course you shall,' said Jacques-Charles

soothingly, his fingers sliding along the keyboard in a tinkling cascade of sound. 'Trust me. In the meantime, let's try 'When night falls', shall we?'

Suzette took a deep breath, waited for the note and sang.

The lesson continued for an hour or more, with repetitions of parts he thought she had not done well and advice from him on phrasing and pitch. Eventually he got up from the piano to pour a little glass of cognac for himself. He offered one to Suzette and she decided to take it. They sat with elbows on the rickety table and chatted.

She had told her dearest friend Gaby that she was paying for her own singing lessons, not relying on Robert Dorville to give her the cash. And this was true, though not exactly the way she implied. The truth of it was she had paid Jacques-Charles twice only. He had become infatuated with his beautiful pupil and she no longer handed over her hard-earned money for the benefit of his advice.

She finished her drink, in the same time Jacques-Charles had refilled and drained his own glass twice. She pushed her chair back and got up from the table and began to undress.

Jacques-Charles stayed where he was, watching with his dark-circled but eager eyes under his great dome of a brow, with a Gauloise dangling from the corner of his mouth, as ever.

She was wearing an orange-coloured taffeta frock with a deep-cut neckline and big buttons all down the front, a belt of grey snake-skin with a gold buckle. When she arrived she had a short velvet jacket with big square pockets, but that had been taken off before she started to sing. Now the frock came off, the big buttons were not designed to be undone, this Jacques-Charles noted with keen interest.

When she was naked, frock and underwear and stockings draped over the cheap wooden chair she had been sitting on, she lay on the divan bed against the wall under the window. The patchwork cover she left on, not wishing to know the state of the sheets. She lay as if posing for a painter, something she had done once or twice in the past to make a few francs, when she was trying for a job at the Folies Bergère.

She was on her side, facing Jacques-Charles, with one superb leg stretched out and the other bent, the sole of her foot flat on the bed, the knee up to form an interesting angle. She was supporting herself on an elbow, her marvellous body revealed in full to her audience of one.

And indeed, here in the privacy of Jacques-Charles' miserable little room, she was displaying more than the paying audience ever saw at the Folies Bergère. When her knickers came off, she had no *cache-sexe* to cover her final secret, her smooth-skinned apricot was in plain view.

'Without doubt, you are the most beautiful woman I have ever seen in my life,' was Jacques-Charles' only comment.

It was only the truth and therefore not a compliment. He got up from his chair and crossed to the divan. Suzette smiled and turned on her back, one knee still raised, her hands behind her raven-black head.

Jacques-Charles sat at the foot of the second-hand divan and smoked a cigarette, just looking at her — though that is a poor way to describe how his luminous brown eyes were devouring her beautiful body, stretched out there for his admiration. And his admiration was wholehearted to the point of being adoration. It was as if his eyes were hands, gliding over her skin to feel it with sensitive fingers.

47

His regard travelled slowly from the black fringe on her brow to her scarlet mouth, then down her little chin and under it to the long neck she was so proud of. Then over her breasts, they had not flattened when she lay on her back − they remained two perfectly matched domes, suggesting poetic comparisons with the golden domes of an ancient Mogul pleasure-palace!

She could feel his eyes caressing her and she became aroused. Jacques-Charles sat still, a trickle of tobacco smoke from the corner of his mouth escaping upwards to the low ceiling. It was the only thing in the room that moved. Through half-closed eyes Suzette watched his face, long, thin and without expression. He glanced downwards, and it seemed to her that with his eyes alone he was stroking her belly. She gave a pleased sigh and opened her legs a hand's-breadth.

He was staring in between those marvellous thighs, savouring the delight of visual appreciation. There came a gleam into his eyes at last. He contemplated her smooth pink petals, he probed them without even touching her.

For Suzette this was a seduction she found to be exquisitely intimate and exciting, though it was impossible to explain why. After all, being looked at was how she earned a living on stage − there was nothing at all arousing about that.

But here, lying naked on Jacques-Charles' wretched bed, while he stared at her with burning eyes and said nothing, there was a strange thrill running through her. She sighed again, feeling the pleasurable sensations in her belly.

Soon Jacques-Charles' seduction by staring was turning into a visual ravishing. Suzette felt the dew of arousal within, as if his fingers were stroking the smooth bare lips at which he was only glancing.

This strange courtship Suzette subjected herself to each time she came for a singing lesson had a powerful effect on Jacques-Charles too, naturally, although he tried to remain calm. His features gave nothing away — his expression was placid and his breathing regular. But in his eyes could be discerned the inner turmoil of his soul, brought about by staring so long, and with open desire, at so much beauty.

And below too — it was impossible to disguise the effect that Suzette's naked body had on his maleness. It stood upright and hard in his thin trousers. Under half-closed eyelids Suzette was gazing at this long bulge of his, accepting it as a tribute to her, one that was sincere.

'Show me,' she murmured — the first words either of them had spoken for ten minutes.

His hands went to his trousers at once, though his gaze never wavered. He continued to stare fixedly at her, his eyes aglow, while he undid the front of his trousers from belt to groin and let his stiff male part jut out. Suzette's heart began to beat wildly. Her breathing became fast and uneven. Her breasts rose and fell in a rhythm to drive a man insane with desire.

Even now he did not move or stretch out a hand to touch her. He sat staring fixedly at her pretty split — the soft lips had parted a little, as if pouting at him, his hand clasped tightly around his quivering length of hard flesh. He did not touch her nor move closer, only his eyes ravished her, growing fiercer as she became more and more aroused.

Her long and elegant legs were wide apart now, freely showing her pink-petalled flower. Her loins were jerking, thrusting her belly up in a nervous little rhythm, and her hands were tightly clenched. It was almost as if she had an invisible lover lying on her belly, sliding into her with fast and regular pushes — a demon-lover in the night, bringing her to ecstasy in her sleep.

Jacques-Charles' clasping hand was sliding slowly up and down his swollen part in a consolatory manner, though he hardly knew he was doing it, so totally engrossed was he in the progress of Suzette's arousal. In the weeks he had known her he had fallen irrevocably in love — a love that was an infatuation. He wanted her every hour of the day and night — she was never out of his thoughts or his dreams. If she lived with him he would keep her naked all day and all night and make love to her until she, or more likely he, collapsed in total exhaustion.

He was a practical man in most things, he knew his dream was just that — a dream of eroticism. It would never come true. She liked him a little, as a teacher, as a friend to give advice on the career she wanted so much. She repaid his longing and his friendship by letting him admire her body when she visited him for a lesson. That was all there would ever be. He shrugged his shoulders mentally and made the best of it.

To say *that's all there'll ever be* was a sort of insult. What Suzette gave him was beyond all price. When she stripped naked and lay on his divan to be admired, she was bestowing upon him, Jacques-Charles Delise, a derelict piano-player, a pleasure of a magnitude and quality that millionaires, Hollywood film-stars and oil sheikhs, kings, princes and Maharajahs, could not begin to imagine.

For this he was enormously and eternally grateful, almost to going down on his knees every day with raised hands, grateful not only to Suzette but to the

Good God who had sent down this glimpse of Paradise into an otherwise drab and difficult life.

Tremors shook Jacques-Charles, his hand moved dreamily on his bounding and purple-headed part. He gasped to hear the stifled little moan which heralded the onset of Suzette's orgasm − her back arched and rose from the patchwork bedcover, her legs were shaking and her heels drumming.

'You are so beautiful, so beautiful,' he whispered, watching the tremors of her delicious belly, the heaving of her breasts.

His clasping hand stroked his taut flesh, its pace increasing in time with the beating of his heart. The tension in his soul and mind was stretched tighter, inevitably coming closer to the point at which it would snap.

It was a Frenchman, naturally, a philosopher of the bedroom, who said that in every *affaire* there is one who loves and one who lets herself be loved. A glance at what was taking place in Jacques-Charles' room was proof of the truth of his words. What happens between men and women when they take their clothes off, however important it may seem to the two people most intimately concerned, is always comical to anyone else.

Here was farce of a high order, Jacques-Charles loved Suzette to distraction, yet believed himself unworthy. She did not love him but she let him adore her naked body, just as if he were a lover. But he never laid a hand on her glorious body, not even at arm's-length with a fingertip. Whether she would have allowed him to go further, to handle her charms, to slide his belly on to hers as she lay on his divan and push his stiff length into her − that was not a question to be answered. It never came to that, because he held back.

By now Jacques-Charles was dizzy from staring at her, almost intoxicated by her beauty. His eyes opened wider, he could wait not another moment. To gasps of intolerable pleasure he spurted into the air, his body shaking furiously as he paid this heart-felt tribute. When the last drop of pleasure ebbed from him, he saw Suzette was calm again and watching him.

'Do you love me, Jacques-Charles?' she asked. This was part of the elaborate game she played with him, although he did not realise it was only that − a game. He took it to be a form of refined affection for himself. Which goes to show how wrong men usually are about women's motives.

'*Je t'adore, ma Suzette,*' he murmured 'awake or asleep, you are always in my mind. You inspire my dreams. If I wanted to, I can never get away from you, not even for a minute.'

'Dreams!' said Suzette, smiling at him with affection. 'Your dreams are made for you like movies by the alcohol you drink. I am sure you see all the showgirls in Paris round your bed, posing for you night after night.'

'No − only you, Suzette, I swear it!'

She could see how his satisfied part became smaller and soft. She never failed to be astonished by the speed of his response, she said nothing about it, not knowing if he regarded it as a blessing or a curse.

'Truly?' she said. 'And what do I do in your dreams?'

'You take your clothes off,' he confessed.

The first time Jacques-Charles had succeeded in bring her to a full climax simply by staring at her body had been an intense surprise to her. She had never heard of such a thing before, if asked she would have said it was impossible.

But there it was, he did it to her twice a week when she came for her singing lesson. She ceased to be surprised and accepted it as normal — normal for him, that is. She didn't think it was likely to happen with any other man staring up between her legs — for instance, Robert.

Not that Robert had the patience to stare at her for five or ten minutes after he'd got her clothes off. He was a man of action, not of dreams and wishes. He wanted to be in her almost as soon as he kissed her breasts. Though why she should be thinking of Robert at a time like this when Jacques-Charles was informing her, for the twentieth time, of her role in his dreams . . .

They were not even very interesting, these dreams of his — at least, not after the first time they were told. They were about making love — what else! — not only in this poor little room of his but in other places, usually public places! Not very nice places, the dens and back streets he had come to know well. He described how in his dream he had her standing her up against a wall in some dark and dismal alley, feeling her breasts through her blouse while he pushed in between her legs.

In these dreams of Jacques-Charles it seemed she never wore underwear. He could push her into a dark doorway, undo a button or two and have her bare breasts in his hands! And pull up her skirt and feel between her legs without hindrance! Did he put his length inside her in his dreams, she asked herself, or was it the same as in reality, exciting himself with his hand?

Well, in dreaming, he could do whatever pleased him most. It embarrassed no one, neither him nor her.

Though he talked freely about his dreams, he never

once said what was going on in his mind when he sat staring at her body, driving her to a climax by the sheer intensity of his desire.

But Suzette imagined they were much the same, that he played out in his head these dreams of his — that while he stared at her with ardent eyes, he visualised himself having her against a crumbling wall in a Pigalle alley, somewhere at the back of the Moulin Rouge.

Men were very strange, she knew, in questions of love-making. They liked to imagine all sorts of outlandish and uncomfortable ways of doing it.

That Robert, for instance, he liked to make love in the bath. It was nice enough when he got going but, compared with doing it in bed, a bath was restricting and inconvenient and usually meant mopping the floor afterwards.

'But you always want me to take my clothes off,' she answered Jacques-Charles. 'You should have become a painter instead of a musician, then I could pose for you.'

'I would paint your naked portrait,' he said instantly, 'not just once, but over and over again! I would never sell any of the pictures, I should need an enormous studio to keep them all in. Imagine it, a studio as big as a railway station, with rows and rows of pictures of you, naked and beautiful, on every wall. I would be overwhelmed, completely devastated, every time I went in! I would explode into ecstasy and collapse unconscious!'

His luminous brown eyes stared at her face, an expression of comic tenderness. His devotions at the altar of her beauty were not finished yet, what had been done so far was merely the curtain-raiser. He bent over her, his eyes half-closed in sheer delight, and kissed slowly all the way down her body, his lips trailing from her long graceful neck to her breasts.

He was down at the end of the divan, kissing her belly hotly, there was no more need for words. Suzette wriggled her shoulders to make herself more comfortable for what was to follow and arranged her legs the way he wanted them. He was on the floor beyond the divan, kneeling and leaning over her. She felt his mouth touch between her thighs, his wet tongue protruding.

He was like a bee with a flower, probing gently between soft pink petals. To Suzette his shiny over-size brow where his hair had receded made his head look like the swollen tip of a giant male part trying to enter her.

And he, Jacques-Charles, what was in his mind while he adored the beauty that obsessed him? Did he see himself in his mind's eye going into his picture gallery and staring in wordless love at endless rows of paintings of her, life-sized and in poses to display her naked charms to the utmost? Did he imagine himself ripping open his trousers and seizing hold of his stiffness, to comfort its longing while he stared about with hot eyes at his own portraits of Suzette?

Who could say what went through the thoughts of a person like Jacques-Charles? The years of booze had fuddled his mind, his dreams had become more real to him than his threadbare life.

Alone in the picture gallery of his mind he could stare his fill at representations of Suzette, naked and smiling, stare at his paintings wide-eyed until his body shook in a fever. Was it only a dream, was it an echo of reality, when in the mythical gallery his legs collapsed and he fell to the floor, rolled in a tight ecstatic ball, his hot desire spurting into his face?

Under the ministrations of that agile tongue of his, Suzette murmured a little in pleasure and let her lustrous eyes gently close, as she gave herself entirely to sensation.

'Slowly, Jacques-Charles,' she sighed, 'ravish me delicately with your tongue, show me you love me . . .'

ROBERT LOOKS FOR CONSOLATION

At about six in the evening Robert Dorville was sitting alone at a table on the terrace of Fouquet's, idly watching the world go by along the Champs-Elysées. Mostly the world went by in pairs, arm in arm, chattering and looking happy with each other.

He had finished his *fine à l'eau* and was staring thoughtfully at the empty glass, considering whether to order another, while he came to a conclusion about what to do that evening. Suzette had made it clear, without words, that the love affair between them was nearing an end. That was a pity, from Robert's point of view, as he had a great affection for her.

Love was another matter, of course, and it usually gave rise to many inconveniences, not to mention grief and mortification. These often outweighed the pleasures of love and always lasted longer. A truly intelligent man, in Robert's summing-up of the situation, shunned love like an infectious disease and made his life happy and content with true affection for a pretty girl of good character.

Or, more precisely, a series of these delicious creatures, for no man could be expected to remain satisfied with one woman for more than a few months. Not when so many of them could be seen every day strolling through the streets of Paris, waiting for a suitable companion to appear.

Naturally, when it was not merely a question of a

57

pretty girl but of an exceptionally beautiful one, like Suzette, regret was all the keener when the affair drew to a close. But there were, it must be said, elements in Suzette's character which made her an enigma to Robert. Even though she had reached the heights of appearing at the Folies Bergère – and when that engagement ended she could get the same job at the Casino de Paris or the Lido – nevertheless she had ambitions.

Her desire to be a singer made no sense to Robert, who was afraid it would lead only to disappointment and heartbreak for her. For this reason he hadn't encouraged her, he knew she held this against him. He sighed at the thought. If, despite all his misgivings, he supported her unreal ambition, she would surely blame him when it went wrong. Robert was well enough acquainted with the ways of women to understand that much.

On the other hand, he adored her and was reluctant to be sent away. At least he could go to the Folies Bergère that evening. He never wearied of seeing her on stage, fantastic in feathers and sequins, her breasts a magnet for the eyes of every man in the audience.

For, though he was her lover and had seen and kissed and felt those breasts so many times, every time he saw her on the stage he experienced a rush of desire. From the moment the orchestra started to play the show's lively theme music and the curtain rose to reveal Suzette and the other showgirls, Robert was lost in a daze of eroticism. He sat through the entire performance with a magnificently throbbing stiffness inside his trousers.

With the house-lights lowered, this condition went unnoticed, generally speaking, though there had been occasions . . . well, to be truthful, several such occasions . . .

One was a few days after he and Suzette had become lovers and he was at the Folies Bergère every evening to admire her on the stage and collect her afterward to take her to supper and then to bed. His passion was running high indeed as he sat silently in the dark, lost in utter admiration of her figure and grace of movement in three metres of sequined train and a tall head-dress of artificial roses and white plumes.

His reverie of delight was brought to a sudden end by a gasp. He turned his head to look, wondering what could have caused so sharp an exclamation of . . . surprise? Dismay?

In the seat next to him sat a lady in her middle years, thirty-five at least, he judged, or perhaps forty, it was hard to be sure in the dim light. She was a foreigner, that was obvious, her frock was stylish and looked expensive, but it was not Paris style.

Beyond her sat a solid-looking man in a dark suit, staring at the stage as if transfixed. Staring at Suzette, thought Robert, a pang of jealousy darting through his heart. Yet, on the other hand, to stare was all this heavy-set tourist could do. Perhaps he was dreaming of what he would like to do with Suzette. But he never would be able to, however hotly he burned.

Whereas he, Robert Dorville, fondled those beautiful breasts and kissed them every day and made love to Suzette in every way that he wanted!

The lady in the electric-blue cocktail frock had recovered a little of her self-possession and was gazing down into Robert's lap. In some accidental manner her attention had been drawn to his aroused

condition. The jacket of his hand-tailored suit was
open, his thighs were apart on the seat, even in the
half-light the long bulge in his trousers was plainly
visible.

The question was absurd but — what was the
etiquette for these circumstances? he asked himself.
Would it be correct to apologise — with a smile, of
course — for disturbing the lady's composure by this
unwanted display of French masculinity, she being
from abroad? Or would it show more panache to give
her a swaggering grin, demonstrating an easy pride in
his natural endowment? Or did one just shrug and let
it go at that?

In the event there was no need for him to make a
decision on so very complex a problem. The lady
reached out stealthily and put her hand flat over the
bulge that had diverted her from the stage, women
took less interest in naked show-girls than their
husbands did and were more practical-minded.

Her hand felt hot through the fine wool of
Robert's trousers and she pressed hard, evidently to
feel the throbbing. She wore rings with large gem-
stones on all her fingers, but it was not possible to
identify them certainly in the dark.

Mon Dieu! thought Robert, if her husband looks
away from the stage for a moment and notices that
his wife is fondling me in this intimate manner, there
will be a tremendous fuss! He will leap up and shout
and wave his arms — perhaps he will even wish to
engage in a fist fight with me! He weighs twice as
much as I do and it looks more like muscle than
blubber.

All the same, it was very pleasant to feel the
strange lady's palm sliding up and down over his
trousers — just a little, not enough movement to
attract unwanted attention. Robert smiled in her

direction, letting his white teeth be seen. Before turning his face back to the stage he winked at her, to show they were friendly conspirators.

Perhaps if he held his programme casually, down on his thigh, to screen her hand from prying eyes? But no – her stylish blue frock was sleeveless, her bare arm was pale-skinned, it must be seen at once by her husband, if he turned his head, how the arm was arranged, where her hand lay . . .

But why trouble oneself about all that? One should do as the poet advised and gather rosebuds while there was time. Thrills of pleasure flicked through Robert and he spread his thighs on the seat. Through all the fondling, he was staring in affection and desire at Suzette up on the stage – she and the other girls were going round and round slowly on a glass carousel, with red and green coloured lights flashing on and off to the music.

He wanted to put his hand up the foreign lady's frock to feel inside her knickers. She had dark hair, a bushy coiffure wound round and held with pearl-headed pins and he guessed she would be somewhat hairy of body. He was fairly sure she came from the lands at the eastern end of the Mediterranean, where according to general belief the women are hot-blooded, darkly passionate and demanding.

If those pearl hair-pins of hers were pulled out gently, in a conveniently private place such as a bedroom, her glossy hair would surely be down to her shoulders. Such round well-fleshed shoulders she had! Under the cocktail frock her breasts seemed formidable in an arousing way, massive and pointed.

The tips would be large and reddish-brown, Robert imagined in the fervid heat of his rising excitement. When they were kissed she would sob in delight.

Her perfume was delicious – *Chanel 5* said Robert

61

to himself. She evidently splashed it on with complete abandon, an aura of sexual stimulation floated around her like an invisible private atmosphere. When she was naked and aroused, the perfume of her hot flesh would mingle with the Chanel to drive a man right out of his mind with desire. No one would be able to restrain his passion, he would hurl himself upon her to ravish her!

Naturally, her legs were shaved, her eyebrows trimmed down to a fashionable curve and her upper lip plucked. But down between her legs, Robert guessed, she would have a thick dark fleece of curls. Very unlike darling Suzette's smooth-shaven petals, but pleasant to finger, no doubt . . . and to retain his faithfulness to Suzette, he could pretend to himself he was feeling between her thighs . . .

Alas for his good intentions towards Suzette, he dare not try to get his hand under the electric-blue frock of the lady next to him. The movement and fumbling would advise the husband that something was going on that he ought to know about.

It was preferable to sit still and do nothing. Nothing, that is, except to stifle a cry of sudden delight as, without proper warning, the pleasure her slow-moving hand was bestowing turned to ecstasy. As Robert spurted hotly into his underwear, an immense effort of will was needed to stop his legs kicking against the seat in front of him.

She was perfectly well aware of what she had done to him, on her broad face there was a furtive little smile. When she took her hand away from his lap she leaned close and whispered a few words, so discreetly that he only just heard *Hotel George Cinq. Madame Sassine. Telephone tomorrow after ten*.

Robert nodded pleasantly and smiled, touching the back of her withdrawing hand lightly with his fingers. He had no intention of making the call, but he saw no point in spoiling her evening by disillusionment. Especially not so quickly after giving him some unexpected moments of pleasure and a sticky shirt-front! She had done her best for him in public, with her husband close by. A certain courtesy was in order, was demanded even.

A girl sauntering along the Avenue des Champs-Elysées on her own in the direction of the Place de la Concorde smiled warmly at Robert at the very moment he waved at the waiter for another drink. He returned the smile naturally — only the most desolate and embittered of woman-haters ignores a pretty girl.

On the other hand, to walk alone on the Champs-Elysées gave a certain suggestion as to her probable profession, and that was the end of Robert's interest in her. It was not that he lacked sympathy for women who made their living on their backs but he personally had no need of their service. He had returned her smile, that was enough.

Except that, to his surprise, she paused, then turned on her heel, left the pavement and came across to his table. There she stood, smiling down at him most charmingly.

'You don't remember me, do you, Monsieur Dorville?' she said with a smile that showed small white teeth. 'Odette Charron.'

The *poules* who promenade along the Champs-Elysées looking for clients do not, as a rule, introduce themselves in this way nor do they often know the client's name. Robert decided his judgement of her had been mistaken and rose to his feet.

'A thousand pardons, Mademoiselle Charron, but just for the moment my memory seems to have stopped functioning. And this is utterly deplorable —

I never thought I'd forget the name of so very pretty
a young lady . . .'

At a loss to place her, he gestured an invitation for
her to sit down, the waiter held a chair for her. When
asked what she would like to drink, Mademoiselle
Charron said she would have whatever Robert was
drinking.

'We met only once, that was for a few minutes, no
more,' she said, putting her smart little suede
handbag on the table. 'It is not surprising you don't
remember me.'

The probability of a pretty girl making excuses for
a man not remembering her were so remote that
Robert knew she had decided to renew the
acquaintance properly – she wanted something.

She was not much over twenty, this Odette, with
clear shiny eyes and a lively manner. She was dressed
well and with style though not very expensively, a
close-fitting two-piece of pastel-pink grosgrain. The
waist was belted in tightly to draw the eye to the
slimness of her waist, her pencil-slim skirt was sleek
over her long thighs. Around her neck she had a
string of large red polished coral beads.

'It was when I did some modelling work for your
father,' she informed Robert. 'You came in to see
him while I was there.'

'Of course! Now I remember! You were wearing
green that day and it was the same colour as your
eyes!'

If anyone asked Robert his profession, he told
them he was a Company Director. This was true, as
far as it went, although it completely misrepresented
his situation.

Robert's father was in the business of making
women's clothes – not a couturier nor a designer,
but a manufacturer of ready-to-wear for others to

sew their label in. His factory was to be found in the
Sentier area, the grid of little streets running south
from the Boulevard Poissonnière to the rue
Réaumur. Here he employed over thirty seamstresses
and other skilled workers.

It had been his intention, Monsieur Henri Dorville,
to absorb his son Robert into the business when his
studies were finished — with a view to handing over
in due course and retiring to the country. But this was
not to be. Robert's natural desire to please his father
was offset by his total failure to develop an interest in
a business career.

Worse yet, to the consternation and chagrin of
Dorville *père* it became evident in a few months that
his son was completely incompetent in business
affairs.

Merely to have him concerned in the running of the
enterprise threatened it with late deliveries,
misunderstood instructions, lost and indignant
customers — in short, imminent and shameful
bankruptcy. Monsieur Dorville put the best face on it
he could and arranged for Robert's salary to be paid
to him monthly on the condition that he stayed away
from the factory and took no part in the business.

The salary was a considerable one, as was fitting
for the son of the proprietor and a Director of the
company, nominal though this directorship was.
And, to tell the truth, tax purposes had much to do
with it. Robert was able to live comfortably and do
whatever pleased him. Being a dutiful son he dined at
home with his father and mother once a week, but
had his own apartment so as not to disturb his
mother with a succession of pretty girls passing
through his life.

And he called on his father unannounced at his
factory two or three times a month to pass on his

brilliant ideas. A constant source of amazement to Robert was his father's lack of interest in these ideas. Not once had he persuaded his Papa to make the wonderful creations Robert invented in his head after becoming inspired by something or other, or more often someone or other, he had spotted in the street or at the theatre or in the cinema . . .

. . . or in his dreams, according to Monsieur Henri Dorville. He no longer attempted to explain to his son that his living was made not by designing frocks for rich ladies but by the manufacture of clothes in bulk for more famous houses to sell . . .

Robert regarded this as a regrettable lack of ambition in his father. But he consoled himself with the thought that *one day* . . . Yes, one day when the old fellow retired to his cottage down in Provence he, Robert, would transform this boring enterprise and establish it as one of the great Paris fashion houses.

Fortunately for the peace of mind of Dorville senior, Robert kept his ambition a secret. Otherwise a fatal seizure would be the finish of him. But Robert was a loving son and he respected his Papa and therefore he never discussed his ambition with a living soul, not even Suzette.

Two or three times a year, depending on how well things were going, Papa engaged a pretty girl with suitable qualifications to impress his wholesale customers by modelling frocks. Not his own creations, of course. Evidently he had been discussing such a showing with Odette Charron the day Robert dropped in.

As Robert recalled the incident, some three months past, she had been wearing a lime-green frock with a white lace collar. It hadn't really suited her very well, she was sure to know that. Perhaps it was a mistake to mention it, although he intended to compliment her on her pale green eyes.

Naturally, he had often wondered if Papa took the opportunity to make love to the pretty girls he hired to model for him. A further source of curiosity was if any of the seamstresses who worked in Papa's factory became his *little friends*. He was only fifty, Dorville *père*, no doubt he had the usual human instincts.

It was surely possible that this charming Odette was a friend of Papa's. Robert looked at her across the table, smiling with pleasure at what he saw. If she wanted anything she was in no hurry to say what it was. On the contrary, she seemed content to sit and chat for hours. He explained that before she arrived he was wondering what to do that evening. Was she perhaps free to join him in . . . whatever they decided?

He gestured vaguely in the direction of the big cinemas of the Champs-Elysées and asked if she had seen the new Danielle Darrieux movie then showing. Yes, she had, and loved it, every second. Then had she seen Simone Signoret in *Casque d'Or*? Yes, that too.

'Me too,' said Robert with a grin, 'twice – I adore her.'

After more talk about the films then showing, they settled on dinner instead. They strolled down the Champs-Elysées, arm-in-arm, taking in the evening bustle and noise, true Parisians out to enjoy themselves. If either had a care in the world, and the truth was that both of them had started the evening with heavy hearts, the oppression had lifted.

They walked together all the way to the Place de la Concorde, where taxi-drivers made continuous attempts to murder innocent pedestrians and force other vehicles to crash, especially the family cars with wives and children as passengers.

Robert steered Odette left into rue Royale, past the imposing Greek colonnade of the Hotel Crillon, before she took it in her head to imagine he was taking her *there*! He had no wish to eat in the company of ancient English milords and their horse-faced ladies, Hollywood film stars with child brides drinking whisky with Lobster Thermidor, or undetected Stock Exchange swindlers dining with their diamond-laden mistresses.

Not even for the sake of the food and the superb dining-room, would he endure that! He was heading toward the Boulevard de la Madeleine. That was where he lived and in consequence that was where he knew a couple of small restaurants. And they knew him as a regular diner and so went out of their way to take care of him properly.

That was important when entertaining a young lady — it made the right impression on her, to see her companion treated with respect. And to be fussed over by an attentive waiter perhaps even by the *patron* himself.

In all, it could be said the dinner was a great success. They ate very well and drank a couple of bottles of excellent wine. Odette was a charming companion — she talked intelligently, she listened with care. She smiled and gestured gracefully, laughed at every droll remark Robert made, her green eyes gazing at him in admiration.

Over a tiny glass of first-class cognac Robert suggested with due delicacy the possibility she might perhaps accompany him to his apartment, which happened to be close by.

'Well,' she said slowly, her hands pressed together as if she was in deep thought, but to let him observe that there were no rings on her fingers, neither wedding ring nor engagement ring.

It was an entirely unnecessary gesture, Robert had taken note of her hands minutes after she sat down with him on Fouquet's terrace. Whatever rings had been on her fingers, it would have made no difference to him.

It was a lively pleasure to him to show off his apartment to an appreciative woman. He had taken care over the furnishing of it and the decor. It had always been an irritation to him that Suzette never wanted to stay with him there during the days of their intimate friendship. The reason for it eluded him but she preferred to take him to her own place by the Gare St Lazare.

With Odette it was a very different story — she commented on his taste favourably, admired the pictures. She settled herself on the sleek black leather sofa, like a cat finding its home in a well-padded basket. When Robert poured two glasses of cognac she kicked off her high-heeled shoes, flexed her toes, and then curled her silk-stockinged legs under her.

There was soft music on the radio, the lights were shaded and romantic, and one thing led to another, as it is supposed to do on these amorous occasions. Soon Robert had his arms about her and was kissing her. Odette responded with enthusiasm. Those green eyes of hers were half-closed in pleasurable anticipation, her glossy red lips were parted for his tongue to enter.

From that it was not long until Robert's hand was down inside the deep-cut top of her pastel-pink jacket and in the cleft of her breasts. He cupped his palm around the warm flesh, but only through a thin brassiere, and decided more radical action would be required. He undid the buckle of her belt and unbuttoned the jacket completely. He reached inside.

'Robert,' she whispered, but whether she meant *please, Robert, do* or *Please, Robert, don't*, that was not a matter to concern him just then. He put his hands on her bare shoulders, he felt the soft smoothness of her skin and the warmth from within her.

He reached behind her back to undo her brassiere. Her breasts were of moderate size but had the appearance of being bigger than they were, and more prominent, because of her small waist. He caressed them, he kissed them, he murmured the usual words women like to hear at these moments of tenderness.

He was planning the next step in his head while he caressed her. It would be impossible to get a hand up a skirt so tightly fitting as hers, it would be better to take her to the bedroom and undress her completely.

After a little while, when she was sighing softly and holding on to him with all her might, he picked her up and carried her into the bedroom. She giggled to find herself hoisted bodily in a man's arms, then she pressed her mouth to his cheek in hot kisses. He lowered her to sit on the side of the bed, observing how the hem of her close-fitting skirt pulled up to her knees. She took off the jacket and displayed her breasts proudly to him.

Her shoes were left behind on the sitting-room floor – black patent leather, shiny with reflected light. Robert went down on his knees in front of her and grasped her ankles lightly. What he wanted was to take her stockings off, he ran his hands along her legs, from her slender ankles to her well-rounded knees.

'You have lovely legs,' he said, which was true but obvious. On the other hand, what else is a man to say to a pretty girl, when he is undressing her?

'I'm lovely all over,' she said with a grin.

Robert wanted to feel the softness of her thighs and that he believed was going to be difficult while she kept her skirt on. He leaned toward her and pressed his lips to hers in a long and unbroken kiss while his hands slid up her skirt, from her knees to the top of her stockings — then a little higher still to lie on the bare flesh of her thighs. She sighed into his mouth when she felt him touching her there.

'I adore this outfit,' she said, when he ended the kiss, 'but the skirt is like a chastity belt. Every young virgin should be bought a two-piece like this by her father.'

'Is it one of my Papa's?' Robert amazed himself by asking — the question was unbelievably trivial, when his hands lay upon warm thighs above stocking-tops.

And besides, did Papa Dorville ever manufacture clothes in such a material as grosgrain?

The skirt fitted so closely that it pressed her thighs tight together and prevented his hands from going further. He kissed her again, harder this time, pushing at her with his mouth and forcing her over backwards. When she felt her balance going she surrendered to him and let herself fall on her back on the bed.

But her legs wouldn't open, couldn't open, and Robert slipped his hands out of her skirt to feel for the fastening he knew was at the waist.

He wanted to see her naked, to see her completely and to kiss all of her, to admire her body. He undid the skirt and took it by the hem to drag it down her legs and off. Now only a pair of thin white silk knickers and her stockings remained. Her belly was round and smooth, with a deep-set button. He kissed it at once and thrust the tip of his tongue into its depth.

First her stockings! Robert undid her suspenders and began to roll her stockings down her thighs, pausing to press kisses upon the warm flesh now and then. Her knickers were small and close-fitting, as they had to be under so tight a skirt. They were of a rich crimson colour and had the tiniest edging of black lace.

From under the sides of this little garment escaped tendrils of dark-brown hair. Robert eyed it in fascination — a nut-brown thatch growing to three or four centimetres down the insides of her thighs. And in a perfect state of nature, untrimmed! It was as if she disdained the sophistication of shorn and tidy groins.

Her armpits were smoothly depilated, Robert noted, her nails were filed and polished, her face made-up with skill, only this precious part of her slender model's body was allowed to remain in the state Nature intended.

The effect on Robert was dramatic, to say the least of it. He stripped her knickers off quickly, parted her legs, and dropped his head to nuzzle his lips and his nose into the wild-growing thatch of hair.

'Ah, I see you like my little fur-coat,' she said, her thighs moving further apart, 'some find it too *sauvage*.'

Robert lay beside her on the bed then, to kiss her mouth and face while his fingers explored her body. His hand glided over her breasts, rolling the tips gently, and he made her draw in her breath in pleasurable little sobs. He stroked her belly, then his touch slid down to her thatch of curls and to the soft lips the curls covered.

How different from Suzette! he thought, with the merest trace of malice in his heart. There was no hair between Suzette's thighs — only flat smooth-as-satin skin and two pouting lips, like a girl of twelve. Whereas with Odette! Ah, the sensory delight to be had of feeling crinkly hair beneath the fingertips, of exploring this veritable thicket of hers!

His probing finger parted warm petals beneath the bush, there the soft flesh was already moist to the touch. He found the bud inside and caressed it delicately. Almost at once he could feel Odette starting to tremble. Her breathing was becoming uneven and her hands gripped his arms.

'Take your clothes off,' she said quickly.

Robert was off the bed in a moment, stripping himself naked — jacket, trousers, tie, shirt. He sat on the side of the bed to rip off his shoes and socks and underwear, then stood up again, turning to face her.

He was proud of his body and had not the least shame in being seen naked. His body was strong and well-shaped, broad in the shoulders, flat across the belly, taut of backside and his legs were muscular.

This condition he maintained by a programme of daily exercise in his apartment. He had big weights he lifted, and a strongly sprung chest-expander he pulled at. Every day he did a hundred press-ups on the carpet, followed by a hundred deep knees-bends, to tone the muscles of his thighs and calves.

As for the male part that now jutted so eagerly upwards to be inspected by Odette, that also received very regular exercise! Whether constant usage improved the fitness and stamina of this particular length of flesh was a matter for dispute, but it was true that a benevolent Providence had endowed Robert more than handsomely.

The part that delighted young women stood at full stretch, a good fifteen centimetres in length, its thickness sufficient to bring a sigh of pleasure from any lady who took it in her hand to feel its strength.

But not so thick as to cause discomfort or problems when it slid into her. What more could any man ask, or any woman?

Odette was impressed by his nakedness. She slithered forward to sit on the side of the bed and clasped his upright stem between well-manicured fingers. Robert sighed in pleasure at the sight of shiny bright scarlet fingernails contrasted against the skin of his most cherished part.

'And how is Jean Jeudi?' she asked comically, using the name heard in the streets, for his hot and quivering stiffness.

'All the better for making your acquaintance, Mademoiselle,' Robert answered with a grin. She shook it as if she was shaking hands.

He liked Odette for her humour — a very rare thing to find in women! It must be some self-protection mechanism in the female psyche, he supposed — they never seemed to make a joke, or to understand one. Suzette was a case in point, that unbelievably beautiful woman had no sense of humour at all — or none Robert had ever discovered.

That must be the reason there were never any women comedians in the variety shows. Except, of course, female impersonators — an exceptionally tedious form of entertainer, in Robert's view. *They* made jokes and tried to be comical. But women they were not, whatever their personal illusions. The real joke was how they exaggerated ordinary female characteristics, which was boring, in Robert's opinion. Why pay to see a man in lipstick and women's knickers make fun of women?

Women were a source of infinite comedy to the man who adored them and did not take them too seriously.

After shaking hands with Jean Jeudi, Odette

decided she must give him a kiss. She lowered her head, the string of red beads around her neck swinging loosely forward, and pressed her mouth to the purple-flushed head in an affectionate gesture. Robert reached out to brush back her nut-brown hair.

She glanced up at him with a knowing little smile, opened her scarlet-painted mouth and took Jean Jeudi inside. Robert stood with heaving chest and shaking legs as waves of pleasure began to roll through his body. Soon he became frantic to crush her against him, to press her beneath him in the last act of love.

He took hold of her under the arms, his fingers gripping deep in the warm and smooth-shaven hollows, to lift her to her feet. His wet part slipped from her sucking mouth, she stood close to him, her breasts flattened to his chest.

She was deliberately squirming against his body to manipulate the upright part trapped between their bellies. Robert reached down her back to get hold of the bare cheeks of her bottom. For a woman with a model's small breasts and slender figure she had a handsomely developed rear. With delight he stroked and traced the fullness and roundness of her fleshy curves.

Her hot belly rubbed frantically against him. She pushed him gently away with her hands on his chest. With an eager look on her pretty face she looked down to where his throbbing length pointed at her. She took hold of it, she pulled him to the bed, and in a moment was on her back with legs open.

'Put it in,' she murmured, 'or in another minute you'll do it all over my belly.'

At once Robert was on top of her, pushing up into her wet warmth. So commenced a night of

unrestrained pleasure, with Odette showing an
eagerness as keen as his own, and a delight in rousing
him again and again.

When, sometime in the middle of the night, his
strength seemed about to wane at last, she made him
lie on his back while she sat over him and brought the
pair of them to renewed ecstasy.

Dawn was showing through the window before
they had exhausted themselves completely and fallen
asleep in each other's arms. It was midday when they
woke up, immediately stroking each other's body,
ready for more lovemaking. But they were too
hungry, pleasure had to be postponed for a while.

They dressed quickly and went out to a brasserie
nearby where Robert often ate. Over a sustaining
meal that was breakfast and lunch together, he found
out what Odette wanted.

She asked him if he knew of any modelling work
going. she was not aware of the slightness of his
connection with his Papa's enterprise, thinking that a
Director must necessarily have much to do with
running the company. Robert said he thought
nothing much was happening just then. Whereupon
she told him how many weeks had passed since her
last job, and that badly paid.

She had fallen behind with the rent and had been
told to move out. Her belongings were with a
girlfriend for safe-keeping, but it had not been
possible to stay with her last night, as her friend had
only a single room and she had brought her
boyfriend home. When Odette ran into Robert on the
Champs-Elysées, she had five francs in her purse and
was hungry.

'But this is dreadful!' Robert exclaimed in distress,
taking her hand across the table. She looked so

young and forlorn then in her misery, so vulnerable.
And so very pretty.

The thought came to him that when they met she
may have been on the look-out for the price of a bed
for the night in a cheap hotel! He congratulated
himself on rescuing so very desirable and intelligent a
young lady from being forced by circumstance into
the degradation of the streets.

'Something must be done!' he declared.

Odette stared at him affectionately with her pale
green eyes, letting him see that she had committed
her Fate into his hands.

'Let's go back to bed,' said Robert. 'It's a good
place to be while we consider how to get you out of
these difficulties.'

'Robert *chéri*,' she said, 'you are so good to me.'

And she sounded very sincere.

SUZETTE AT A PARTY

Armand Regence started as a song-and-dance man back in the twenties. He had a way with him, he stood out from the many, many song-and-dance men doing the rounds of the Paris music-halls. He had a cheeky expression, a *joie-de-vivre*, a charm. So did all the others, of course, but in Regence the stock-in-trade of variety performers was to be seen at its absolute peak.

Very naturally, he became popular and was able to command big fees for his appearances. In the 1930s he was invited to make a movie at Paris-Cine, a musical with the standard boy-meets-girl plot. The production was of little worth, except for the songs Regence was given to sing, but it spread his fame to America.

In 1939 he was invited to Hollywood, just in time to miss the war. Not that he would have been required to be a soldier – he was already well past forty. It was his good fortune that while he was making musicals in Hollywood he avoided the inconveniences of living in Paris under Nazi occupation.

He made three smash-hit musicals in ten years, becoming very rich and an international star. But as he said to reporters at every interview, he was a Parisian and his heart was in Paris. In fact, the phrase pleased him so much he had a song composed for him with those very words. This he recorded – in French as well as the charmingly accented version of

English he had been taught to speak by the best coaches in Hollywood. Both versions sold millions of records.

He returned to Paris in triumph after the war was over, sang a few songs, collected enormous fees and returned to Beverly Hills. Wherever his heart was, that was where he had his home.

Now and then, to keep his name revered in France, he agreed to do a few weeks at whichever Paris entertainment spot offered the best terms.

After six weeks at the Folies Bergère he was about to return to the United States. He gave a party for the cast and as the women far outnumbered the men, they were told to bring a friend.

Suzette decided not to take a man friend, she wanted a chance to talk to Regence's song-arranger, a legendary hit-maker. This was someone who knew how stars were made and Suzette was hoping to wheedle some free advice out of him. A boyfriend hovering about her would be a hindrance. And so she asked Gaby to go with her, unconcerned by what nasty tongues might say.

The reason for this was her increasing alarm at Gaby's latest boyfriend, Lucien. He seemed to have plenty of money to spend, though he never explained how he got it. He was a lively lover, said Gaby, and amusing to be with. And yes, he was a fetishist, and not in the least furtive or embarrassed by it — in fact his bedroom games were often highly entertaining.

All of which may have been true but it was Suzette's opinion that Lucien Cluny was a very dubious type. She would prefer it if Gaby found another boyfriend, as good-looking, well-dressed and open-handed as Lucien, but with a recognisable way of making a living and not so secretive.

The party was on their evening off, there was no

performance and most of the next day to sleep it off. In general, parties for the cast take place backstage at the theatre, but to flaunt his importance and wealth Regence held this one in the vast and impressively expensive apartment he rented. This was on the Boulevard Lannes and overlooked the Bois de Boulogne, naturally.

Suzette decided to wear her white chiffon — the contrast with her jet-black hair was stunning. It left her shoulders bare and as they were superb, she liked to show them off. Another reason she liked the frock was the way the fragile material clung to her breasts, close enough to show their marvellous shape while covering them decently.

In her experience men liked that. Their imagination needed a jolt, a close-fitting frock over bosom and bottom did it. Loose frocks that hid what was inside them were not worth wearing, in her view, whatever big name was on the label.

They arrived at the Boulevard Lannes and went up in the lift to the apartment where a large radiogram was playing in the sitting-room. As was to be expected, it was Armand Regence's voice that warbled away on the record. The carpets had been taken up for dancing and the furniture moved aside. Ten or fifteen couples were on the floor and, though the party had been going for only about an hour, some couples were very closely entwined with thighs pressed together and hands caressing bottoms.

Suzette waved to a friend or two and kissed a few on the cheek. Then, with Gaby trailing behind, she made for the champagne to get a glass before greeting the host. Regence stood at one end of the long room in a circle of hangers-on and flatterers. He was wearing a dinner-jacket, though none of the other men did — perhaps it was a symbol of superiority.

His internationally famous features had been given a facial — creamed, patted, massaged and steamed to get rid of any slight pudginess. His toupee was marvellously natural, his belly most expertly corseted to a youthful trimness.

He was also celebrated as a lover, of course — the archetypal Parisian lover, according to the publicity stories — the suave and debonair seducer of thousands, pretty girls and young wives alike. He was the Frenchman every foreign woman would leave home for. Armand Regence had his way with them so neatly and swiftly that they dreamed of it for the rest of their boring lives.

He kissed Suzette's hand with style — backstage in the past six weeks he had patted her bare bottom several times when the showgirls were leaving the stage and he had been watching in the wings. Everyone in the cast knew he had an eye on Suzette, even the stage-hands knew it. Some offered her advice on how best to proceed, according to whether they thought her advantage lay in taking her knickers off for Regence or in rebuffing him.

She had not discouraged him, knowing herself to be safe from the annoyance of unacceptable advances. Regence had married four times, in Paris before the war to a tap-dancer and three times since in Hollywood. These later marriages had been to American starlets whose ages had decreased successively as his had increased.

But alas, a whisper backstage said the great French lover was in some difficulty these days. He still did it, of course, but not without assistance. That being so, he remained faithful now to the three secretaries who formed part of his entourage when he travelled. Not one was a day over eighteen. It was a question of great interest backstage what their secretarial skills were.

They were from French Indo-China, the secretaries, a trio of flowerlike little Oriental beauties. Conjecture had it they had been trained from earliest youth in the secret arts of the Far East, those arts which pleased Emperors in the good old days of whenever-it-was. Be that as it may, the three of them were very precious to Regence.

Suzette basked in the sunshine of his smile and listened with amusement to his charming overtures, in them she recognised the touch of an expert. She flirted with him, which pleased him and made him chuckle. He bestowed upon her the supreme accolade of pinching her bottom through her thin chiffon frock.

But it was all a game and both knew it. Eventually he turned his attention to someone else, having exhausted his repertoire. Suzette drifted away gracefully. She saw Gaby had acquired two or three admirers and needed no support. The next question was, where was the celebrated song-arranger?

There was laughter from the dancers and Suzette moved closer to see what was going on. She stood next to Angelique Brabant, one of the Folies Bergère show-girls, a svelte brunette with large eyes and a mouth set in a permanent pout. Angelique's good looks compensated in part for her lack of intelligence, but she was good-natured.

'What's happening?' Suzette asked. 'Why are they laughing?' She slipped an arm into Angelique's in a friendly gesture which brought a scowl to the face of the man standing next to her, his arm around Angelique's waist.

'Have you met Jean-Pierre?' said Angelique,

happily missing her boyfriend's surly manner. Suzette nodded to him, he was not worth the effort of offering her hand.

There was no reason now to ask what had caused the laughter. Miss Hetty was dancing with one of her *boys*. Hetty was a star – an American and a singer, greatly popular with Paris audiences for her outrageousness. She sang sentimental love-songs and in very competent French. Her songs were romantic to excess, so much so that their sugariness would have choked a sophisticated audience in other circumstances.

Hetty went on stage soberly dressed in shiny black satin, her bosom decently covered and with several kilos of imitation diamonds draped round her neck and wrists. While she sang, her boys posed in a line behind her. These so-called boys were in their middle or late twenties, chosen for the magnificence of their physiques. Stripped down to their underwear they resembled Greek athletes at the original Olympic Games!

For Hetty's act they certainly were stripped down. They wore skimpy fake leopard-skin briefs, shiny black top hats, starched white cuffs and black velvet bow-ties around their thick necks. They took up silent poses behind Hetty and made their muscles ripple and bulge, their oiled skin gleaming golden under the lights.

With so much nude masculinity on show – shaven muscular chests, massive thighs, bulging leopard-skin briefs – the spectacle gave a *double-entendre* to the innocent words of Hetty's songs and audiences found her effrontery amusing.

Parlez-moi d'amour she sang very sweetly, and the boys thrust their loins forward to aim their leopard-skin bulges at her. *Je t'aime* she warbled and the boys stood with feet apart and legs astride to make their monstrous thigh-muscles twitch and roll.

Gentlemen in the audience laughed, ladies with them stared at the leopard-skin bulges and thought their own thoughts.

Backstage, naturally enough, tongues wagged. Most of the cast believed Hetty made use of her six boys in bed, a different one each night. Some insisted this was not so, the boys were surely selected for their lack of interest in women, they went to bed with each other. Some maintained Hetty had all six boys in bed with her, every night.

Whatever the truth of that might be, Hetty was dancing with one of them — Anatole Something-or-other — to a mournful Armand Regence love-ballad on the radiogram. Her boys were enormously tall and she was petite, half a metre shorter than Anatole. She looked like a little blonde doll in his arms.

She had made Anatole take off his jacket and his shirt so she could stroke his bare chest while they danced. On stage Hetty never touched any of her boys, nor did any one of them approach within two metres of her.

To see her now caressing Anatole so openly aroused a buzz of speculation. It was right, after all, that she made the boys be her lovers! One at a time or several at a time, that was the only question.

The quicker wits among the watchers realised she was playing a different game altogether. It had been natural enough for the publicity people to leak to the newspapers the most sensational show-business story since Armand Regence's most recent divorce, namely that international celebrities Armand Regence and Miss Hetty had fallen madly in love. They were inseparable by day and night — the most passionate of lovers since . . . well, since anyone you cared to mention, all the way back to Antony and Cleopatra.

Newspaper readers liked that sort of thing, it was very good for business all round. The facts were otherwise, for what have newspapers to do with truth? Regence and Hetty disliked each other intensely and never spoke. If her name was ever mentioned in his presence, he shrugged and said that regrettably there was an audience for the less sophisticated type of entertainment. And when Hetty spoke of him, it was to dismiss him as a second-rate old has-been.

Now she was making a mockery of his song and of him. A fixed grin appeared on his pampered features when he understood what she was up to. To save face he pretended he found it amusing.

A roar of laughter greeted Hetty's actions. As Regence on the record sang huskily, 'Let me embrace you, my darling' Hetty put her hand down the front of Anatole's trousers and groped about in there.

Again, 'Let me embrace you, *chérie*' sang the radiogram and Hetty undid Anatole's trousers and pulled them open. She was clasping his advantage, making sure everybody saw what she was doing.

'Americans!' said Angelique's boyfriend with a heavy sneer, 'they have no finesse!'

'What do you think, Suzette — are Hetty's boys all left-handed or does she sleep with them?' asked Angelique, her pretty brow furrowed with the effort of thought.

'There's never been any doubt in my mind,' said Suzette. 'I'm certain they put all the pillows on the floor in her hotel room to make a huge bed and get in together, Hetty and the six.'

'But that's an orgy!' said Angelique, a catch in her breath. 'Imagine it — to lie in the dark with six naked men round you. All those hands feeling you at the same time! Its unbelievable — truly unbelievable!'

The boyfriend gave Suzette a bleak look. To annoy him further she squeezed Angelique's arm confidentially and said:

'But consider how fantastic it must be, to be ravished by six strong men at the same moment! One in the usual place and five others burrowing in wherever they can!'

'Look how hard Anatole is!' Angelique murmured.

'That and five more like it!' said Suzette, delighted to see how red in the face Jean-Pierre had become. 'Thick and strong.' And to put him in his place, she went on:

'Imagine it, at the supreme moment, not just a warm dribble,' and she stared pointedly at Jean-Pierre, 'but a great hot flood all over your body!'

As the indignant boyfriend began his tirade, Suzette moved on and left them to reconcile their differences. She strolled from room to room round the enormous apartment, greeting friends and exchanging frivolities. Some she liked, some she did not, some she hardly knew, but here they were, the people she worked with — the stars and the showgirls, the dancers, the acrobats, the jugglers and illusionists, the unhappy female impersonator, the costume designers, the frauds, the fast-talkers, all the glittering company that assembles around a theatrical production.

She did not see the man she was looking for. Where was this song-arranger Armand Regence relied upon? Where was Raoul de Montmilieux-Pontillard, as he called himself? A name like that had to be bogus, and the man himself was a charlatan — no doubt a provincial school-teacher kicked out for fumbling the little girls!

But he had this ability to take indifferent words and tunes and transform them, develop them into something new which even Armand Regence with his cracked voice and fast-fading charm was then able to turn into a million-selling hit record!

She found him at last, in the star's own bedroom. She guessed it was that because the bed was broad enough for three or four people and had peach-coloured satin sheets and a canopy.

Raoul de Whatever was lying on it full length, his jacket off but his shoes on. Evidently he was asserting himself – proving he had a right to do whatever he wanted. Without him there were no more hits for Regence, never again! So let him complain if he dare, the old ham!

He was a big round-faced fat man, this Raoul, with dark hair greased back shinily. He had kept his big horn-rimmed glasses on, even lying down. He had a girl sprawled on each side, both stripped down to their knickers.

One girl held a glass and was tipping champagne from it into his open mouth. She was a red-haired and cream-skinned beauty, not a member of the cast, probably someone's girlfriend brought as a guest.

The other girl was one of Armand Regence's oriental lovelies. Her skin was the colour of dark honey. How slender her body was – almost boyish in narrowness of hip and flatness of chest! It was hard to imagine what special charms the three *secretaries* had for Regence.

She held an almost empty bottle, this lotus bud of the East, and she was pouring a stream of frothing champagne into Raoul's open trousers. His white shirt was pulled up over his fat belly and a bird's-nest of wet dark hair was plastered to his skin about a small limp item. His trousers were soaked through and a large wet patch was spreading on the satin bedcover.

All three of them were giggling, all three were drunk. But Raoul de Wherever-it-Was was not too drunk to know when Suzette came into the room and stood there staring at him.

'Ahah!' he crowed, pushing his glasses up the bridge of his nose with a forefinger. 'I know you – you're Suzy – and you've got a lovely pair of *nichons*! Best pair in the show! Get your clothes off and join the party. I want a feel of them!'

Suzette shrugged. There was nothing to be done – in his state there was no sensible advice to be got, she would prefer a toad in her bed to him.

He was too ridiculous, crowing over his little victory, doing Regence down in this petty way! She laughed – at him for his simple-minded buffoonery and at herself for thinking he would ever condescend to help her.

She slipped out of the room while he burst into a choking fit of coughing, brought on by talking while champagne was being poured down his throat. The naked girls shrieked with laughter, the honey-skinned one with the champagne bottle was stuffing it into his trousers.

Back in the big sitting-room Hetty's display was over and more people were dancing. Evidently Regence had given orders to remove the stack of his own records from the radiogram and play something else. A couple of men asked Suzette to danced and she did. The second was a man she hadn't seen before. He was about thirty-five, dark complexioned, good-looking and well-dressed, though conservatively. He was not a member of the cast, he said he was financial adviser, whatever that might be, and his name was Blaise Fulbert.

He danced very nicely and he talked well. He held Suzette in a light, yet reassuring manner, and he told her he attended the performance at the Folies Bergère often. Well, perhaps once a month and he always looked for her on the stage. He thought she must be the most beautiful woman he had ever met. He informed her that to find himself dancing with her was a dream come true!

Suzette found him agreeable. A financial adviser must surely be a person of means. Who would listen to advice from a man who couldn't make money for himself? But leave that aside, he had an air of reliability rarely to be found among the theatricals she worked with. And besides, he was charming.

Having met so fortunately, they stayed together. Blaise went for more champagne, they stood chatting and laughing as men and women do when they are making up their minds about each other. First impressions were favourable, before too long Blaise had an arm round Suzette's waist.

They retreated from the dancing and in a long passage outside of the main sitting-room they leaned casually on a silk-lined wall while they exchanged some details of their life stories — only a flattering selection, as was sensible. They were drawn back to the dancing by hearing little exclamations of surprise.

It was a night for public displays of private emotion: Hetty showing what she thought of Armand Regence; Raoul de Fat-belly displaying his inflated view of himself. Heaven alone knew who else had removed the mask and shown the secret face beneath it. Perhaps something was wrong with the champagne to provoke these episodes of contempt and detestation —' Regence was known to be mean. Now it was the turn of Francine Mesuet to show the world that she despised her professional partner.

Gilles and Francine were acrobatic dancers. Which is to say, they appeared on stage virtually naked – Gilles in the tiniest buckskin briefs he could cram himself into without exposing his masculinity completely, Francine in a tiny spangled *cache-sexe*, her breasts bare. To suitably romantic music from the orchestra, Gilles lifted Francine up over his head with one hand and they took up artistic poses – his hand under the small of her back, her arms and legs thrust straight out, his hand under her thigh so she sat upon his palm with her knees bent and her arms raised high . . . and so on and so on.

As a display of fine balance and acrobatic skill it might be thought impressive. The true appeal of their act lay in letting the men in the audience study Francine's lithe body in curious positions – upside down, prone with her feet apart and her legs toward the audience – whichever way Gilles held her. The women out there gloated over Gilles' slender strength.

At present Francine was dancing with a Hungarian juggler who called himself Sandor. She was in a short black frock, fitted very tightly, and she was pressing her body to Sandor's in a manner that left no doubt as to what she wanted him to do.

'She dances with such passion!' said Blaise, a friendly arm about Suzette's waist again.

'For a virgin, yes,' said Suzette with a smile.

'Surely not! Her stage partner – what's his name – must be in love with her. Where is he, anyway?'

Gilles was not to be seen, which was fortunate. Francine was swaying her supple body against Sandor so hotly that a flush of excitement had come to his face and a gleam to his eyes. It was evident to all watching that, before the night was over, their bodies would be pressed even closer together, without the hindrance of clothes, bare breasts on bare chest, his belly on hers and her thighs open for him.

Suzette explained to Blaise that it was not Gilles' custom to sleep with his partner. Nor with any other woman. He was badly thought of in the theatre — not because he was left-handed as a lot of the men were — but because he treated Francine as if she were his personal property, an object he had paid for over the counter of a department store.

But the only use he had for her elegant body was in their act on stage, stripped down to her little *cache-sexe* with the spangles and lying gracefully in his grasp.

Such a sad waste was the verdict on Gilles of the female cast backstage. There had even been futile attempts to convert him. A friend of Suzette's in the line-up, Jasmin Bonaventure tried and got as far as drinks in a bar with him. Jasmin had big and very nicely shaped breasts, the tips so dark she painted them pink before she went on stage.

She could have painted them screaming violet for all the good it did her with Gilles.

'He's so good-looking,' she complained sadly to Suzette. 'He can get into bed with me any time he likes — if he wants me to lie face down for him, I'll do it!'

If Francine went to Sandor's flea-bag hotel after the party and abandoned herself to his embraces all night, Gilles would not be jealous. But he would be furious, because such an act of independence would be a threat to his control of her life. He didn't want her himself but he didn't want anyone else to have her.

Everyone had heard their frequent rows backstage through the dressing-room walls, Gilles shouting at

Francine, she sobbing. Everyone knew of the humiliation he inflicted on her after she had been out of his sight for an hour. There, in the dressing-room they shared, he would make her undress to her knickers and stand under the overhead light, while he examined every last millimetre of her body.

He had a great and abiding fear that she would leave him and run off with another man. He looked for evidence she had been making love, he searched her body for marks of teeth or nails.

He pretended his concern was that the marks of love would show when she was on stage. Perhaps the lingering trace of a bite on her shoulder would be visible or the imprint of fingers on thigh.

There never were any such marks to be found. Gilles refused to believe it but Francine was pathetically loyal to him. And it was the opinion of Suzette that she was still a virgin. All the same Gilles would fly into a rage, call her obscene names and threaten to beat her. He never actually did beat her, but the threat was bad enough to make her burst into tears.

As for his own lean and muscular body, he took care that it was never marked by the casual lovers he picked up in bars and took home with him. He made Francine massage him every day, to keep his muscles supple and his skin in good condition. For this he stripped to a tiny posing-pouch. He lay on his bed, legs apart and arms out from his sides.

He added to the sexual humiliation with which he controlled Francine by compelling her to undress at this daily ritual — to take off her frock and stockings, and massage him wearing only her knickers. Women's breasts held no interest for him but he insisted on hers being bare. The reason was cruel. Moderate as Francine's breasts were in size,

when she leaned over him to massage him they swung
to her movements. Gilles would make unpleasant
remarks about them, exclamations of ridicule.

She tried to ignore his comments, though they still
brought a dull flush to her cheeks. The problem was
she owed everything to him, of that he constantly
reminded her and she knew it to be true. Without
Gilles, her youth and prettiness and prospects would
all have drained away in the back streets, in poverty
and frustrations.

Gilles had found her in a cheap dance-hall and
spotted her potential. He persuaded her to run away
from her family and move into his tiny apartment.
He taught her his acrobatic skills, cursed her and
rehearsed her sixteen hours a day, until he made her
into the perfect partner for him. Their success in
various cabarets, culminating with their run at the
Folies Bergère, was reminder enough of her debt to
him.

She was nearly seventeen when he found her and in
her innocence she imagined he would be her lover as
well as her dancing partner. She learned quickly he
was not interested in her sexuality. In fact, most
nights of the week she lay alone on a divan in the
sitting-room, while in the bedroom Gilles amused
himself with the latest pretty young man he had
brought home.

When Gilles spread himself on his back for his
daily massage, Francine would kneel over him bare-
breasted, her hands on his flesh, a little golden oil on
her palms. She loosened the muscles very carefully,
working up his neck and down his chest. At first he
kept his eyes on her, staring at her with mockery,
making sharp comments on her dangling breasts
above him.

She massaged his flat belly and his muscular

thighs, and by then his eyes would be closed and he would be lost in dreams of his own. What the dreams were, that was his secret. What vivid pictures played in his mind, that was none of Francine's business.

But she was able to guess what film was playing behind those closed eyelids, for as she worked on the long thews and tendons of his inside thighs she could see the stiffness growing inside his black silk posing-pouch.

All she could do was to stare at the quivering outline. She had seen his male part, many times, both hard and soft, when he dressed and undressed, but she had never been allowed to touch it or hold it in her hand. When she dug her fingers deep in the muscles of his thighs and inflicted pleasurable pain on him, he would gasp, his concealed part growing longer and harder. It jerked up from his belly in the black silk pouch.

She heard his soft moaning when his excitement rose to a peak and her thumbs dug cruelly into his flesh, twisting and turning on the nerves. Then his loins bounded up off the bed, he cried out mindlessly and spurted into the posing-pouch. Francine saw his excitement emptying into it, a wet stain spreading over the thin black material.

When he became tranquil again he licked his lips and told her to leave him in peace to doze for half an hour.

One day, Francine had solemnly vowed to herself, Gilles was going to get the greatest shock of his life. It would be when she found another partner with an act she could join, then she could leave Gilles without destroying her career.

On that day, before breaking the gleeful news, she intended to give him a last massage. She would behave as docile as ever — in fact, she would spin it out longer than normal, and take perhaps half an hour to work her way down from his neck to his thighs.

By then he would be viewing in his mind's eye the naked body of some boy or other and he would be hard and ready inside his little pouch.

She knew him well, after five years of this mental torment he had inflicted on her. And when she saw he was two heart-beats away from spurting, she was going to snatch at the posing-pouch with one hand and jerk it down, grab his twitching part and flick it up and down furiously!

It would be too late for him to stop her. His desire would be gushing out to the heavy beat of her hand, surging up over his twitching belly! He could cry *Stop that*! as loud as he liked, he would have no choice but to endure a humiliating orgasm brought on by a woman – for the first and only time in his life!

It was not impossible, Francine thought with feline pleasure, to imagine him bursting into tears as he surveyed what she had done to him – the wet trickle on his skin. And she, in only her knickers and on her knees between Gilles's splayed legs, she would push out her breasts in pride for the first time and laugh at him! That was the very moment, while he was sobbing in shame and squirming in unwanted ecstasy, to tell him she was leaving him and going off with a new partner.

And as a final insult – getting her own back for the years of mortification at his hands – she would spit on his bare belly, her saliva mingling with his own outpouring.

'Francine has changed,' said Suzette, watching how she clung to Sandor. 'After tonight she will not be a virgin. Gilles must beware.'

'Come and dance with me like that,' Blaise suggested.

So they danced closely and Suzette felt a stiffness pressing against her and a hand lightly stroking her bottom through her chiffon. He kissed her very pleasantly and she let him put his leg between her thighs. After two or three minutes of that the music became irrelevant and the other dancers an inconvenience.

They slid out of the crowded sitting-room, their arms around each other's waist, in search of a secluded place. In spite of the number of people at the party there must be, in an apartment as huge as this, a room with a key to turn in the door to allow them to be alone for a while.

But the bedrooms they tried were already locked — except for one, and it was in darkness when they entered. The light from the passage spilled in to show an interesting and unusual scene — five people rolling about together on a bed. Fingers fumbling at each other, trousers wide open with stiff parts jutting out, skirts up round waists and knickers pulled down to reveal tufts of brown curls, hands caressing the cheeks of pale bottoms and a tongue lapping at pink lips between parted thighs.

'*Oh la la*!' Blaise whispered, his arm tightening on Suzette's waist.

A cry of surprise came from the bed and a spurt of creamy desire onto the top of a silk stocking. The stocking-owner rolled the man underneath her, thrusting her belly at his spurting part.

Suzette turned away and Blaise closed the door and followed her. He thought she was offended by what she had seen and began to apologise, saying he had had no idea what was going on. But the reason was that one of the women on the bed was Gaby, her

frock up round her waist and her knickers down
round her long thighs. Suzette had no wish to
interrupt her friend's pleasure.

'Let's go to my apartment,' Blaise suggested,
taking Suzette into his arms to kiss the tip of her
perfect nose.

BLAISE FALLS IN LOVE

In the Boulevard Lannes, Blaise's car was parked with its nose close up to a tree. Suzette saw it was a large black Citroen limousine, new and shiny. Blaise opened the door and settled her comfortably, tucking in her legs with gentle gallantry — and at the same time taking the opportunity to run a hand lightly over her knee. She smiled at him and for just an instant he gripped the soft flesh of her leg above the knee, under her frock, and squeezed. He got into the car and started the engine, looked at her with his eyebrows raised.

'Where do you prefer?' he asked. 'My apartment or yours?'

'Where do you live, Blaise?'

She had no intention at all of going to his place, not on the first evening they met. That would be to surrender far too much of the initiative to a man who was as yet only a casual acquaintance.

But naturally it was interesting to know about him and, when she understood him better, she would visit him at home. It was revealing with unmarried men to see what style — or lack of it — they lived in. But, until then, it was for him to go with her to her apartment.

'Boulevard Haussman,' he said, 'the western end.'

'It's early,' Suzette said, 'take me for a drive through the Bois de Boulogne.'

It was hardly midnight. Armand Regence's party would go on for hours yet, until practically no-one could still stand on their feet.

Blaise backed away from the tree and turned up the Boulevard toward the Porte Dauphine entrance into the Bois. It was a warm and pleasant night, an encouragement to be up and about, taking in the pleasures Paris had to offer. Suzette wound the window down to let a breeze ruffle the fringe of jet-black hair on her forehead.

They turned into the Bois and Blaise drove with only one hand on the steering-wheel, the other resting on Suzette's knee. The gear-change lever was up out of the way on the dashboard with the dials − there was nothing to stop him embracing her in due course, there were no mechanical barriers or other annoyances.

He drove across the Bois to the Allee de Longchamp and turned down it.

'No, no!' said Suzette. 'Not here − there's a tart standing under every tree. It's like Montmartre without the neon signs. Turn off somewhere.'

Eventually he found a quieter and less frequented area, after driving about for a while. But when Suzette suggested he should pull over and park, he became slightly agitated.

'Parking's not allowed after dark,' he pointed out. 'I'm sure there are police patrols.'

His reluctance was a reminder to her that he was not a member of her world of glamorous make-believe. He was on the fringes, perhaps, because of his professional usefulness as a financial adviser to Regence or the management or whoever it was who had invited him to the party. But this Blaise Fulbert was first and last a solid citizen, a man who paid his rent when it was due and never lit a cigarette near a *Défense de fumer* sign.

But now and then, if temptation was strong

enough, might he not permit his sense of duty to
bend a little? And there could be no doubt at all
about it, beautiful Suzette in the moonlight was a
temptation no one but an elderly judge could resist.
Not only in moonlight, but in broad daylight, for
that matter!

Blaise parked as unobtrusively as he could manage
beneath a tree and turned off the engine. After a
moment, he turned off the lights as well, and eased
himself round in his seat to face Suzette. She sat
demurely in her white chiffon, knees together and
hands in her lap. After all, Blaise was the man – it
was up to him to make a start.

For a slow beginner he did well eventually. His arm
was along the back of the seat, round her shoulders,
his head came close. He covered her face with quick
kisses, his breathing was almost a caress itself on her
cheek and mouth. He kissed her throat to feel the
tiny pulse under his lips, he kissed the long neck she
took such pride in. He kissed behind her ears, on her
eyelids, at her temples.

Suzette lay comfortably in the circle of his arm and
let the excitement build up in her. Now he had begun
he was bold. Through the chiffon of her frock his
hand played over her breasts, learning their opulent
shape, caressing the buds he could feel through the
thin silky material.

She felt a gentle throbbing between her thighs, a
first hint of moistness, and a pleasurable tremor in
her belly. Blaise told her she was the most beautiful
woman he had ever met and his hand was under her
frock, lifting it above her knees. He laid a hand flat
between her warm thighs, where the slickness of silk
stockings prevented him touching bare flesh.

'Ah, Blaise,' she murmured, her voice a little
shaky from the delicious sensations his kisses and his

touch caused. His hand slid up higher, above her suspendered stockings, and now it rested easily on bare skin, very high up, almost touching the lace hem of her knickers.

'*Chérie, chérie!*' he sighed, his fingers climbing that last centimetre or two, pushing her thighs apart. Then his hand was inside her knickers, moving gently and arousing her. She heard him gasp loudly to find she was smooth-shaven between the legs.

'Oh, oh!' he said, his baritone voice quavering with strong emotion. 'But . . . but . . .'

'But yes, Blaise,' she murmured, parting her legs wider.

It was some moments before he recovered the power of rational speech, even then his voice was shaky.

'But of course,' he said, 'it is because you wear only a tiny *cache-sexe* on stage. I understand. *Bon Dieu* – all the evenings I have watched your performance and never guessed you were nude between the thighs, under the sequins. Ah, such pleasure!'

While he was babbling away his fingers played feverishly over the smooth lips that had caught his fancy. Suzette lay back in the car seat as far as she could, her legs spread.

For her, Blaise's reaction of surprise was nothing new. Every boyfriend made the discovery at the beginning of their intimate acquaintance and all but two had expressed amazement.

Some liked it, some did not. But that's how she was and they had no say in the matter. At the beginning, two or three years ago, when she had first shaved the thick black fleece between her legs in preparation for her first appearance on stage, it had felt very strange. But strange in a pleasing way. She felt very conscious of the nudity under her *cache-*

sexe. There was a private thrill in the thought the audience could stare at her breasts as much as they liked, the women in envy, the men with something stiff down their trousers, but there was an ultimate secret they did not know. A secret that was hers.

Alone that first night she revelled in her secret. In bed she lay with her legs open and reached down to feel the smoothness of flesh between. The touch was very pleasurable, she caressed her denuded softness gently, not trying to bring on her crisis, but enjoying the slow slide of fingertips on sensitive flesh.

It seemed to her that the pleasure she felt was flowing along two separate routes. There were the little thrills experienced by the bare lips she was caressing, the thrills that ran up and through her belly. There was also a different sort of pleasure the touch imparted to her fingertips. Not quick little thrills but long throbs of pleasure, they passed up her arm, the slow throbs, to her shoulder, then into her breasts, making the buds hard and from there down inside her. The two streams of delight met in the core of her body, as if they were electric currents along different cables. Where they met, they set up strong vibrations of near ecstasy.

When the vibrations reached a certain intensity, like a note sounded by a violin – long, insistent, sustained – she opened the moist petals and stroked inside with a most delicate touch.

Down there, down between her thighs, down inside her belly, a melting sensation of extreme pleasure began. There beneath her finger the flesh was slippery and the little bud was firm.

So wet, so wet she thought as the orgasm came closer. Now she flicked her fingertip rapidly over the yearning bud, until her back arched off the bed in convulsive delight.

For the first few weeks after she began to shave off her dark curls, the urge to touch herself was constant. She would do it at night, if she had no boyfriend in bed to pleasure her, and again when she woke up alone in the morning. It was a compulsion, not to be taken seriously, a childish curiosity. brought on by the strangeness of smooth-shaven skin and combined with her passionate nature.

She became accustomed to her new condition after a few weeks, and no longer felt eagerly to savour the strangeness twice or more a day. She forgot she had ever been different − that there was a time when she boasted a richly lustrous fleece between her perfect thighs, a stunning complement to the jet-black hair on her head.

The only times now when she touched herself there, to revive that double flow of pleasurable sensation, was when she spread her legs to remove any sign of hair sprouting on her alabaster skin. The touch of warm suds, the cold steel of the razor, they together excited her to use her fingers on this sensitive spot until a climax calmed her again.

Blaise Fulbert was one of those who found her bare condition a delight. He caressed her for the longest time before pressing his finger in to touch the delicate pale pink interior and the little bud that throbbed gently under his touch.

'Suzette, Suzette . . .' he sighed, as if dying.

She put her arms round his neck and pressed her mouth to his in a kiss that was intended to comfort him for the time being. That is until they arrived in due course, when she was ready, at her apartment in the rue de Rome. He could have her knickers off then and feel her and kiss her all he liked. For hours, she hoped, long night hours of kissing and touching and loving.

104

She had taken a liking to Blaise and she wanted him to ravish her with love, until neither of them could continue. Then they would lie side by side on her bed, limp and content, their arms lightly about each other – he drained dry, she wrung-out with passion fulfilled. Ah, the very thought of it! They would sleep in each other's arms then and even in their sleep be half-aware of the closeness of their embrace, of bare skin on bare skin. They would sleep only until Nature reasserted itself, their strength renewed, and they were ready to love again.

But it was not comfort that he needed, this Blaise, however tenderly it was offered. He pushed two joined fingers deep into her slipperiness, making her gasp into his open mouth, 'Blaise!'

His other hand grabbed her wrist hastily and pressed her palm between his legs. She felt the hard bulge jump under her hand as his loins shook and lifted.

With a little shock of amazement Suzette realised his crisis had arrived unbidden – he was spurting wildly into his clothes, soaking his underpants. She was amused and confounded to think feeling between her legs did that to a man. What a fool he must feel! If he was too shamefaced about it he might drop her off at home and vanish, which would be a pity.

In sympathy, she pressed her hand tight against his trousers, feeling his throes decreasing, the jerking slowing down. He was kissing her again, although less wildly now, his tongue touching hers.

Without stopping the clinging kiss, she flipped his trousers open to slip her hand inside. His shirt was wet and warm to her fingers. She felt underneath it, finding the soaked patch on his underwear, the slipperiness on his belly.

She clasped his upright part in the palm of her

hand — and a frisson of astonishment ran through her. The size of it seemed to her enormous! It was still hard, the head was uncovered and sticky, but the bulk was formidable!

He began to apologise, which made her smile in the darkness.

'What have I done!' he gasped, sounding put out. 'It's never happened to me like that before — what must you think of me!'

Suzette laughed, not unkindly. She said she felt flattered to have had so dramatic an effect on him. She still held his imprudent part in her hand and could detect no sign that it was becoming any softer, or any smaller. On the contrary, it bounded in her palm as if to draw attention to itself, not at all abashed by its display of impatience.

'What I think of you,' she said, 'is that you should take off your underwear — it's soaked. Let's go to my apartment where we can make you comfortable.'

In truth, Blaise's comfort was not a matter of importance to her then. What she wanted was to see him with his trousers off to confirm what her hand suggested in the dark — that there was a sight well worth seeing between his legs. Something that was 'large and long, thick and strong', as the old rhyme said.

She withdrew her hand, Blaise started the Citroen and made for the way out of the Bois. He was not certain where they were and made a blind tour of the available roads before finding the Porte d'Auteuil. He turned up the Boulevard Suchet, between the elegant apartment buildings.

Of course, when they reached the Gare St Lazare and the rue de Rome, there was nowhere to park. The inhabitants had gone to bed, leaving their cars standing locked and dark on both sides of the street, crammed into every cranny. Suzette showed Blaise where she lived and had him drop her there – she had no wish to sit beside a fuming man circulating in hope of finding a space.

'Do not be long,' she said as she got out of the car, kissing his cheek and bestowing a pat on his still-hard bulge.

Did it remain permanently stiff? she wondered, climbing up the stairs to the second floor. That was an interesting thought.

She remembered being told the famous writer Guy de Maupassant experienced a permanent stiffness. He had given a demonstration of his talents before eye-witnesses, by having six tarts in the space of an hour. To Suzette's way of thinking he might as well have saved his money by having the same tart six times and asking for a discount. But men were never logical about these things.

Not that she remembered reading anything written by Monsieur de Maupassant, this story about him was told her by a boyfriend who said he too was a writer. André Dubas, his name was, a nice enough man in his way. He wrote for the theatre, dramas of wit and passion about modern life. Or so he claimed.

But he never found anyone to put them on. Perhaps he had told Suzette of Monsieur Six-Times-An-Hour to convince her writers were special people, himself included. She was eighteen at the time, impressionable perhaps. But although she liked André she could see he had no prospects in the theatre. In the end he became so discouraged he abandoned writing entirely and got a job selling insurance.

This question of permanent stiffness did not apply to André himself, his capacities were average. Nevertheless, he seemed to think it admirable and desirable. Suzette had another view. It would be far from convenient to have a boyfriend with that ability. Much as she enjoyed lovemaking, there were times when it was inappropriate. Who wanted a man nuzzling his stiff thing against her, like a puppy seeking for attention, when she was manicuring her nails or shampooing her hair?

All the same, thought Suzette, unlocking the apartment door, it would be fascinating to meet such a man — if there was one!

The apartment was dark and empty. Gaby was still at Regence's party unless she had gone home with someone — perhaps one of the men on the bed with her. Or someone else entirely, if the ones in the bedroom had exhausted themselves too much to continue.

As a way of finding a more acceptable boyfriend than Lucien, this multiple activity in Armand Regence's back bedroom did not recommend itself to Suzette as well-planned or intelligent. But then, Gaby was scatterbrained, she always had been and always would be — infuriating though it often was, it was part of her charm.

Twenty minutes passed before Suzette heard Blaise at the door and went to let him in. He gave her a glance of reproach, as if the impossibility of finding a place to park was her fault.

She dismissed his mood with a kiss and thrust a small glass of cognac into his hand. His absence had been useful, she had had time to powder her face, freshen her lipstick and brush her glossy black hair. And to check with a long and slender middle finger that her little cap was securely in position.

Blaise was not in a mood to sit down and drink and talk. Even with the annoyances of parking, during his absence from her his interest had revived. And truth to tell, Suzette was in no mood for further delay — she was impatient to see the stiff part she had felt, the headstrong member which at the merest stimulation had gasped out its flattery so naively.

They were standing facing each other, close together, glasses in their hands. Suzette reached out to touch Blaise, to run her fingers over that fascinating bulge in his trousers. And it was hard! She gave him her glass to hold and with both his hands occupied she had him at a certain disadvantage. She unbuttoned his jacket — the well-tailored jacket of his expensive but very conservative midnight-blue suit.

She opened his trousers and pulled his damp-fronted shirt out of the way, then she slid her hand in through the slit of his soaked undershorts. With a firm hand she gave his stiffness a squeeze and brought it out where it could be seen.

At the sight of it she uttered a little sigh. Her impression had not been mistaken, Blaise was as impressively proportioned as she thought — long and thick and like a bar of steel in strength. In her hand it stirred eagerly, hinting at the power that could be unleashed.

But Blaise seemed to be embarrassed by her regard, or perhaps he thought himself freakish to be provided for more generously than the average man on the Metro. At all events, he got rid of the empty glasses and took Suzette's hands. He pulled them from his quivering part and swept her into his arms to kiss her.

All things considered, she thought it best to show him where her bedroom was. She made a silent promise to herself to have a good look at his oversized part later, when he was more at ease with her. It made no difference whether he was shy about it or not, she meant to handle it for as long as it amused her.

She had earlier switched on the discreet bedside lamp, giving a warm and intimate look to the room. Blaise sat her on the bed and went down on his knees on the carpet to raise the skirt of her white chiffon frock. He clasped her knees, her thighs were together, but he bent right down to kiss the smooth and supple flesh above the tops of her silk stockings.

He forced her knees apart with strong hands – she struggled against him for a little while, the pretence of being compelled always excited her. Then with a long sigh she submitted to his greater strength and let her knees open wide. His hands slipped between to stroke the insides of her thighs, to touch the white silk of her knickers, the thin silk concealing her split peach. His fingertip tracing the smooth lips, Suzette shuddered with sudden delight.

Then he was pulling her knickers down, her legs closing as he slid them to her knees and to her well-shaped ankles. When he had them off she parted her legs again to reveal all to his burning stare. As if transfixed, he sat on his heels, his mouth hanging a little open, almost unable to comprehend the beauty of all he saw. There were the pink petals between her thighs, smooth and hairless, bare and accessible to him!

She was able to understand and to share the emotions he felt because of her appreciation of her own body, most particularly that delicious secret part of it. How often had she sat on the edge of her bed, her knees apart, a wooden-backed hand-mirror held in one hand to reveal her secret to herself!

With pride she parted her legs wider yet to Blaise's piercing stare, it was as if she could almost feel the

110

heat of his gaze. For a moment or two it was like being with Jacques-Charles, in his sordid little room in Montmartre. He too stared between her thighs with hot eyes, so devotedly he could make her react to his intense lust by sliding into orgasm.

But now she was with another man, one who was endowed magnificently, and she wanted to feel that thick and solid part of his thrust into her. With dear Jacques-Charles that was never the question, he was formed very moderately, if ever he became bold enough to want to slide into her the sensations might be a mild disappointment.

But with Blaise — she was certain it would feel like a brutal ravishment when he plunged into her! Tremors of anticipation ran through her belly. She was moist and slippery already, just thinking of it!

First she must get him moving, he crouched there on the floor as if mesmerised. It was evident he had not before seen a grown woman smooth-shaven between the legs, the effect on him was too devastating. His superb stiffness was sticking out of his wide-open trousers, it twitched rhythmically, the huge head purple and shiny with engorged desire.

Blaise was lost in some curious reverie of his own and unless something were done, his emotions might carry him to the point where he spurted his strength on to the floor — which would be annoying in the extreme! Once could be amusing, twice would be an insult. He needed to be prodded into action. But discreetly, of course, not to offend his male pride.

'Kiss me, *chéri*,' Suzette murmured.

He gasped at that, then put his head between her legs to kiss her. The touch of his wet tongue was exquisite, it sent throbs of pleasure through her and made her tremble — but that was not what she

111

meant. She had intended him to kiss her mouth and give her the chance to steer events along the path she preferred.

It must be admitted what he was doing was indeed delicious to feel, if it had been Robert and not Blaise she would have been content to let it continue, to let him kiss between her thighs until the crisis of sensation arrived.

But with this unknown Blaise it seemed necessary to postpone these intimate expressions of adoration until he had proved his ability in the usual manner. With that in mind, she gripped the dark brown hair over his ears and pulled his head away from her — until he was staring up into her eyes, his face flushed and his expression bemused.

She pushed him away and stood up. He remained crouched down. He wrapped his arms round her legs and pressed his cheek to her belly through her frock. When he saw she was taking her clothes off, he returned to his senses and released her. She pulled her rustling chiffon frock over her head while he stared up at her in doglike devotion. Then he rose to his feet, the idea at last getting through to his pleasure-fuddled brain, and began to rip off his tie and his midnight-blue suit.

At last they lay naked on the bed together, Blaise murmuring over the beauties of her pointed breasts. Under the pressure of strong emotion he had forgotten that he had seen them before, though at a distance, when she was on-stage at the Folies Bergère with the other eleven showgirls, their *nichons* hanging out to entice and captivate the audience.

But this was very different, this was not a theatre, there was no audience, he was close enough to Suzette to touch and to kiss those marvellous breasts, to caress them and enjoy to the full the warmth and texture of her adorable flesh.

Which was all very well, but he continued his caresses beyond any reasonable length of time, till Suzette guessed he was once more in danger of drifting away from the real world into some dream-state of his own.

She rolled on to her back and reached down to grasp his stiff part, it was throbbing heavily. She used it as a handle to pull Blaise on to her belly. Hearing his gasps of pleasure, she held the swollen head in her fingers to guide it between her parted thighs.

Now came the moment of truth! Blaise's 'large and long, thick and strong' was about to slide into her!

For a moment or two the huge smooth head paused, almost as if kissing the soft lips between her thighs. Then with a cry that might be triumph or amazement or gratefulness, or another less recognisable passion, Blaise penetrated her with a strong push, a redoubtable thrust that took him as far in as he could go.

Suzette shrieked to feel the solid thickness forcing its way deep into her, filling her fuller than she had ever known with any man before, fuller than she believed humanly possible. The sensations were overwhelming. A solid length of hard flesh was stretching her to the very limit, packing her belly cram-full, full to bursting!

Her loins bucked, her long back arched, her belly shook – she writhed in instant orgasmic ecstasy.

Blaise heard her cry and misunderstood. He tried to pull out, thinking he was hurting her, he took her throes to be pangs of pain, not delight.

Apologies came pouring from him, the words meaningless to her in this frenzy of pleasure. She felt his movement of withdrawal and sank her scarlet-painted fingernails deep into the flesh of his bottom to stop him.

Blaise jumped and gasped, then started a strong and rhythmic thrusting. Suzette met his thrusts with jerks of her belly, her knees drawn up to open herself for him. Her superb breasts were crushed under him, spread beneath his chest.

He sighed her name. He felt her smooth-skinned belly heaving under his. He felt her slippery warmth swallowing his oversize length with each plunge, accepting it joyfully.

'More, *chéri*, more,' Suzette cried out, fingernails clawing his bare bottom, her breath hot on his ear.

He responded gallantly, till with a great jolt that made the bed beneath them creak, he fountained his rapture into her. Suzette moaned and squirmed under his weight as she attained a second peak of ecstasy, her legs kicked in the air above him.

When they were tranquil again, lying side by side and looking into each other's eyes, Blaise resumed his apologies, sounding abashed and making Suzette giggle. Two marvellous orgasms in the space of a few minutes – she still felt a faint lingering quiver of delight – and he was begging her to pardon him for his brutality!

She learned that Blaise was by no means overjoyed by the size of his male part. On the contrary, he was embarrassed by it and had reached the age of thirty-five convinced that it inflicted pain and suffering on normal women. Suzette listened astonished and also amused to this account. She asked him what he did to enjoy the relief of his natural desires, in these circumstances.

He confessed that after difficult experiences years ago with the woman to whom he was engaged to be married, he had given up all hope of normality. But by trial and error he discovered he could make love without problems to women who were the mothers of several children.

'There is a natural enlargement, you understand,' he said to Suzette, who was struggling to stifle her laughter.

'My poor Blaise,' she said, astonished that so intelligent a man could be so innocent in respect of women's abilities. 'When you were younger you must have had a very restricted circle of friends.'

'It's true,' said he. 'I was brought up very strictly and was eighteen before I had a girlfriend. The most daring thing I ever did with her was to put a hand up her jumper while we kissed.'

'And your fiancée, what was she like?'

'A charming girl, the youngest daughter of a close friend of my parents. It was they, really, who arranged everything. But I was twenty-three and had been with a woman by then — though only a tart I picked up, outside the Gare du Nord. She was big and much older than me and things went very well — with the tart, I mean, not my fiancée. Naturally, I wanted to make love to Yvette just to make sure she and I could be happy together.'

'Well?'

'Disaster! An absolute disaster! She screamed and hit me in the face when I tried to put it in. Not that I was insensitive, I assure you. I went about it with the utmost care, knowing the problems involved. But she became hysterical and told me it was too big.'

'*Oh la la*! Such a fuss about a little lovemaking!' Suzette said with all the sympathy she could muster. 'Was that the end of the engagement to be married?'

'Yvette refused to speak to me again after that afternoon. We each told our parents some convenient lie or other and that was the end of it.

115

Since then any girlfriends I have had were all the mothers of two or three children. Not mine, of course. You understand what I mean.'

Suzette pushed him over on his back and took in hand the part in question. It was limp now, but even in a slack condition the thickness and weight were impressive. Though it had given her a most ravishing climax, she would not want to accommodate it too often. This enlargement Blaise spoke of might be acceptable to the husbands of women with several children, but it sounded as if it would be a disadvantage to herself in her dealings with future lovers.

One more time — that was all she would permit Blaise tonight. if that was inadequate for his desires, she would calm him by other means. In her hand she felt a thickening and a growing as he responded readily to her touch. She stared down in wonder to see the mighty head swell and uncover itself. The column of hot flesh in her palm hardened as it expanded.

'Suzette — there is something I must tell you.'

'What then?'

'I've fallen in love with you, *chérie*. I want to marry you. You are the only woman in the world for me!'

The thought was absurd of course and, worse, inconvenient. A tiny frown appeared for an instant on Suzette's forehead under her fringe of shiny black hair. She had brought him here for a night of romance and passion and the fool was talking of love and marriage!

'Perhaps we may talk about that in the morning,' she said, as her hand slid up and down Blaise's upstanding mightiness, 'but for now, lie still and let me see how big it will grow . . .'

ROBERT AND MADAME SASSINE

After two and a half days of Odette's company, besides the two nights between, Robert Dorville began to wonder if it had been entirely prudent to invite her to stay with him. It was just till she found employment, of course, but it was only now he understood that might take a long time.

Naturally, it was exciting to take her to bed. The nights had been spectacular, it had been necessary to remain in bed until midday to recover. And, in some pleasantly inexplicable way, he found himself making love to her on the sofa in the afternoons, Odette was so keen. But . . .

The problem was, it was much like being married, a condition Robert regarded as unnatural. For him, that was. For others it might be suitable. Certainly he was not pleased to be informed she intended to go to her friend's apartment that afternoon to collect all her belongings. That had a formidably permanent resonance to it. It introduced a sombre note into an enjoyably frivolous affair.

Apart from making love to her, he liked her, of course – liked her a lot. She had style and vivacity. In bed she was enthusiastic, in restaurants an appreciative companion, in the cinema a hand-gripping fan of movies Robert himself enjoyed, on café terraces a light-hearted chatterer who made time pass most agreeably.

But this plan to move in with him – only temporarily, as she insisted – disturbed Robert.

Naturally, now he had assumed some sort of responsibility for her, he couldn't just kick her out into the street, suitcase in her hand. He thought of offering her enough money for a week in a modest hotel and two meals a day, while she looked for a job. Instinct warned him she would burst into tears and make a scene of unpleasant proportions.

So he agreed to her suggestions with as good grace as he was able to manage and decided to visit his Papa. Even if Papa had no immediate work for Odette, perhaps he could be persuaded to telephone round his colleagues in the business and find out if anyone needed a model just then.

Odette suggested she go with him to talk to Monsieur Dorville Senior, but Robert shook his head and said it was better if he went on his own. Papa might take it in his head to invite him home for dinner with Maman, he said, and if it became very late while they were talking, he might stay the night there, in his old room.

So Odette was not to worry if she did not see him that night. He gave her a spare key to his apartment, enough money to buy food for a meal. What Odette thought of this rigmarole she kept to herself. Then with a kiss on her cheek, off he went.

Much as he liked Odette, he wanted a rest from her. And if he decided later on that he wanted to sleep alone, he was free now to do so. Apart from all that, Madame Sassine was in Paris. She had asked him to meet her that afternoon and the course of events afterwards was unforeseeable.

Their casual first meeting in the Folies Bergère audience was some months past. At the time, after he had recovered from her unexpected manipulation of his emotions in the dark, he had no intention of ever seeing her again. It was only a passing *event* he told

118

himself, a frustrated woman seizing the advantage when she found a good-looking man sitting next to her in a condition of sexual arousal. He laughed at himself and put the occurrence out of his mind.

But having dismissed her from his thoughts, next day he woke up thinking about her, in a state of high arousal. He therefore gave some consideration to *for* and *against*. This wasn't easy at all, mainly because he couldn't think what to put on the *against* side of the ledger. He knew precisely what was on the *for* side, of course, a fine-looking, big-breasted, very willing woman of exotic origin, waiting for him with her legs apart.

What hot-blooded young man could resist, when the proposition was put in those terms? Even though the beautiful Suzette was his girlfriend and she was more than willing to satisfy all his desires, It was well known a man needed variety. Tedium could ruin even the most devoted love-affair.

In consequence, it was with the very best of intentions that he made a telephone call to the Hotel George Cinq and asked for Madame Sassine's suite.

When she came on the line her voice was deep and sensual — he had only heard her whisper in the dark before this. She had a voice to thrill an imaginative man and it thrilled Robert. He felt it hinted at passion, dark and smouldering passion, furiously energetic love-making, impossible satisfactions.

Robert's nature was very romantic, of course. He explained that they had met at the Folies Bergère, where he had been seated on her right. A spontaneous little event had made itself evident, he said, an event that was charming and of a delicate intimacy. He hoped that Madame Sassine had not forgotten. By way of reply he heard a sigh of pleasure and this was followed by an order to present himself at her suite promptly at three o'clock.

There was, of course, a misunderstanding in the making. When Robert arrived at the appointed hour Madame Sassine opened the door herself and invited him into a very lavish suite. Robert kissed her hand. He was wondering why she was wearing an amber-coloured silk dressing-gown when a visitor was expected.

His intention was to take her for a saunter in the sunshine, as far as the Place du Trocadero perhaps, and sit with a drink on a café terrace.

They could talk about themselves to each other while admiring the Eiffel Tower on the opposite side of the Seine, that superb upthrusting emblem of French virility. A little later on, when the mood was right, maybe they would take a taxi to his apartment to resume the game they had played the evening before — the game she had instigated when she had put her hand between his legs.

But that was not the way of it at all. The instant the suite door was shut behind him, Madame Sassine took his arm and led him past a sitting-room with excellent reproduction Louis XV furniture into a large bedroom. Robert felt this was rushing things a little. He didn't even know her first name.

But then, he considered, Madame Sassine was a foreigner, from somewhere at the eastern end of the Mediterranean, lands of the olive and lemon, where the women are hot-blooded, demanding and darkly passionate.

And they were also businesslike, it seemed. She took a packet of new banknotes from her dressing-gown pocket and gave it to him with a pleasant smile. Then at last Robert realised Madame Sassine believed he was a gigolo she had picked up.

He handed the money back with a curt bow and a few words that informed her very clearly of her insulting mistake. He strode from the bedroom, hardly knowing whether to laugh or snort in indignation. She came trotting after him, fast on her feet for a lady of her plumpness, put a hand on his arm and pleaded with him to wait a minute, to give her a chance to apologise.

He refused, of course, his honour had been impugned and there could be no acceptable explanation, no possible words to wipe out the slur. He continued toward the door. At least, he fully meant to, as a matter of principle.

But he couldn't help noticing how Madame Sassine's amber silk dressing-gown had, in her agitation, opened a little on a pair of breasts of splendid proportion and a creamy-skinned texture. This was a sight to make Robert ask himself if she was wearing anything at all under her expensive-looking dressing-gown.

Besides, it was only reasonable to hear what she had to say — and to allow her to apologise to him. Perhaps her mistake was to some extent understandable, he had permitted her, after all, to take certain liberties in the darkness of the Folies Bergère performance. And in another half-minute he was seated on one of the excellent reproduction Louis XV sofas, while Madame Sassine poured him a glass of very good champagne.

She sat down beside him and they raised their glasses to each other and to a better understanding. Her tale was a sad one and Robert found it touching. During the telling she made no effort to close her silk dressing-gown. The reverse happened, for she used her hands to gesticulate a great deal while she spoke, those hands that had rings with gem-stones on all her fingers, the constant movement eased her dressing-gown further open.

Eventually her big soft breasts were almost entirely bared to Robert's gaze. And when she crossed her legs, the slippery silk fell away to uncover an extent of creamy-skinned thigh he found pleasantly distracting.

As he had guessed, she and her husband were from the Levant. Monsieur Sassine was a businessman of importance and this took him to Paris and Madrid and New York constantly. It was his custom to take Madame along with him. Not because he would miss her, alas, for she told Robert freely that Monsieur Sassine had an excessive interest in young girls these days, blonde girls for his preference. And not much above the age of sixteen, for choice. Much of his time in Paris and other cities was passed with girls of this type, when he was not lunching or dining with businessmen like himself. If he encountered a temporary lack of sixteen-year-old blonde girls he found it possible to make do with sixteen-year-old boys, so long as they too were blond.

In short, Madame Sassine was a neglected wife! Another man might have left her at home to look after the children while he jaunted from city to city in search of business deals, wealth, and a supply of willing sixteen-year-olds. But Madame Sassine's own family were important in their own right. And for this reason, to give no offence where he could derive profit, Sassine took her abroad with him. It was on the understanding she would pass her days shopping and sightseeing and not bother him too much or ask where he had been.

She was not yet forty, Ariane Sassine, and still attractive, but unfashionably plump. Her blood was hot, her urges strong. What could she do in these unfortunate circumstances, alas, except amuse herself with handsome young men? Not regular lovers, who would demand attention when it was inconvenient, but charming young men whose favours were readily available for cash.

Robert nodded sympathetically and said it was tragic so fine a woman should be forced to look for the type of man who sat around at big hotels, waiting for lonely ladies. He had himself observed them in action, these types, making flattering remarks they knew to be untrue – though in the case of Madame Sassine, he hastily added, the compliments would be true!

She accepted his words graciously and said it was interesting and remarkable that there were so many handsome men in Paris, young and able. How delighted she was to have the rare privilege of making the acquaintance of one who was not selling his services – namely Robert. She asked how he made his living and was quite impressed to hear he was a Director of a company making clothes for women.

And Robert responded by declaring himself delighted to meet a lady so charming and intelligent as Madame Sassine. She smiled and informed him her name was Ariane. To demonstrate to her how very privileged he felt, Robert pulled undone the bow that held her sash around her waist and the silk dressing-gown fell open.

His question was answered: Madame Sassine was wearing nothing at all, not even the tiniest knickers, not even a pair of silk stockings, under her dressing-gown.

Her big, beautiful plump body was fully exposed to Robert's eager gaze – all that creamy-white skin and those melon-sized breasts, her round belly and heavy thighs! Robert kissed the reddish-brown tips of her breasts, put his hand between her thighs and kissed her warm belly. In due course he let her lead him to the bedroom again and this time he stayed, there was no more talk of offended honour.

Since then they had met each time she had been in Paris with her husband. Robert had become genuinely fond of her and looked forward to her telephone calls announcing they had arrived that day and were, as always, at the Hotel George Cinq.

On that first occasion together Nature had seized control of the situation and they had made urgent and extensive use of the broad bed. Since then he had never made love to her in the hotel, he was nervous Monsieur Sassine might return unexpected and when he was least required. For this excellent reason Robert always took Ariane to his apartment.

That would not be possible today, of course, not with Odette staying there. But although Ariane assured him that her husband would not return for hours, even so he did not intend to take a risk. Once, two years before, Robert had been with a girlfriend when her husband turned up before he was expected. The row that followed was bitter and nasty, it had led to punches being thrown (though missing) on both sides. Never again!

When Ariane telephoned they arranged to meet at the Cafe de la Paix. That was within strolling distance of his apartment − rather too close, now the circumstances were changed. It was possible that Odette, left to her own devices, might go there to sit and watch the world go by for an hour.

Robert wished to annoy neither her nor Ariane, he enjoyed the company of both too much. He left a message at the Hotel George Cinq for Ariane, to say he would be at the Dome in Montparnasse at three.

That seemed far enough away from his apartment to be safe from an accidental sighting by Odette and any consequent tears and brouhaha.

He was also fairly certain there was little chance of running into Suzette at the Dome. But then, it seemed to him he had no chance of seeing her again anywhere. That was a pity, because he was half in love with Suzette and sad she had lost interest in him. Very sad, in fact, though he hid it from himself quite well and got between other women's thighs.

Broken hearts were very much out of fashion, even for such a romantic as Robert.

Ever since someone had told him that the Dome was a favourite spot for writers and intellectuals, Robert had entertained a good opinion of it. He hoped if he went there now and again he might himself be taken for an intellectual, he looked as intelligent as many. He might in consequence be approached by a beautiful young lady or two, with an interest in improving the mind. And, naturally, the body must be also considered.

So far nothing had happened. Robert was beginning to think he had been misled – he never recognised anyone at the café who he could categorise as an intellectual. Mostly they were men with beards and tweed jackets, smoking pipes. Their companions were all too often women who displayed no interest in grooming and a plain taste in clothes. Some of them wore spectacles. This made them of limited interest to Robert.

Even if it was true, as he remembered reading in a magazine, that Professor Jean-Paul Sartre discovered the Secret of Being, Life and the Universe sitting here on the Dome terrace with a small glass of Pernod, understanding this momentous secret did not seem to make his followers happy, to judge by the solemnity and plainness of their appearance at the café.

As far as Robert understood it from the magazine, Professor Sartre taught that there was no secret to teach. Life was completely without meaning, it seemed – we live, we die, that's it. Perhaps it was not to be wondered at if his disciples looked glum.

Ariane was at the Dome before him. He spotted her sitting at a table on the terrace, under the awning, looking magnificent. She was wearing a grey and sage-green silk frock and long black suede gloves. And a square hat that seemed to be made of black velvet and jet beads.

She bought clothes in every city she was taken to – Paris and Milan, Madrid and London, New York and Chicago. She seemed to believe them equally stylish if they were equally expensive. Robert had endeavoured to explain that Paris was the only possible place for a woman to buy clothes, but she had found it hard to grasp the logic of his argument.

She beamed at him when he reached her table, she offered her hand to be kissed. There was a glass in front of her and Robert ordered *fine à l'eau* for himself. They chatted as old friends, then she asked him why he changed the rendezvous and he explained she had been to the Café de la Paix before and he thought it of interest to her to see another part of Paris.

After an hour and two drinks Ariane began to exhibit signs of impatience. She touched Robert's hand, she smiled at him in her most sensual manner, she made her breasts roll under the silk of her frock. She was ready to move on, to Robert's apartment, and to his bed. And he had the problem of Odette.

'There is a small difficulty, *chérie*,' he lied, 'a water pipe has burst in my apartment and there are

126

workmen there to repair it. There will be days of cleaning up and drying out before it is inhabitable.'

Ariane shrugged and smiled insouciantly, her invitation even more manifest.

'There is no difficulty, Robert, we can go to the hotel.'

'No, I don't think so,' he said. 'You know my feelings about that — I could never submit so adorable a person as you to the shame and reproach if Monsieur Sassine found me there.'

'Then what do you suggest?'

'Something extraordinary — something to astonish you, Ariane. This *quartier* of Paris has many small hotels that offer rooms for a few hours without questions asked or passports and papers of identity being required. If we stroll through the Luxembourg Gardens towards the Boul-Mich, we shall find what we need.'

Ariane stared at him with immense accusation in her dark eyes, her full lips quivered before she could find words.

'You wish to take me to a place where common street-women go with men?' she said at last. 'Do you despise me so much? Am I a whore in your eyes?'

'No, no, no!' Robert said hastily. 'I adore you and respect you, dearest Ariane! I thought a little adventure into unknown Paris might amuse you — but I see now the idea was a little too bizarre. We shall say no more about it.'

'But I have a lot to say about it!' said she, indignant and determined to assert her right to speak out. 'You have insulted me, Robert, you have degraded me by your suggestion. If I were a man I would produce a revolver and shoot you dead.'

Robert had an uneasy feeling that she spoke the truth, those born in her country had a reputation for blood-feuds continuing for generations – and for hasty action with firearms and daggers in public places, when they considered their honour slighted.

He glanced uneasily at Ariane's handbag on the table, it was large and expensive, easily able to contain a weapon that might inflict a dreadful wound on him, or even kill him.

'But you are a woman,' he said in a winning tone, a look of admiration on his face, 'a beautiful and desirable woman, with a woman's heart to forgive a man so on fire to make love to her that he casts about for the nearest secluded place, without any thought for its reputation. Forgive my lack of care – it was my burning desire to undress you and kiss you from head to toe, to crush you in my arms and throw you down on your back . . .'

'Is this true, Robert?' she murmured, her eyes softening.

'Every word, I swear it!'

'You truly desire me so much?'

'With every fibre of my being!'

'You are hard?'

'Like an iron bar,' he said.

This was totally untrue. The apprehension he experienced had caused the part in question to shrink to its smallest between his thighs. In his mind there lurked an unnerving thought that Levantine ladies enraged might very well launch their attack at the most important male part. He remembered a dreadful story he had read in a newspaper, of an Egyptian lady who had dealt with an unfaithful lover by biting his length right off!

'I forgive you, *chéri*,' Ariane said, her face aglow with love and desire, or something similar. 'Quick, quick, pay the waiter and let's go! I too am on fire for your embrace!'

Robert slid a banknote under the saucer and led her, his arm linked with hers, from the Dome terrace and toward the nearest taxi stand. Her perfume was delicious, now he was close to her, waves of it wafting about her entire body — evidently she was a great contributor to the profits of the House of Chanel!

'Where are we going?' he asked.

'To the Hotel George Cinq, where else?' she said simply, and that was the end of the discussion.

On the pavement and in broad daylight she was unable to touch him. But as soon as they were in a taxi and speeding along the Boulevard du Montparnasse, she threw herself into his arms and thrust a questing hand under his elegant ice-blue jacket. While her red-painted mouth pressed hotly to his, she felt the front of his trousers, searching for the bulge.

She had his assurance he was stiff with desire — to discover otherwise would put an unpleasant strain on the reconciliation they had achieved. Robert was aware of her capacious handbag on the seat beside her, who could say what was hidden in it? To be murdered or maimed in a crime of passion, travelling in a taxi, seemed an absurd Fate.

Happily, he was ready for her intimate inspection. During the brief time they had walked from the café to the taxi stand, his arm in hers, he had put his other hand into his trouser pocket. Through the thin lining he had stimulated his dangling part with busy fingers. By the time they got into the taxi it was becoming stiff. He gave a final flick up and down as he sat close beside Ariane, his arm round her, waiting for her to check the truth of his words.

At the hotel they went straight into the bedroom of the empty suite. In a way Robert found impossible to explain to himself, the balance between them seemed to have changed. As he saw it, he was Ariane's lover and she respected him as such, being a man the initiative was his. But not today, not this afternoon, not at this moment, in the hotel suite bedroom.

She flung handbag and hat on to the dressing-table, wrenched his jacket off his shoulders and ripped open his trousers — all while he was standing between the door and the bed. She was on her knees in front of him, his stiff part half down her throat, her fingers circling his hairy pompoms.

'Ariane, Ariane . . .' he murmured, feeling his knees quake to the thrills of sensation running through him.

He took her head in his hands, meaning to pull her away from his hard-straining part and undress her, before easing her onto the bed. She pushed his hands away furiously and made a noise deep down in her throat. It was not precisely a growl but it was undoubtedly threatening.

She was treating him as a gigolo now, as if she paid him for his services and could do what she liked. When Robert realised this, objections rose up in his mind, his emotions revolted, he experienced anger and a sense of humiliation.

'No, no, no! I will not be treated like this!' he stammered out, and seized her head again, twining his fingers in her long and glossy dark hair.

Yet his nerves were responding to her assault, the lapping of her tongue on the uncovered head of his engulfed length and the forceful sucking of her mouth. Huge throbs of pleasure beat in every part of his body. He was swaying on his feet, his mind in a whirl, knowing he was being raped, so to speak and unable to stop it happening to him!

In this conflict of opposed emotions, neither he

nor she had, nor could they have in their state of
arousal, the detachment to recognise the element of
farce in what they were doing there in a hotel
bedroom. Ariane's busy fingers crept in between his
spread thighs, he felt her tickling between the cheeks
of his bottom, her fingertip pressing the knot of
muscle there.

'Ariane, no . . .' he sighed.

The crisis took him fiercely and his body jerked to
the gush of his desire into her mouth. Her face turned
up to stare at him in his extremity of ecstasy, her
cheeks flushed, her dark eyes gleaming with victory.
Robert sighed and squirmed as the throes of pleasure
faded away in his belly, aware that she had daunted
him and broken his will. She had asserted her
personality over his, things would never be the same
between them. That was his farcical interpretation of
what Ariane had done to him.

She got to her feet, leaving his sticky part hanging
out of his trousers, and she calmly removed her
elegant sage-green frock. Robert sat down limply on
a Louis XV chair by the bed, crushed in spirit by her
easy triumph over him. That was how he saw it, he
did not understand he had invited her assault.

She pulled her ivory silk slip over her head and
threw it on the floor and took off the sizeable
brassiere that supported her large soft breasts. When
she bent down to take off her silk stockings her
breasts swung free, almost prompting a flicker of
new interest in Robert.

She stood close to him while she pulled out her
hair-pins − the pearl-headed pins she always wore −
and let her long shiny hair cascade down onto her
shoulders. Robert sighed silently to himself, to
unloose Ariane's hair had aroused him every time he
had been with her. There was something enormously

sensual about freeing those soft hanks of hair from the pins and letting them fall like a curtain.

Sometimes in the past, when they were together in the bedroom of Robert's apartment, he found great pleasure in playing with her hair, running silky dark tresses between trembling fingers. To see her sitting naked, her creamy-skinned breasts uncovered for his eyes, to stroke her unpinned hair, Robert found this to be very exciting. Even now, though she had undone her own hair, not allowing him the privilege, it was still so sensual a sight for him that his dejected part twitched.

She was looking at him with a malicious glint in her eyes — or so it seemed to him. Without a word, she bent down to take off her black satin knickers, thrusting out her formidable bottom, letting her breasts hang and swing almost under Robert's nose. She threw the knickers into his face and his mind registered they had been drenched in Chanel 5 before she met him at the Dome.

In another moment she flung back the bed-cover and was lying on her back with her legs apart. Robert sat with her perfumed knickers in his hand, unable to speak a word. He was paralysed by the clash within him of indefinable emotions set in motion by Ariane's extraordinary stance toward him. He felt anger and despair, humiliation and resentment, foreboding and shame.

But staring at her as she lay naked, could it be there was a hint in his loins of a very familiar emotion? He meant never to have anything to do with her again. But was there a hint of excitement in his blood?

Ah, that creamy-white skin of hers — there was so much of it! To the tongue it was warm and smooth. To lick her from her throat to the cheeks of her bottom rendered hours of delight.

Those superb and powerful breasts, russet-tipped – they rose like the peaks of twin mountains to be conquered by an intrepid adventurer. Her broad and curving belly formed a platform to support a man while he burrowed into her innermost secrets!

And such thighs she had! So round and full and well-fleshed, satin-skinned and delicious to feel and to kiss! And, like her breasts, it was marvellous to slide his hard-standing part between them and mimic the action of making love!

All of Ariane's body, in its size and plumpness of flesh, was made for pleasure And there, between the thighs that were open for his gaze, there lay the ultimate delight, the secret altar itself: a bush of strong and crinkly hair that framed a pair of long pinkish lips. To the eye of affection they pouted forward in a promise of incredible pleasure!

'Why are you keeping me waiting, Robert?' she said sharply. 'Take your clothes off and come to me.'

That was how she spoke to the gigolos she brought into this bedroom, he thought bitterly. She hands them the money and they put it in their pocket – and she can tell them to do whatever she wants. *Get your clothes off, Jules. Kiss my breasts, Emile. Lie on my belly, Antoine. Put it in, Jean-Claude. Do it harder, Raoul. Do it to me again, Raymond.*

While these dark and rancorous thoughts were passing through Robert's mind, he was undressing. Ariane lay on her back at her ease, her feet well apart, her arms by her sides. Her head was turned on the pillow to watch his progress in taking off his clothes. Then he was naked. His knee was on the bed, he paused, uncertain of his new status, or how he should proceed.

In some extraordinary manner Ariane had put him

in the wrong. She had made him feel guilty — about what he couldn't begin to decide. She had increased his uneasiness almost to paranoia by raping him with her avid mouth. She had victimised him and had forced his subjection to her. Now he truly felt as if he was a gigolo, bought and paid for. He was not a person at all, merely a length of hard flesh to rub her itch and gratify her lusts.

Ariane gave him no choice in the matter. She reached up with both arms to take him round the neck and pull him down onto her broad belly, her mouth was hot in a clinging kiss of desire.

'I am yours, Robert,' she gasped, 'take me!'

Nothing could be less true, he thought, in a spate of anger. It was very obvious he was hers and it was she who was about to take him. But did it matter? The male part she had drained a few minutes ago was stiff again, she was holding it tightly and steering it up between her legs.

She drew in a long and shuddering breath as he slid deep into her, then threw herself heart and soul into the love-making. In seconds, before he had thrust into her slippery warmth not more than five or six times, she was gasping and panting in ecstatic orgasm.

'Yes, yes!' said Robert fiercely.

He was overjoyed she was at his mercy now. He thrust hard and fast, ravaging her tender flesh in his lust for revenge.

Ariane did all that her hot nature prompted. She writhed and she wriggled under him, she shrieked and clawed and bit. And it continued — it was not over in a matter of a few seconds! With her thighs raised and wide open, her whole body shaking to his savage thrusting, she grasped Robert hungrily.

He had excited himself beyond reason in inflicting

this long ordeal of pleasure on her, he stabbed his stiff part into her as if it were an assassin's dagger. Stimulated so immensely and for so long, Ariane's throes went on and on, until the powerful sensations became more than she could bear. With a last wailing shriek she fainted away and lay as if dead.

If she had truly died, there was no stopping Robert now.

'Take that! That! That! Bitch, bitch, bitch!' he screamed in a sexual frenzy, the violence of his thrusting made her limp body flop about beneath him, as if still aware of what he was doing to it and taking part in the ravishing.

There came a last shriek of triumph from Robert as he spurted his raging emotions into her, barely conscious himself of what he was at.

When calm returned to him at last he lay shaking and sweating on Ariane's belly. He saw her eyes were closed, her skin pale and he heard her breathing was shallow. In sudden terror he rolled off her limp body, to rush to the bathroom for water to splash her face and bring her round.

He sprinkled cold water on her forehead, brushing back the tousled dark hair. He sprinkled water on her wrists, where the pulse beat very faintly, between her great breasts and on their reddish-brown tips, hoping that the shock of sudden chill might bring her to. He ran back to the bathroom to refill the glass and splashed water on her soft belly and in her Chanel-scented groins.

To Robert in his panic it seemed a very long time before her dark-brown eyes slowly opened. She stared up at his face with a certain vagueness at first, collecting her thoughts. Her tongue licked out and found a drop of water at the corner of her mouth – and Robert raised her with an arm under her shoulders to hold the glass to her lips and let her drink from it.

She lay back again with a faint smile, her hand roaming over her belly to investigate the wetness there.

'Are you all right, Ariane?'

'That was stupendous,' she said softly.

She reached out to take hold of his limpness, she gave it an affectionate squeeze.

'You are a very good lover, Robert – outstanding! You made me undergo *the little death*, the climax so profound it takes away the senses and is like dying. In my country women go crazy over men who can do it for them. That was the first time I ever felt it.'

'You gave me a scare,' he said, deciding to take his leave as soon as she seemed fully recovered. 'I think you should sleep a little now.'

The wandering Monsieur Sassine might be on his way back even now, to bath and change for whatever entertainment he proposed for that evening.

'What an absurd idea!' said Ariane, reading Robert's thought in his eyes.

She tugged at his slack part, bringing him closer to her.

'He won't be back until late, if that's troubling you.'

'But suppose you're wrong?' he said.

She brushed aside his feeble evasion with a flicking gesture of the hand that was not gripping his rising part.

'Do it to me again, Robert,' she said. 'I refuse to let you leave me now I know what you can do. I must feel that fantastic sensation again. Lie on my belly and kiss me while I make you hard.'

SUZETTE SINGS CHEZ BOBO

Jacques-Charles suggested to Suzette she had a try-out, singing in one of the bars where he played the piano two nights a week. Naturally, she said it was impossible, she had no songs and no clothes to wear.

'Then sing stark naked,' he said with a grin, 'I guarantee it will get their attention. As for songs – you have all the songs ever sung by Piaf and Mistinguett – and every other singer that Paris has taken to its heart in the past fifty years.'

'They are not my style. You know that.'

'Yes, *ma chérie*, but while we are waiting for your own style to announce itself, it will be good experience to entertain an audience with songs they know and like, someone else's or not.'

In spite of her objections, Suzette had decided instantly she would seize this opportunity. But no beautiful woman agrees at once to anything a man suggests. First she says *definitely not*.

Then she raises his downcast spirit by saying *perhaps* – and a man of intelligence knows that he has taken a huge step toward whatever his goal may be. After a while she says *if you insist*. In the end she smiles and says *yes, of course*.

Knowing this, only a fool expects to travel all the way from *non* to *oui* without passing through the intervening stages.

As for this matter of clothes, Jacques-Charles advised her to be prudent, to dress very simply for the place he intended to take her. Simply, she demanded? What did he mean by that? She should dress drably, was that it? A dark pullover and a thick woollen skirt? Black cotton stockings and flat-heeled shoes?

This discussion between them was conducted while she lay on the scruffy bed in Jacques-Charles room. At the end of a lesson he took his reward by adoring her beautiful body to orgasm and solacing his bounding part with a few strokes of his hand. That was all it took to make him spurt, he was so aroused by staring at her naked body.

Suzette was lying contentedly on the divan, her emotions were tranquil. But this placid frame of mind disappeared instantly at his suggestion. She sat up, her breasts swaying exquisitely to the gestures with which she emphasised her words.

When they had progressed from *absolutely not* to *well, yes* they quarrelled over which songs to sing, as might be expected. And when that was eventually agreed, he asked her to be there next day at three to rehearse the programme.

Only a few hours after the rehearsal, her debut as a singer would take place! Suzette found the thought breath-taking.

'On stage with my clothes on, for the first time,' she said.

The miserable bar Jacques-Charles had chosen as the scene of Suzette's first public appearance as a *chanteuse* was located up a Montmartre backstreet, a place no tourist ever found. Called Chez Bobo, it was no more than a dingy cellar under a crumbling building.

Its first use had surely been to store bundles of firewood or discarded ironmongery. A few dim electric light bulbs had been strung round the walls and ramshackle little tables and chairs set out for the customers. A zinc-topped bar and a small stage made of loose and unswept planking completed the amenities.

The piano was shamefully ancient, some of keys had lost their ivory and what remained was cracked. As for veneer, much of it had gone a long time ago. On the nights Jacques-Charles did not play, an accordionist squeezed well-known tunes out of a wheezy old box.

A man who played drums maladroitly was there at times, though his attendance was unpredictable. Some evenings he accompanied the piano on his worn-out drums, to the annoyance of Jacques-Charles. On other evenings he forced his accompaniment on the accordionist, who was normally too far gone in drink to care.

Not that it mattered to the regular clientele, who paid very little attention to the music anyway. They drank cheap spirits and even cheaper red wine, in formidable quantities, and if the profit on that seemed little enough to provide Bobo with enough to live on, it was generally believed he had a ten-percent arrangement with tarts coming into his bar to find customers.

Needless to say, Bobo did not propose to pay Suzette for her appearance on his splintered platform. He agreed she could sing when Jacques-Charles suggested it but, far from offering a fee, he was insistent the pianist ought to pay her himself.

'She's your girlfriend, not mine,' he said. 'Pay her in bed or pay her cash, that's up to you, Jacques-Charles.'

Ah, how very happy Jacques-Charles would have been if Suzette had been his girlfriend! The afternoons she came for a singing lesson and let him make love to her in his curious way were the high points in his life. He was madly in love with her. The joy of hearing her voice and of looking at her − this was a sacred rite for him.

When she took off her clothes and let him see her naked, let him gaze at her marvellous body − it was like getting drunk on finest cognac! After she came for a lesson, he was in a state of grace for the rest of the day, lying on the bed she had lain on. Although he was as sober as a lawyer, the visions in his head whirled around like a fairground carousel.

Next day, alas, the hangover was just as evil as one brought on by alcohol. Worse, because it was a nagging pain within the heart, not the head, and aspirin was useless against it. He was like a drug-addict, existing from one fix to the next, waiting in anguish for Suzette to come to his room again.

For her first appearance as a singer, it goes without saying Jacques-Charles chose the only night of the week the Folies Bergère was closed. When the rehearsal in his room ended, there was no curious love-making that day, he was just as nervous as she, though hiding it well. He cooked an omelette and they shared it with a bottle of good wine, then he made her rest for an hour.

They arrived at Chez Bobo at eight, when he was due to start playing the piano. Suzette gazed round in horrified disbelief at the rat-den in which her career as an international star was in theory to be launched. She was introduced to Bobo and this did nothing to improve her opinion. He was a fat, sweaty and small-eyed gangsterish-looking type, with rolled-up sleeves and badly stained trousers.

But her friends were there to give their support, which made her feel a little more cheerful. Gaby was there, naturally, and Blaise. He was wearing a suit like a banker, even though she had warned him not to. If he was robbed and assassinated — this Fate seemed probable in such dire surroundings — then responsibility must be his alone.

A few friends had turned up from the Folies Bergère, but not too many, because Suzette didn't want everyone laughing at her if things were wrong. There was Angelique and she had brought her awkward boyfriend, Jean-Pierre.

There were two of the other show-girls — Jasmin and Yvette — they being on good terms with Suzette. And Francine, who looked as happy as a young bride with her Hungarian juggler, Sandor. He had a contented look about him too, evidently their *affaire-du-coeur* was developing to the satisfaction of both. Of Gilles the dancer there was fortunately no sign.

The whole contingent of supporters sat together, three little tables had been pushed close for them. In their bright clothes, except for Blaise, and in their chatter and laughter, they were set apart from the down-at-heel and morose customers at other tables.

The arrival of new business in Suzette's wake put a gleam of greed in Bobo's watery eyes and this explained his polite greeting to her. Polite for him, that is. She did not know it, but a more customary approach of his to women entering his bar was to ask them to step into the kitchen with him, for a quick bang up against the wall.

Blaise was buying drinks for the whole party and no one was bothering to keep a tally, except Bobo and his barman, and they intended to multiply the eventual bill by ten at least. But what of that? All the party were enjoying themselves and Blaise in particular, to find himself in the company of so many lovelies. All were being nice to him for the sake of Suzette. A handful of francs more or less had no significance for him.

Jacques-Charles was seated at the disgraceful piano on stage, wearing the light brown suit that in the daytime hung on a wire coat-hanger behind the door of his hovel. What could one say? It was respectable enough in its way and still clean, but so old that surely he had bought it before the war.

His hair was brushed back to lend emphasis to his great dome of a forehead. The impression of a professor having a night out was marred by the drooping cigarette in the corner of his mouth and the smear of ash down his jacket. His hands ran along the keyboard and anyone who was listening, if there were any, knew at once the pianist was a man of true talent.

The drums were there on the stage but the drummer was absent — and for an excellent reason. Jacques-Charles had bribed him — he got rid of him for the evening by a simple ruse, he gave him the price of a cheap tart. It would have been cruel to expect Suzette's singing to compete with a madman thumping to a rhythm of his own.

A ripple along the keyboard, a greeting of *Bonsoir, Mesdames et Messieurs* from Jacques-Charles and the night's entertainment began. No one paid attention to his greeting and it would have surprised him if anyone did. He played two or three well-known tunes, nothing requiring effort, to settle the audience into a proper state of mind before Suzette came on.

She was sitting among her friends, at the side of Blaise, who was trying to reassure her with well-chosen words. She sipped a little cognac from his glass and prepared herself mentally for her debut. From the depths of Bobo's dirty cellar to the height of the Olympia music-hall was an unattainable distance but, as the proverb says, every journey starts with one step.

It goes without saying her clothes were by no means as dowdy as Jacques-Charles had mockingly suggested, but she had dressed with restraint. There was no use distracting the cellar-rats of Chez Bobo with anything stylish, she considered. She wore a silk blouse in banana-yellow that went well with her black hair, and a grey linen skirt fitting closely enough to show off the shape of her bottom.

Jacques-Charles seemed to have been playing for only a minute or two, yet he was already announcing her – to the applause and cheers of her friends. And, she noted with a shudder of dread, to the apparent indifference of everyone else in the bar!

'Welcome Mademoiselle Suzette,' he was saying, 'a new singer who will be a star one day soon.' He told them they were fortunate to have this opportunity to hear her – that the time would arrive when they would stand in a queue to buy a ticket to hear her sing! Never in his years on the Paris musical scene had he ever once encountered so enchanting a singer and so enchanting a voice.

And so on, as is customary on occasions of this sort. Around the room conversations continued undisturbed, eyes stared dully into glasses of wine, tarts rubbed their hands on the thighs of possible customers to interest them.

Praise her as Jacques-Charles might, the moment arrived when Suzette had to stand beside him at the piano and perform. Gaby led the applause, strongly backed by Blaise, Angelique and Jasmin, and the Hungarian juggler put two fingers in his mouth and whistled in loud and sustained encouragement.

Naturally, there was no spotlight to illuminate the

singer, only a naked light bulb dangling on a dusty wire above the so-called stage. Jacques-Charles took a swallow from the glass of pastis standing on top of his rickety piano.

'Nice and easy,' he said to Suzette in an undertone, fingers poised over the cracked keys, 'just glide through it while you warm up.'

She began with '*La vie en rose*', pitching her voice carefully, not overdoing the emotion, but giving enough to carry the song. It needed concentration, this singing, it wasn't possible just to glide along. Jacques-Charles knew that very well. He said it to give her confidence.

Suzette had confidence, of course. Anyone who appears more or less naked on stage six nights a week must have confidence. But her confidence resided in her power to enchant with her body, a very different thing from belief in her ability to get and hold attention with her voice. But she did not lack courage and she sang three songs very prettily.

She was looking for someone in the audience to sing to, that being the advice Jacques-Charles had given. 'Make it personal,' he had said, 'pick someone and sing to him, sing with emotion, as if he were your lover. After a while, pick another. Make everyone feel you are pouring out your emotions solely for *him*.'

She could sing to Blaise, of course, but that seemed to miss the point, he was her lover. It was too easy. And besides, she didn't want him to misunderstand and begin to babble of eternal love and marriage again, as he tended to. There was no time to be involved in domestic bliss if she was to become a star.

She needed to find someone else to sing to. It was not easy, the cellar was so dim the customers were only shadows beyond the first few tables. Perhaps it was as well, those she could make out were unpromising, with bleary eyes, sagging faces, unshaven chins and cheap clothes! It required a superhuman endeavour to address words of love and longing to specimens of this type.

There was one possible, sitting at a table near the wall on his own, a dark-haired man of not more than twenty. He appeared to be very slender inside his roll-neck pullover and dark jacket. Suzette thought he might be a sailor from a motor-barge — the fleet bringing cargo up the Seine from the Rouen docks.

He had a sensitive face, at odds with his rough clothes, and large dark eyes that never wavered for a moment from Suzette's face. She sang to him and he responded to her — with open adoration! It reminded her of lying on the tatty divan in Jacques-Charles' room, undressed and accepting the adoration he felt. And revelling in his burning glance that seemed to penetrate her.

So much so that she was glad to have her clothes on while she was singing Between those ardent eyes and her beautiful body were layers of protection — thin, fragile silk and satin, it was true, but a guard against ravishing eyes. The dark-haired man over by the wall — the intensity of his gaze made Suzette quite sure he was stiff inside his trousers and that made her smile.

Jacques-Charles had caught some tiny change in her voice and recognised it, he stared round at the audience balefully while he played, seeking for the source of her sudden emotion.

Naturally, he spotted the dark-haired man staring at Suzette. He recognised that stare, it was a facsimile of his own burning stare when she undressed for him. With jealousy in his heart he glared at the interloper, fully prepared to kill him. But to no avail, the other man had no eyes but for Suzette and he didn't even notice he had incurred the pianist's anger.

It was during '*Paris je t'aime toujours*' that a quarrel began between some of the Chez Bobo habituals. A man who looked like a battered prize-fighter threw the dregs of a glass of red wine into another man's face. The aggrieved person stood up and took him by the throat. The table next to theirs was kicked over in the squabble, with a crash of breaking glass. Loud shouts arose from those whose drinks were spilled, cries of anger and abuse, threats to join in the fight.

Suzette fell silent, staring wide-eyed at the apparent murder being committed almost within arm's-length in the cellar. The person being strangled was retaliating by kneeing his murderer between the legs, causing him to howl, but not to release his death-grip.

Jacques-Charles had seen all this before, and worse. He took no notice, but played on resolutely.

'Sing, *chérie*,' he said to Suzette. 'It will soon end.'

Bobo spat on the floor and came out from behind the bar, fat, ugly, wrathful, evil-eyed and aggressive. He had a short way of it with malcontents, he grabbed each combatant by an ear and he cracked their heads together.

'*Voilà*!' said Jacques-Charles. 'That settles it.'

Bobo dropped the brawlers over their table, they lay slumped and moaning, only half-conscious. He waddled back to the bar, giving Suzette a truly hideous leer in passing and spoke to her in his customary hoarse shout.

'Get on with it, girlie, don't let this riffraff put you off. Come and see me in the kitchen when you've done. I'll give you something special.'

By a superior effort of will, she picked up the

thread of the song again and finished it. Her friends applauded noisily and enthusiastically, but from the rest of the audience came a response that was muted — a solitary clap or two and a hand smacked onto a table-top. The man in the roll-neck pullover didn't applaud, he sat staring at Suzette as if dazed.

Before Jacques-Charles could start to play again, she touched his shoulder and said she must have a moment to recover. Those lustrous brown eyes of his gazed up at her in adoration and he nodded. He launched into his usual repertoire of tunes and she went to sit with her friends. To steady her courage, she accepted a glass of cognac pressed on her by Blaise.

He had a bottle of doubtful cognac from the bar on the table before him, and champagne bottles, it being beyond the ability of the barman to keep pace by the glass.

'We must leave here at once,' he said to Suzette, patting her knee in sympathy. 'It is monstrous to think of you wasting your talent in this pig-sty of a place. Your singing teacher must be out of his mind to bring you here. Finish the glass and I will take you away.'

To be truthful, Suzette was tempted to accept his advice. She hoped for better on her first outing, a modest triumph at least — not this indifference from strangers. But she guessed that if she ran away now, she might not have the courage to sing again elsewhere and to a different audience.

A hand rested heavily on her shoulder from someone who stood behind her chair. She glanced round and up and saw it was one of the tarts. She was a heavily built woman of at least forty, thickly made-up with orange face-powder over her wrinkles and crimson lipstick. The vast bosom inside her dark-red pullover hung over Suzette like a sagging balcony.

She had a man in tow — a thin stick of a man with a moustache and not much hair. He was dressed fairly shabbily, like a clerk with a wife and family and too small a salary to support them. Evidently the tubby tart was taking him to the nearest flea-bag hotel to relieve him of his anxieties.

'Give it up, girl,' she said in a friendly manner to Suzette, wafting a smell of liquor over her, 'you'll never make a living singing. Stick to what the good Lord gave you — you won't ever go hungry while you've got that between your legs.'

'And why won't I be a singer?' Suzette demanded, insulted by the criticism of her performance.

'You haven't got the voice. You've got to be able to belt it out and half-deafen them, that's what they like. You'll never do it, though you've got the chest for it.'

'That's not the only way!'

'Right you are, girl — there's a better way, and it's a lot easier. On your back, five minutes work and money in your hand. You stick to that and you won't go far wrong.'

The indignity of being taken for a tart took Suzette's breath away for a moment or two. Blaise looked shocked. Gaby burst out laughing and Suzette joined in.

'Thank you for the advice,' she said to the tart, who looked puzzled by the hilarity. 'You do it your way, auntie, and leave me to do it mine.'

'Please yourself,' she said with a shrug, and gathered in her patient customer with a arm like a leg of mutton. 'If you don't want that nice-looking man you're drinking with, I'll have him as soon as I get back.'

Off she went, leaving Blaise goggle-eyed in

indignation, and everyone round the table laughing at him.

'The voice of a true critic,' said Suzette acidly. 'I'll give it one more try.'

Jacques-Charles was playing '*Printemps*', no one was listening. Before Suzette could go back on stage to sing again, there was an altercation near the bar. The origin of it was obscured in darkness and billowing cigarette smoke, but a bellow from Bobo attracted general attention. A thin tart in a white raincoat stood with an elbow on the bar.

Bobo leaned over to give her a punch in the ear that knocked her to the floor. The pimp standing next to her was too scared to protest, he turned on his heel and left in a hurry.

'What was that about?' Blaise asked, twisting his neck to peer into the dimness. He sounded a little drunk.

'*Merde*!' said Suzette in dismay. 'This place is incredible I must have fresh air before I sing again.'

He wanted to go with her, but she preferred to be alone for a few moments. Out in the narrow street it was dark and deserted, only a street-lamp on the wall down at the corner shedding any light. Suzette walked slowly along the cobblestones – there was no pavement in so narrow an alley. She was not going anywhere, merely giving her eyes and her lungs a rest from the thick fug down in Bobo's death-trap.

'Mademoiselle!' a voice called behind her.

It was a man's voice, a young man's voice, well-spoken, polite. She turned and saw it was the man in the roll-neck pullover three steps behind her – evidently he had followed her.

'You are beautiful,' he said. 'You sing like an angel.'

'Tell me your name.'

'Michel.'

He took her arm gently, seeming hardly able to believe he was speaking to her face-to-face.

'Where are you from, Michel?'

'Fécamp. I am a student.'

He led her in the direction away from the street-lamp, going further into the warren of narrow and twisting lanes that were the old original Montmartre. She went along willingly, pleased to be with the one stranger who had responded to her singing.

There was a dark doorway with a broken stone step — he pushed her carefully into a corner of it and stood close. He had long eyelashes like a girl, Suzette noted, and full lips. But there was nothing girlish about the way he kissed her, with his hands over her breasts.

His touch made her tingle with desire and sway just a little. He held her face and tilted her head back while he kissed her throat. Then his hand was under her skirt, up between her legs. For so slender a man he was stronger than a casual glance might suggest, he gripped Suzette between the thighs with a strength that melted her heart completely.

He kissed her again, his other hand behind her as support, he bent her over backwards, his strong grip between her legs never relaxing. She was aroused and felt herself becoming wet, so wet he felt her moisture on his palm, through her thin underwear.

He gripped her tighter still, his mouth crushing down on hers until she felt she was floating in space, far removed from the world, floating through a cotton-wool cloud that cut off vision and deadened all sound from elsewhere. She felt she had entered a state of Nirvana, her breathing suspended, her heart beating faintly, distantly.

She did not hear footsteps coming closer on the

cobbles and Michel disregarded them. Out of the gloom a man approached, his face a blur under the brim of his hat. He glanced into the doorway and saw the couple hugging each other. His interest was clear, he stared hard at them, thinking his thoughts, wishing himself in Michel's place.

But he kept moving, though his pace slowed when he came level with the doorway. In the narrow lane he could have reached out and touched Suzette's face as he went by, but with a last long look over his shoulder he continued on down the street, toward the distant lamp.

Of all this Suzette knew nothing — her awareness was between her thighs, concentrated on Michel's grip there. He held tight, held her secure, declared his possession of her with that grasp more than if his male part had been inside her.

Suzette could feel an orgasm was racing toward her like a big saloon car about to run her down. She was pinned to the wall by its bright yellow headlights, trembling and mesmerised while it accelerated at her. Her belly shook, her breath was hoarse in her throat, she was flung headfirst into ecstasy.

'Mademoiselle . . .' Michel murmured, *'je t'aime.'*

He reached with both hands under her thin linen skirt to pull down her knickers. He took them off and held them flat between his palms to feel how wet they were from her excitement. He put them in his coat pocket, he felt up her legs again. She sighed to feel his warm hands clasp the bare cheeks of her bottom and test between his fingers their superb texture. He stroked those cheeks lovingly, his palms sliding over the smooth flesh.

Suzette wanted him inside her, she was ready for him, she was slippery with desire, her belly was

quivering to feel him push into her. She hoisted her
skirt up to show him the smooth-shaven petals that
lay between her thighs.

'Mademoiselle . . .' he sighed, and dropped on
one knee on the stone step to kiss them. Finding them
smooth-shaven and bare to his lips caused no
reaction, as it usually did with men. Perhaps he was
too dazed by his good fortune to even notice!

But that was all he did, kiss her soft petals. Suzette
waited impatiently to feel his tongue press its way
inside to find her little bud, but other than a
respectful kiss, nothing happened.

Was he hard inside his trousers? she asked herself.
How could he not be, after what he had done to her?
Did he want her? She took his shoulders and urged
him to stand up. She felt with trembling fingers the
front of his rough trousers.

Yes, there was an interesting hardness there! She
sighed in relief at this discovery, just as Michel
pressed his mouth hard to hers in a determined kiss.
In a moment she had his trousers undone and his stiff
length of flesh in her hand, rubbing it to make it
grow bigger yet.

He reached down to grip the hem of her skirt with
both hands and raise it to her waist. Suzette rested
her back against the wall of the doorway and moved
her feet apart on the stone step. She guided him
between her parted thighs as he bent his knees for a
second, then straightened them to push up inside her.

He was not as over-endowed as Blaise, this Michel
who called himself a student. He slid easily into her,
without the threat of *enlargement*, without giving
Suzette a feeling she was being filled too full. Yet it
was delicious, his strength inside her.

His belly was pressed close to hers, his tongue was
between her lips, he made fast little thrusts below,

using his hips to slide his hardness within her. Suzette closed her eyes, she had forgotten where she was, in a dark little street, standing in a doorway, in full sight of anyone who chanced to pass by. In her belly she felt the exquisite throbs of fast-approaching ecstasy and there was no room in her mind for any other consideration.

At the moment of crisis she opened her beautiful eyes to look into Michel's long sensitive face – and dark as it was, she saw there an expression of mute adoration. Her wet tongue slid into his open mouth and she dissolved into a long orgasm. Her throes tipped Michel into ecstasy with her, he spurted furiously, his hands up inside her silk blouse to grasp her breasts.

When he had finished, she eased herself off his impaling part and kissed his cheek.

'*Au revoir*, Michel, I must go now.'

'But why?' he stammered, sounding very young and hurt. 'Stay with me! *Je t'aime*, mademoiselle.'

'I have to go back and sing. Walk with me to the door, but do not come in with me.'

They parted with a kiss at the entrance to Chez Bobo. Suzette picked her way through the gloom and litter and cigarette smoke to the stage. Jacques-Charles was playing a sad little melody she did not recognise, in keeping with his mood. She smiled at him, her confidence restored, and he played for her to sing.

It was ridiculous, she thought with a secret smile, absurd to an unimaginable degree, to stand in a doorway, back against a wall, for a complete stranger! But how marvellous it had been, what exquisite sensations she had experienced when he pushed up her and spurted hard!

If Jacques-Charles even guessed, he would be

enraged. The thought of a younger man casually taking what he himself longed for with all his heart but could only worship with kisses! It was sad, of course, and very comic. Poor Jacques-Charles!

She was well into the song, '*Si tu m'aimes*', before remembering her knickers were in Michel's pocket. Her sudden little laugh disrupted the song for a moment but then she continued, better than before.

ODETTE FINDS A JOB

Odette Charron had early on discovered that
modelling ready-to-wear clothes for manufacturers
was reasonably well paid, though continuity of
employment was haphazard. But in her eyes a worse
disadvantage was the sad lack of glamour and high-
life. Not for her the catwalk at Dior or Chanel, to be
studied, admired, and envied by very rich ladies,
twittering to gigolo escorts.

Nor could she hope for recognition by writers of
the world's fashion press, sipping free champagne
under their absurdly big hats. The shows in which she
was the star usually took place in draughty
showrooms attached to factories and her audience
were the highly critical buyers for wholesalers or
provincial stores.

She had another occasional source of income, in
modelling for artists. Not the type who paint nude
portraits for sale through galleries, but commercial
artists drawing for magazines. And as nothing much
happened after Robert talked to his father, Odette
paid a visit to the agency who sometimes found her
work.

She had given them Robert's telephone number to
call if there was a job for her, but only discouraging
silence followed.

However, everyone's bad luck changes eventually
and this turned out to be Odette's day. In the agency
office up three flights of stairs Madame Drouet
greeted her warmly. She said she was at her wits' end

— she was desperately afraid she was losing a most important account, because the model booked for the job had not arrived.

Her frantic call to the model's apartment revealed — horror of horrors! — she had run away with a married man to Corsica.

Or so said a disgruntled male voice on the telephone — and it was the voice of the man with whom Annette had shared her life for eight months past. But the uncertainties of Annette's loves held no interest for the client, who naturally was furious at the delay to his important work. And every other model on the agency list was out on assignment!

'Then why did you not telephone me, madame?' Odette demanded in a voice indicating her displeasure at being overlooked.

Madame Drouet explained that this particular artist asked for underwear models. She rolled her eyes upwards to suggest a less innocent significance to her words.

'He is a *voyeur*?' Odette asked. 'A molester? A rapist?'

'Who can say? Annette never gave me a straight answer when I asked her. But she never complained so, whatever he wanted, she did not find it offensive. I know you have never done underwear modelling before, Odette, but if you take on this job, you'd be saving my life.'

'Does he pay well, whoever he is?'

'His name is Laurent Breville and he pays top rates. For that he demands exceptionally pretty models.'

'Then obviously it is me he requires.'

Less than half an hour later Odette was in the studio of this Laurent Breville, a large and pleasant room with big windows in his apartment off the

Boulevard Edgar-Quinet. About the walls were cork-
boards to which were pinned pictures — samples of
his work. They were all watercolours done in a
sketchy and slapdash impressionist technique of
women in high-fashion lingerie.

Odette noted he paid little attention to his models'
faces, a dab of red for the mouth, two dots for
nostrils a line or two where the eyes should be. But
the style and colour of the hair were carefully
painted, that formed part of the overall effect which
was to focus the eye on the garments.

Breville was not quite what she expected — though
she was not sure just what she had expected. From
the hints and nudges of Madame Drouet she had
pictured Breville as a middle-aged pervert, a leerer, a
slobbering lecher, with piggy little eyes and no hair
on his head. An ogre drooling over pretty young
models posing in Givenchy knickers!

In fact he could hardly be thirty, a tall and slender
man with a faintly annoyed expression. He wore an
expensive pullover with a pink silk scarf knotted
loosely round his throat and elegant trousers of dove-
grey flannel. His appearance and the apartment
suggested a man doing well for himself. No
struggling artist in a miserable attic here, not at all,
this Breville evidently had money in the bank!

He looked Odette up and down in a professional
way.

'Well, you've got a model's long body and legs,' he
admitted at last, 'a neat backside and not too much
bosom. You'll do for now, if Annette really has
disappeared. I have to complete this job by
tomorrow, so I haven't much choice. It's for *Vogue*.'

It was not the most flattering greeting Odette had
received, but at least it meant she was working again.
She smiled at him and asked if he made many

drawings for *Vogue*. All the time, he said, waving an arm at the water-colour sketches pinned round the walls. And also for *Harpers Bazaar* and most of the other important magazines.

'I thought they used photographs,' said Odette.

'That too, but photographs are expensive to set up, and also expensive to print,' said he, as if everyone understood that.

'Besides, the camera is merciless,' he went on. 'It shows the imperfections that are better not seen. For example, when it is a question of a range of garments like underwear, it is more effective to commission me to produce colour sketches.'

'And your speciality is women's underwear?' Odette asked.

'I am the expert!' he answered with pride. 'In the whole of Paris I am regarded as the top artist for underwear. The great designers and makers turn to me for beautiful pictures of their latest creations.'

Odette thought he was about to be carried away and deliver a long speech in praise of himself and his genius but he glanced at a heavy gold wristwatch, shook it hard and looked at the dial again. In an irritated way he said the morning was already half over. Odette took the hint at once and asked how he wanted to begin.

'The garments they sent round are over there on the chaise-longue,' he said. 'We'll start with the slip, I think. You can undress behind the screen. Please hurry up.'

The chaise-longue was an elaborate piece of furniture, gilded and carved, all pale pink velvet and richly polished dark wood. It was the sort of thing that was far too fancy for anyone's house but the mistress of a vulgar scrap-metal millionaire, but it

was exactly right for a film-set or as a prop for
fashion sketches.

On it, in layers of rustling tissue-paper, lay
matching sets of underwear in different colours —
slips, knickers, brassieres, foundation garments. She
enquired which he wanted first and he told her the
blue. She took the blue set behind the screen and
began to undress.

The screen was another extraordinary piece,
antique-looking, foreign-looking, valuable-looking.
it was made of red leather, mother-of-pearl and
polished brass, with hand-painted peacocks. Not
even the greatest expert could have put a date and
place of origin to it. It was fake, of course, theatrical,
absurd, made for show. In Breville's studio it looked
just right.

Behind this magnificent screen was a small gilt
chair, and Odette draped her clothes on it as she took
them off. She was not sure what was usual on these
occasions and called to the artist over the screen.

'Do you want me to keep my own underwear on
under the slip or wear the set that goes with it?'

'The set, of course,' he said crossly. 'I've no time
to waste while you keep darting behind the screen to
change knickers.'

She stripped completely naked and put on the set
— Breville had called it blue but the word didn't do it
justice. The blue was an intense sapphire and, by
contrast, it made her flesh glow like alabaster. The
slip was high-waisted and knee-length, with a deep
edging of lace. Under it the knickers were flimsily
chic, with more lace, the brassiere was a wisp of silk-
satin in the same astonishing blue.

Odette ran a comb through her hair and checked
her lipstick in a tiny mirror in her handbag, not that

Breville cared if she had make-up or not as he ignored faces in his work. But she felt better when she looked good. She stepped bare-foot from behind the screen, the uncovered wooden floor hard and unyielding.

Breville was sitting on a high stool with his knees up, feet on the cross-stave, behind a large drawing-board that swivelled from upright to horizontal. He had arranged it at the angle he preferred, sloping down towards him, but not too much for water colours run very easily. His head and shoulders were visible to Odette above the top edge and his feet below the bottom. He had pinned a large sheet of paper to the board and was impatient to make a start.

He had evidently thought out how he wished her to pose.

'Stand sideways to me,' he said, 'your feet well apart, as if you are walking toward the door over there. Good, now turn half toward me, keeping your feet where they are. A little more. Now put your arms up as if you're holding a mirror and are brushing your hair. That's it! Stay like that.'

He worked very quickly, dashing down an outline in charcoal, then dragging brushfuls of water colour across the thick paper. In twenty-five minutes he produced five sketches of her wearing the beautiful sapphire-blue slip. Four showed her standing, to display the slip's long and graceful line, and for the other he asked her to sit on the chaise-longue sideways, with her knees up and her arms round them.

He worked in silence, this Laurent Breville, not like some of the artists she modelled for who liked to chat as they daubed. Odette spent the time mainly in admiring herself. The blue slip was exactly the style of thing she ought to wear every day — it represented the chic and luxury she knew she deserved.

Her skin looked gorgeous beside it. And the way it hugged the line of her thighs was very flattering. She needed to make the acquaintance of a man able to provide her with the clothes and jewels that would set off her looks, who would take her to the fashionable restaurants and install her in an apartment in a good part of Paris.

She liked Robert Dorville and was appreciative of what he was doing for her. It was three weeks now since she had moved into Robert's apartment and shared his bed. He took her to eat in pleasant little restaurants and to cinemas and dancing. In bed at night he overwhelmed her with pleasure. She had never before had so many marvellous orgasms in so few days!

But Robert was never going to fall in love with her and give her all the luxurious things she wanted. Not even if he could afford them, which she doubted — at least not while his Papa ran the business. And there was a bigger stumbling-block. Robert, she had discovered, was more than half in love with a show-girl.

Her name was Suzette and there was a photograph of her hidden at the bottom of a drawer, underneath Robert's shirts. Although the *affaire* was at an end and he had never once mentioned it, Robert still had strong feelings for Suzette, it seemed.

Meanwhile, the speedy success of Breville's endeavours at his drawing-board much improved his temper. He smiled at his work, though not at his model. At least he sounded affable when he said he was ready to move on to the next pose, and asked her to take off the slip.

Odette didn't retire behind the screen for this, not after he had complained earlier about wasting time.

She eased the slip over her head and draped it over the screen, shook out her hair and turned to face him, her long slender body clad only in the sapphire-blue knickers and brassiere.

'How do you want me?' she asked.

Breville was occupied with drawing-pins and sheets of paper, he spoke without looking at her.

'Start on the chaise-longue,' he said, 'an elbow on the back and one knee up − a very casual pose.'

Odette did as he said. After five or six minutes had passed she turned her head to see how he was getting on and if he was ready for a new position yet. He was staring at her from above the drawing-board, his face flushed, his eyes fixed as if in a trance.

'Monsieur Breville?' she said softly. 'Shall I move round?'

There was no answer, and suddenly she knew where his gaze was fixed − between her thighs, where little tendrils of dark-brown hair showed, out past the lace edging of the blue knickers. She had completely forgotten her riotous thatch, being accustomed to seeing it every time she dressed and undressed.

Totally natural though it was to her, she knew very well what the effect on men was.

'I completely forgot!' she exclaimed. I hope you don't find it displeasing. I've never posed for underwear before.'

Breville became even redder in the face, realising it was no secret where he was looking. He struggled for a moment or two, regained his composure, and said something in reply.

'I don't understand,' he said faintly. 'You shave underneath your arms. But this . . .'

'Under the arms for show,' said she, pleased by the strength of his emotion. 'As to *this*, Monsieur, since you ask, I prefer to remain in a true state of Nature.'

His eyes were fixed on the brown fleece that grew for several centimetres down the insides of her thighs and he made a gurgling sound.

'Where is the problem?' said Odette helpfully. 'Leave it out, just as you leave out my face. Fashion magazines don't want to have pictures of the hair between a woman's legs, or even under her arms. The pictures they print show women looking as waxed and unreal as dummies in dress-shop windows.'

Breville said nothing, he continued to gaze at her, his eyes almost popping from his face. Odette decided to be offended by his attitude, she was reasonably certain he went with men, not women. To disconcert him she leaned casually against the pink upholstered back of the flashy chaise-longue and spread her legs and displayed more of her curly brown mat.

Still he said nothing, although his face was scarlet and his eyes insane. Odette found the situation, whatever it might be, amusing. On an impulse she jumped up and in three long strides she was beside the drawing-board. Breville's hands until then had been shielded from her sight by the tilted board. Now she saw he had opened his trousers and was holding his stiff part tightly, as if afraid.

'*Oh la la*, Monsieur Breville!' said Odette. 'Is this how you treat your models?'

Evidently this was what Annette Lillot had declined to inform Madame Drouet at the modelling agency, her best client liked to give himself little thrills in secret while looking at models in silk underwear! Well, it was nothing out of the ordinary, tame really, to what Odette came across when she modelled for garment manufacturers in their showrooms. Most of them were twenty years older than Breville and by no means as good-looking.

Breville tried to stuff his male pride back into his trousers out of sight. Odette put her hand quickly on his wrist and held it, preventing his shame-faced cover-up.

'Let me see what you've got,' she said and he blushed hotly.

The apparent sophistication of the fashion illustrations and madly expensive pullover from the rue du Faubourg Saint Honoré had faded. In a quavering voice he begged her not to mention it to anyone. What she saw was a moment of weakness, he insisted, unfortunate but nothing more. And in a sense she was to blame, his lapse was due to the sight of . . . of her . . . her untrimmed . . . But at this point he seemed lost for a word.

None of this made sense to Odette. Why should he, who was so well-established, so independent, give a *sou* for the opinion of anyone? But he astonished her then by explaining he had only a week past become engaged to be married.

'Truly?' said Odette with a dubious smile. 'I thought your interests lay elsewhere and the sight of my body upset you.'

He understood her meaning and assured her she was wrong about him. He was not in the least left-handed, he maintained warmly, he was engaged to a charming lady, her name was Marie-Louise de Beaucourt-Villiers.

Naturally, as an intelligent person Odette would understand that if word of his momentary foolishness ever reached the ear of Mademoiselle de Beaucourt-Villiers, or if her parents got to know of it, then the engagement would be broken off.

'I understand,' said Odette.

Indeed she did, to her mind he was trying to

wriggle his way into the minor French aristocracy.
He yearned for *cachet*, this sketcher of women's
underwear. That raised possibilities in her agile
mind. She intended nothing so common or so
criminal as blackmail, but a little discreet persuasion
was another matter.

'Mademoiselle de Beaucourt-Villiers is a proud
and jealous lady, I'm sure,' Odette said in a very
friendly manner, 'and naturally she knows that a top
artist for important magazines needs models in the
studio, undressed down to their underwear.'

'I have sworn utter faithfulness to her. But every
time we meet she asks the same questions, who has
been to model for me? Did I become excited while I
was sketching them? Questions like that. It is
embarrassing, to be accused in this way, but I love
her and she needs constant reassurance.'

'Poor man,' said Odette, her busy mind examining
the ways of benefiting from what she was hearing.

It seemed obvious to her his fiancée was plain, to
become so worried about pretty models. After all, if
she was beautiful or rich as well as of good birth, why
would she consent to marry a commercial artist,
however successful? On reflection, Odette thought it
unlikely Mademoiselle the Fiancée was young, either.
It explained a lot about Breville, if he proposed
marriage to a plain woman ten years older than
himself, because of her name.

Odette smiled at Breville in an understanding sort
of way. It calmed his fears and he smiled back warily.
But his smile vanished when she undid his belt and
pulled up the front of his shirt.

'What are you doing?' he gasped.

While they had been talking his upright part had
started to droop. Odette's hand circled it and he
sighed a feeble word of protest or two, the half-

hearted *No* that indicates the exact opposite. The hand he had stroked himself with fell loosely to his side, making way for Odette. She held his slackening flesh with a firm touch, to restore hardness to it . . .

'Why is it in your magazines the women are like dummies in a window?' she asked lightly. 'Can you answer that?'

His only reply was a sharp gasp of guilty pleasure.

'The purpose of these magazines,' said Odette, handling him with a light touch now, 'is to show beautiful clothes. And the reason for women wearing beautiful clothes is to stun men. And the reason for that is obvious. Off come the beautiful clothes, off come the silk knickers and *voilà*!'

'It is very uncivilised to be so direct,' Breville murmured. 'We conceal these realities with marvellously designed clothes and silk underwear.'

With a quick movement Odette stroked up and down, to make him grow as stiff as he possibly could. Her fingertips slid on the smooth skin and over the purple head. He squirmed on his stool, his nerves set on fire by the caress.

'But when you catch a glimpse of the real *me*, inside the silk underwear, my poor Laurent,' she said, awarding herself now the intimacy of using his first name, 'you become aroused. You pull out Jean Jeudi behind your drawing-board and play with him.'

'It is not pretty to be so hairy,' he murmured, hardly able to speak. 'It ought to be trimmed, that would be much better.'

Odette chuckled to feel the tautness and strength she held. A scheme was formulating itself in her head but it required some care. So far all was proceeding well, Breville was staring down into his lap, fascinated by what was being done to him, to see his

male pride being caressed. His eyes were wide and his
mouth hung open.

She reached up with her left hand to push her
forefinger into his open mouth. His lips closed on it,
and he began to suck, as if at her breast.

'You are a strange man, my poor Laurent,' she
murmured. 'I've never heard of anyone being so
faithful to a fiancée before, as you claim to be. You
must be truly and desperately in love with her. That's
the most romantic thing I've ever heard.'

His eyes turned to her, a bewildered look in them.

'But when you looked between my legs, even
though you believe I am hairy and ugly, you started
to play with Jean Jeudi.'

He couldn't answer with her finger in his mouth,
but his eyes — a pale golden-brown, she noticed —
were set on her face as if in dumb appeal.

But for what? she asked herself. What appeal?
What does he want from me apart from this simple
pleasure he is getting? If he wants me on my back, he
can ask. More likely he is appealing for my silence.

She smiled into his eyes, knowing she had the
answer to her riddle. Laurent was begging her not to
compromise his fidelity to his absent fiancée. He
wanted the pleasure of the moment but he was afraid
of the temptation. She could feel his anxiety in the
touch of his hand as he put it on her bare thigh and
began to stroke her smooth flesh.

It was a strangely furtive stroking. She guessed he
wanted to feel the thick dark-brown hair between her
legs but dare not in case he became carried away and
did what would afterwards cause him regret.

Odette's hand moved very slowly — she meant to
impress on him her superiority, her desirability. And,
when he was eventually ready for the thought, her
availability. On the right terms, of course. But for

now she meant to let his pleasure last and last until his nerves could stand no more. Let him pant and writhe — she was not yet ready to consider permitting him to achieve the peak he was straining to reach.

'Your fiancée, she must be beautiful,' she said, her voice as tantalising as she could make it. 'When you make love to her it is marvellous — yes?'

Her finger in his mouth gagged his reply. He nodded his head, his eyes fixed on her face.

'And I'm sure you make love to her very often,' Odette said. 'Very very often. Every day. Or more than that. Twice every day? Nod your head if I am correct. Yes, I guessed so. Does she come to the studio and undress? Does she lie down on the chaise-longue with her legs apart? Does she shriek at the climax or is she a silent one?'

Laurent moaned lightly and took hold of her wrist to pull her blocking finger out of his mouth.

'You mustn't speak of her like that,' he said, hardly able to speak himself, his breath ragged in his throat.

The slow rhythm of her fingers on his bounding flesh was now an exquisite torment of sensation. Odette knew it and refused to allow him to escape into the brief ecstasy his whole being cried for. When she had finished with him, he would remember her!

'Then I won't speak of her at all,' she said, smiling at him while her fingers sent little tremors of pleasure like electric shocks through him, 'though I know she comes here and takes her knickers down. She lies on the chaise-longue by the screen, you cannot deny it. How hairy is she between the legs? Is she like me? Or thin and patchy?'

'No, no, she is beautiful . . .' Laurent sighed, very nearly at the end of his tether.

Odette bent down to take his jerking hardness into her mouth. He cried out and squirmed on his stool. But she did not let him escape her yet, her wet tongue flicked over the smooth head and he sobbed with pleasure. She straightened her back and clasped him in her hand again.

'Is she coming this afternoon to lie down for you, Laurent? If she is, I must stop doing this, or you won't be able to make love to her. What would she say if you weren't able to go hard enough to get up her? Would she think you had been unfaithful with another woman? Even if you haven't?'

The sensations gripping Laurent Breville had carried him far beyond all possibility of rational speech. He stared blankly at Odette, his mouth open, cheeks flushed dark red. His whole body shook and his loins were jibbing forward.

Odette took his hand and pushed it into the lace-edged leg of the sapphire-blue knickers. His open palm rubbed, trembling, over her thatch of nut-brown hair and his twitching fingers explored its extent and texture. When he had felt it thoroughly, he touched the soft lips concealed in her fleece.

It was time, Odette judged, time to finish him. She cast all restraint aside. Her clasped hand beat up and down strongly and without mercy. Laurent uttered a wail like a tom cat on a roof by night and his passion spurted furiously.

The violence of it made clear to Odette that he had not been with his fiancée for some days — not to make love to. No wonder he reacted so strongly to the sight of her curls round the lace edging of the blue knickers.

He twitched and moaned, spurt after spurt leaping from him, spattering across the thick paper he had pinned on the drawing-board.

When he grew calm again she winked at him and tucked away his wet and shrinking part. Then she fastened his trousers.

'Not a word to anyone,' she said. 'It is our secret. Not that you have been unfaithful, no one could accuse you of that. But a certain prudence is always wise.'

'You are a very intelligent woman,' he said, much friendlier now than half an hour before, 'and a good model.'

'Except for one thing, it seems,' said she. 'You made it very clear that it is not pretty to be hairy. This never bothered me before but I have no choice but to listen to advice from an important artist like you.'

'For underwear work and for swimsuits and beach wear, it is essential,' Laurent told her, pleased to be able to give advice of a professional nature to a very pretty woman. It gave him a feeling of being in command, which was mere self-deception, of course . . .

'You said it would be better trimmed,' Odette reminded him.

While she was talking she pulled aside a leg of the knickers to reveal most of her nut-brown mat of curls. Laurent stared at it in open fascination, evidently he had seen nothing to match it, not in all his thirty years.

'But trimmed how?' Odette asked him. 'I don't know how to go about it. How shall I trim it?'

They discussed the question for a little while before Laurent arrived at the conclusion that a simple demonstration would be far easier than a thousand words. Odette encouraged him in this thought and what followed was only natural − he led her to his bedroom to show her what he meant by *trimming*.

But first she had to take off the expensive underwear sent to him for sketching. She followed him naked through the apartment from studio to bedroom, her own clothes over her arm. It was a large and pleasant bedroom, one she would be happy to sleep in, furnished in the best of *Vogue* magazine taste. The bed was broad and low, with a padded silk coverlet over it.

On the bedside table there was a long-stemmed pink rose in a tall crystal vase and three new books, the latest novels that all the best people were reading that month. A large square water-colour hung on the wall opposite the window, a peaceful country landscape with trees and a river bank.

While Odette was examining the bedroom fittings, Laurent was in the bathroom to collect the necessities for what he planned. He came back with a large towel, threw aside the silk coverlet and spread the towel on the bed.

'Lie on that,' he said, 'and I'll show you what can be done.'

She arranged herself as he asked, her feet on the thick woven carpet, her back on the bed, her shoulders propped on two soft down-filled pillows, so she could watch what he was doing. It amused her to see him taking this little comedy so absolutely seriously. There was a frown of concentration on his face as he knelt between her widely parted thighs with a pair of scissors, a copper bowl of warm water, a shaving-brush and a safety-razor.

This is ridiculous, she told herself, struggling not to laugh and spoil the moment. But how intent he is!

He combed out her fleece, making it look even larger than it was. When he'd finished and put the comb down, the brown curls seemed to stretch a long way down the insides of her thighs and halfway up to her dimple of a belly-button. Now he was at work with the scissors, snipping round the edges of her curly thatch to reduce the size. Between her legs, on the thick white towel, commas of hair were accumulating.

When he'd cut enough, he took the shaving-brush to lather her from belly-button almost to her knees. The soft sweep of it on the tender lips he was planning to expose was arousing, it made Odette sigh a little and close her eyes to savour the touch. He was very adept with the razor, gliding it over her skin without a scratch or a nick, a consideration of supreme importance when the sharp blade was so close to her most intimate parts.

He washed off the remaining lather with warm water, clipped a few stray hairs with the scissors, then he raised his golden-brown eyes to her face for the first time in ten minutes.

'There!' he said proudly. 'What do you think?'

He had tamed her wild and exciting thicket, he had reduced it to a well-clipped heart shape that fitted neatly in between her slender thighs and left her belly bare almost down to her pink lips. For Odette it was no improvement at all, on the contrary, she thought it uninteresting.

But that was a private opinion. Laurent was absurdly proud of his handiwork and to humour him she praised it extravagantly. She ran her fingertips over the short-clipped heart, saying how witty and delightful a thought it was, an inspiration! By this means she drew his eyes back to her shorn charm.

He was on his knees, hands on her thighs to support himself, while he gazed at what he had achieved. Clearly, the effect on him was exciting. But it was impossible to understand men or to guess what aroused them, thought Odette, observing the flush of emotion on Laurent's cheek and the long bulge apparent in his expensive dove grey trousers.

'Am I pretty now you have trimmed me?' she asked.

'You are beautiful,' he murmured in an abstracted way, as if his thoughts were too deep to be disturbed by conversation.

Odette spread her thighs a little wider, her invitation very clear. With a long groan Laurent ripped open his alligator-skin belt and trousers and out jumped his stiff length, nodding up and down like a mechanical toy. In another instant he slid it deep into Odette, who closed her eyes and smiled secretly to herself that she was making great progress with her scheme.

'This is dreadful,' Laurent gasped as he thrust in and out to a rapid rhythm. 'I love Marie-Louise − I must not be unfaithful to her! Save me, Odette, make me stop before it's too late!'

'But of course I won't let you be unfaithful to her,' Odette said and locked her legs over his back, holding him tight and urging him on in his forceful thrusting.

'But you don't understand − I love her!'

'I know you love her, Laurent, you love and adore her, your beautiful young fiancée! This has nothing to do with her, what you are doing to me now, trust me.'

'I can't help myself,' he moaned. 'When I saw that beautiful *little heart* I created between your thighs I lost all control! Unless you help me, Odette, I am lost!'

'I'll help you,' she said, feeling how firmly he was driving into her, carrying them both quickly toward the crisis. 'Do not despair, be happy, I will help you, Laurent!'

She pulled loose the pink silk scarf from out of the top of his fine pullover and held on to the ends, using the scarf to drag his head down toward her. His pale eyes were staring down with a curious expression of not understanding what was happening – or not wishing to know! She pulled his mouth down to hers and in the kiss that followed, all words were forgotten.

And not only words – also forgotten were the qualms and pangs of conscience that troubled him. With his mouth on hers and his tongue pressing between her parted lips, he thrust like a wild animal and spurted his passion into her. Odette bucked beneath him as she was gripped by a fierce orgasm.

When the ecstatic sensations began to fade, she congratulated herself on her achievement that morning. From now on she would insist on being Laurent's regular model. When he wished to play with Jean Jeudi behind his drawing-board, she would wear flimsy knickers and pose by the chaise-longue for as long as he liked. A daily session ought to keep him happily dependent on her.

And to forestall any sign of restiveness, she planned to show him her neat *little heart* very regularly – she was confident he would play Cupid and pierce it with his arrow every time he saw it! That would very conveniently stir up his feelings of bad conscience about his silly fiancée.

Those uncomfortable emotions of his ensured Odette the upper hand in their arrangement – the arrangement he knew nothing of as yet. From now on Odette was in charge of a vital part of his anatomy, she intended to ensure it was kept well used.

Naturally she would also insist he paid her the top rate for models – and also recommend her to other commercial artists he knew. Her luck had changed, she was at the beginning of a new, a fascinating new career! Perhaps the catwalk at Dior was not out of her reach, if she made the right contacts.

'Laurent,' she murmured, pressing her cheek close to his and holding him close to her with her legs, 'that was very nice.'

'I shouldn't have done it,' he said mournfully.

His voice was heavy with futile self-recrimination.

'Nonsense,' said Odette, 'there is no question of *should* and *shouldn't*. And no reason to feel guilty, none at all. Set your mind at rest, Laurent. Lie here on the bed beside me and I will explain it to you again.'

'Odette,' was all he said, but with gratitude.

BLAISE MAKES A DECISION

It was true Suzette was impressed by the personal dimensions of Blaise Fulbert. Not one of the men she had known intimately came up to Blaise in this respect, but to be impressed was not the best foundation for a lasting acquaintance. Mont Blanc is impressive when seen for the first time but who would want to set up home on its slope?

For Blaise himself his personal development was the source of mixed feelings of pride and shame. The pride was in having more than anyone else, the shame in the inconvenience it caused him. In his experience, few women and no virgins wanted to risk the possible damage of penetration by him. He was given to brooding about his *problem*, quite often − at least once a day.

These bouts of brooding had the invariable effect, strange as it was, of bringing on a stiffness, drawing his attention even more closely to his *problem*.

If he was alone when this took place, he had a compulsion to open his trousers and let his stiffness out, where he could see it. He meditated over it in a melancholy way, on the absence of true love and lasting happiness in his life, for he believed in these things and he thought everyone was entitled to them.

Often enough these fits of introspection came on him when he was not alone. This was inconvenient. Other methods then had to be devised to control the situation.

If he became hard when he was travelling on the

Metro, he got off at the next station and went up to prowl the street till he found a suitable tart. Tarts never squealed when he pushed it in them. Not even when he slammed in and out in a fury that he, Blaise Fulbert, a man of substance and importance, was reduced to this second-rate fulfilment by a miserable quirk of Nature.

Sometimes it happened in his office, when he was glancing at documents, and his attention would slip away from the intricacies of financial investments to the pleasures he felt were denied him. This was very inappropriate, of course, there being no time for day-dreaming on personal matters when money was at risk.

Yet that formidable length in his trousers refused absolutely to recognise office-hours or set times. It rose upright when it chose to do so, without any reference to Blaise's wishes. This caused him considerable social discomfort and embarrassment.

In the cinema it occurred regularly, alone or not. Soon after the lights, went down, the story on the screen lost its interest for him and the characteristic brooding started, accompanied by a feeling of tightness and constriction in his underwear.

When he was at home, of course, he experienced none of these difficulties. Off came jacket and waistcoat, he flipped open his trousers and, like a lance, his monumental hardness jutted out. For the rest of the evening he remained like that, walking from room to room, staring out of the windows, lost in thought. In short, Blaise was obsessed by his well-grown part.

He thought about all the women he had fallen in love with in the past, the women with whom he had started to make love, only to be repulsed.

This rejection of him sometimes happened the very

first time, when his new love experienced the raw sensation of being burst open by his huge maleness forcing itself into her. Sometimes it happened even earlier – more than one woman saw him naked for the first time, took fright when she held him in her hand and refused to let him try.

He had of necessity become a lover of tarts and married women with their *enlargement*, as he referred to it – the result of having children. They accommodated him without the calamitous results he dreaded. But the satisfactions of being the lover of someone else's wife were necessarily temporary, also infrequent. A wife and mother had more urgent calls on her time. She needed excuses for being away from her family, in order to meet a lover.

The essential secrecy of these liaisons gave Blaise trouble, for by Nature he was a cautious man. Ingenuity was required to find excuses and reasons to allay a husband's suspicion. More than once suspicion had hardened into grim certainty and Blaise faced angry men thirsting for revenge over the abuse of their marital rights. In these predicaments there was only one thing to do, deny everything and go away for a week, till calm was restored.

All in all, Blaise was by temperament the type who preferred to have a wife and family of his own and live in domestic peace and happiness. But ever since the fiasco with his fiancée when he was much younger, he had abandoned this aspiration. It was out of his reach, he believed, a freak of Nature had consigned him to a life of love affairs.

When he met Suzette Bernard his forgotten hopes had revived, though not for long. She was young and very beautiful, not the wife of anyone and had no children. Yet there had been not the least difficulty in making love to her. She had accepted him in full and gave every appearance of enjoying his penetration.

Perhaps, Blaise concluded, there existed in some women a sort of natural *enlargement*, either permanent or temporary.

Unhappily for him, their very different way of life meant it was ridiculously difficult for them to be together. Suzette was on stage at the Folies-Bergère every evening of the week except one. As an important financial adviser Blaise had an office in the rue Réaumur, near the Stock Exchange, and three employees including Mademoiselle Lenoir, his secretary.

His clients expected him to be there when they telephoned. It was impossible to leave the office to meet Suzette, except once or so a week. To be with her it was necessary to wait until the show was over at the Folies and take her to supper and dancing and afterwards go to her apartment, to make love, at two in the morning. Blaise was not a night bird – next day he dozed at his desk and became bad-tempered.

As for Suzette's evening off! That had all changed, she had no evenings off any more. Her frightful debut as a singer in an atrocious bar her drunken pianist friend found should have put an end to her ambition. But no, on the contrary, she was more than ever determined!

The pianist, suitably prodded, now arranged for her to sing in other bars and cafés every week! Suzette said this was the way to get the experience she needed before tackling any of the big venues. Blaise attended loyally every time, not enjoying it but pleased to think he would be able to go home with her after the performance. And it was always her apartment they went to, she had only been to his twice.

Her various friends from the Folies-Bergère no

longer came to hear her sing. Presumably they felt
they had given sufficient evidence of their friendship
by turning up at Chez Bobo, except Gaby – the
dancer she shared the apartment with. Gaby was
there every week without fail and she brought her
boyfriend, a little fighting-cock of a man named
Lucien.

Lucien Cluny made Blaise uneasy. His clothes were
too showy, for one thing, and his dark hair too
glossily waved. But worst of all was the mystery of
his occupation. He had money to spend – he
thought nothing of pulling out a wad of banknotes at
least five centimetres thick to pay a bar bill. If
questioned about his profession, he appeared to have
an attack of deafness. And when the question was
repeated, he told a joke instead of replying.

Evidently Lucien was a criminal and it troubled
Blaise to be seen with someone who might perhaps be
nabbed by the police. By association, a shadow of
doubt might be cast upon Blaise's own business
integrity! The consequences of that were fearful to
contemplate. But there it was – if he wanted to be
with Suzette and take her home after she had sung,
he had to put up with the unwanted presence of a
crook.

Though not for much longer, thought Blaise
gloomily. The fact was, his love affair with Suzette
was fading out. Soon it would be finished
completely. Much as he adored her, he saw that her
determination to become a star left little scope in her
heart for anything else.

A lover she wanted, yes, but not a lover who
monopolised her time and attention. She required a
lover who was there only if she wanted him and who
vanished when she had other things to do. For Blaise
the end was in sight, his romantic nature was still set

upon a love affair of operatic scale, despite the setbacks of the past.

He lived just off the Boulevard Haussman, not far from the Parc Monceau. The district was a suitably plush setting for a man of his importance. The apartment building was a lavish nineteenth century edifice, modernised in every way possible, and the tenants were well-to-do families whose lives were conducted in a quiet and orderly manner. There were no noisy parties late into the night, no perambulators left in the hall.

Blaise was on good terms with several of his neighbours, none more so than Monsieur and Madame Lafon, whose apartment faced his own across the internal courtyard. Lafon was an interesting man, by Blaise's standard, a lawyer of importance who concerned himself with commercial law and advised on business ventures.

But, to come to the point, the person with whom Blaise was on truly excellent terms was Madame Lafon. The way in which this close friendship came about was unusual and improbable, to say the least. It had started one evening more than a year earlier, when Blaise was supposedly working at home, studying papers his secretary had put into his briefcase.

After a snack of cold meat and a single glass of wine, Blaise settled down to read the documents and all too soon he slipped into a fit of brooding on the inequities of life that condemned him to a solitary existence. He had no particular girlfriend at that time, his last being away with her husband and not likely to be back from Belgium for months.

He wandered restlessly around his apartment, work forgotten. He had changed out of his business suit on returning home, into a casual shirt and trousers. As was usual on these disconsolate occasions 'large and long, thick and strong' had been liberated. It was poking fiercely out of his open trousers.

Lost in depressing thoughts, Blaise stood looking out of the window at the well-kept courtyard below. He was quite oblivious to his condition, which was not suitable for public exhibition. As luck would have it, Madame Lafon was at the window of her apartment across the courtyard and she saw the overgrown insignia of virility protruding from Blaise's open trousers.

What is a respectable married woman to do when confronted with an exhibitionist – the degenerate type who lurks in a shabby old raincoat behind trees in the Luxembourg Gardens waiting to spring out whenever a young woman approaches, his raincoat held open?

For that is how the situation necessarily presented itself to a casual and unprejudiced observer. An observer who could have no knowledge of Blaise's obsession. What is she to do? Scream and run away, calling for the police?

Or attack the perpetrator with her umbrella, if she carries one? Jab his offensive male part with the ferule and put him to flight? But all this is hypothetical, since it was not in the Luxembourg Gardens, not even in the Parc Monceau, where the confrontation took place.

What Madame Lafon did was to wave at Blaise through the glass of the window. He was too deep in his downcast ruminations at first to notice her, but when he did he waved back politely. He knew her by sight, of course, he said *bonjour* to her and her husband if they met going in or out of the building.

Madame Lafon was a good-looking woman in her

middle thirties, the same age as Blaise, more or less. She wore her hair long — it was an interesting shade of dark chestnut-brown. Some found her a little too heavily built for smartness but she succeeded in dressing elegantly. This particular evening she was wearing green, from what Blaise made out across the courtyard.

He turned away from the window to pour himself a drink and to continue his mournful reflections. To him it was so natural for 'long and thick' to be exposed when he was at home alone that it simply did not occur to him he was guilty of an exhibition, and before a respectable married woman!

He poured himself a glass of white wine and was sipping at it when the doorbell rang. He was not expecting anyone and guessed it was the concierge with a message or a package left for him. He reached the door and his hand was stretched out to open it before he shook off his despondency and returned to the normal world — and saw he was in a state of indecency.

He did up his trousers and opened the door. To his surprise, there stood Madame Lafon in a silk foulard frock, a jade-green tint that set off the pretty pink flush on her face.

'*Chéri*!' she exclaimed, and threw out her arms in a dramatic manner. 'I am here!'

So affectionate a greeting from a woman known only by sight is guaranteed to astonish any man. Blaise was duly astonished, he was also slightly alarmed, wondering what this portended. A moment later he knew. She pushed into the apartment and closed the door behind her, put an arm round his neck and kissed him.

Her other hand groped at his trousers, ripped them open again and seized hold of his stiffness.

If the situation was reversed, if Blaise — or any other man — had pushed his way into a woman's apartment, a married woman, mother of three small children, not a close friend but almost a stranger, put his arm round her and kissed her, fumbling under her skirt to feel between her legs — then this would have been a police matter! It might well have been reckoned an attempted rape, with appropriate punishment.

But a good-looking woman doing this to a man? There was not a magistrate in Paris who would take the charge seriously. Women do not rape men, it was as simple as that. And besides, Blaise was finding it most enjoyable to have his male part massaged so enthusiastically. He returned Madame Lafon's kiss willingly and led her into his sitting-room, she holding on to his handle the entire time.

There was a misunderstanding, of course. She had seen him at the window with his fleshy monster sticking out and thought he was trying to entice her in a crude sort of way. His small wave of acknowledgement she interpreted as an invitation. Her husband was out and the maid had put the children to bed. Madame Lafon was an adventurous woman, she had taken note before of her handsome neighbour, Monsieur Fulbert. He was good-looking and well-dressed. She accepted the supposed invitation.

Blaise was unaware of all this. He thought . . . well, he wasn't sure what he thought of this remarkable turn of events. Except that he thought Carole Lafon was beautiful and desirable. They sat on the beige washed-silk sofa and he adored the pale cream tint of her skin, her long chestnut hair hanging to her shoulders and her abundant breasts.

He held her close to him and stroked her breasts

through her jade-green frock. He kissed her a hundred times as his hunger for her body grew furiously. And Carole? She was three-quarters of the way toward a marvellous orgasm just by holding 'large and long.' She was desperate to be taken the rest of the journey to Paradise. She pressed her mouth to his, her hot tongue searched between his parted lips, her clasping hand slid up and down his distended flesh.

This had always been a nervous moment for Blaise. He too was in an intense state of arousal, his male pride leaping within her hand. Carole's frock was undone and down round her waist to let him open her brassiere. He pressed her back on the sofa and put his lips to her breasts, exciting her to a frenzy. In truth he feared what might happen when he slid 'thick and strong' into her, or tried to.

But the direction of the proceedings was no more in his hands than their informal introduction had been! Carole ripped off her knickers and lay on her back on the washed-silk upholstery, her thighs well parted. She pulled him between her legs and put the smooth swollen head of what she held to her wet lips.

'*Chéri*!' she gasped, and it was only the second time she had spoken since he opened the door.

Blaise paused for a moment in anguish of mind — would she cry out and wince when he pushed in? That for him always had the same effect as sticking a pin into a toy balloon — it made him shrink and grow soft in seconds. And was the end of friendship.

He drew in a breath, braced himself and pushed slowly, ready to desist if she squealed. She sighed and opened her legs wider — there was no tightness to trouble him! In fact, Blaise slid easily and pleasurably into her!

'Carole!' he exclaimed, in delight. 'Oh Carole!'

'*Chéri*,' she murmured for the third time, 'more, more!'

Blaise thought he must be dreaming. Only in dreams did he slide deep into capacious and beautiful women like Carole – rare and marvellous dreams induced by too much champagne, satisfying dreams from which he awoke with a sticky belly and wet pyjamas.

But Carole was real, this was truly happening and he was in her to the limit! His entire twenty centimetres of hard flesh was sunk into her! He was sliding in and out to sensations of delight! And Carole clung to him, with eager hands while she urged him on with 'Harder! Faster!'

That was how it started between them – in a misunderstanding. She adored size and he had it in abundance. He wanted a girlfriend with a certain *enlargement*, she had it in good measure.

Inserting this into that proved highly satisfactory and their love-affair developed. Blaise was careful to become acquainted with Monsieur Lafon the lawyer, as cover for when he dropped in on Carole at times when Lafon was absent and the children were in the park with the maid.

They were lovers for a month or more before discovering their first encounter arose from a mistake. They were lying naked on Blaise's bed, deliciously content after making strenuous love, and Carole said in an affectionate manner she was so very glad he had waved Monsieur 'Large and thick' at her through the window that day, from which ensued this fortunate train of events.

To which Blaise replied in bewilderment, 'I don't understand.'

They discussed it and Carole laughed when she realised how the mistake came about. Blaise joined in the laughter, although he was decidedly uneasy. It could have been someone else, not Carole, who had seen his *exposure* through the window. Someone who felt outraged at the innocent sight, who would cause trouble for him. He resolved secretly never again to walk round his apartment with his trousers open, unless the curtains were drawn.

Whatever Carole may have believed, Blaise himself was gloomy about how long this *affaire-du-coeur* would endure. Based on his past experience with married women, he knew how easy it was for them to revert to domestic fidelity when they became sated with a lover. He also realised, if vaguely, that he was a difficult person. The overall trend of his nature was toward a pessimism women usually found trying.

But the rift between them, after months of intermittent pleasure, had another cause entirely. Carole had not by any means become bored with him, she was as passionate as ever. The trouble was that Blaise met Suzette at Armand Regence's party. His interest in Carole lessened. This she noticed and resented.

She accused him of betraying her with another woman. Perhaps not a logical point of view for a married woman to take but it had a certain truth in it that disconcerted Blaise. He lied, of course, he assured her there was no one else, he adored her to distraction and so on, in the normal way of unpleasant scenes between disillusioned lovers.

Carole knew better. And the situation deteriorated week by week. Blaise still wanted to make love to her on evenings when Monsieur Lafon was out but she grew more anguished. Eventually she was furious enough to stage a noisy and heart-breaking row. She called Blaise names he found hurtful and distasteful. When she had reduced him to a quivering hulk of shamefaced evasion, she stormed out of his apartment redfaced, declaring he would never see her again.

And there the matter rested for three weeks. In that time he didn't lay eyes on her once, she avoided the times he might be entering or leaving the building, and she persuaded her husband to take her out every evening she thought Blaise was at home.

It was when he found himself wandering about his apartment in the old way, his trousers undone, his thickness sticking out like the bowsprit of a sailing-ship, that he realised how much he missed Carole.

The *affaire* with Suzette had tailed off, that was undeniable. Her life was too different from his, there were no compromises possible, no halfway meeting-point.

Blaise sat down in his kitchen, on a wooden-backed chair, and with morose eyes contemplated the fleshy column sticking up out of his trousers. Solemnly he cursed it for the unending trouble it brought him. He had been drinking more than usual that day, starting when he left his office and went to the nearest bar in a perplexed mood, continuing over dinner, which he ate alone at a little restaurant he often went to, and then at home.

By ten in the evening he was in an impossible state of mind. He blamed himself for antagonising Carole and he pitied himself that Suzette had lost interest in him. Through his mind ran the disasters his oversized equipment had led him into in the twenty or so years since he first took an active interest in girls.

In his drunken state it did not seem unreasonable to speak to 'long and thick' — angry words, words of exasperation, words of resentment. His temper rose so high that he threw his glass of cognac at the swollen offender! Most of the liquor went on his trousers and soaked in at once but Blaise felt he had made his point. A little later he fell fast asleep, his arms cradled on the kitchen table and his head on them.

When he woke he had an atrocious headache and it was five in the morning. He ached in every joint. The pride and bane of his life was at rest, limp and dangling. Blaise got up, unsteady on his feet, to stagger into his bedroom. He fell face down on the bed, still dressed, and slept again, certain of one thing – he must be reconciled with Carole.

Easier said than done, of course. She was still indignant and hurt by his treachery. It was impossible to send her an armful of red roses every day, not with Monsieur Lafon there. He wrote notes and letters but they were never answered. He didn't know if she read them or threw them away when she saw his writing on the envelope. He telephoned every day but always got the maid, she informed him Madame was out, even when he knew she was in.

With misgivings, he attempted the method that first drew her to him. He stood at the window late in the evening, his mighty advantage exposed and upright, the whole length pressed against the glass. If any of the other tenants in the building saw him, the concierge would hear of it in the form of angry complaints. This was an expensive building in a superior neighbourhood, the occupants expected to live in decency and dignity.

If Carole caught a glimpse through the window of what Blaise was humbly offering, she gave no indication. And the third time he stood there, feeling like a perfect idiot, his warm flesh on the cool glass, he was horrified to see another face appear at the Lafon window – the maid who took care of the children!

The distance was too great and the light insufficient to make out the expression on the maid's face. With gasps of dismay and fright Blaise leapt back into the room, swivelling round to get his back to the window and conceal his shame. This incident was highly upsetting – in his anguish of mind he put on a hat and a jacket and went out, to stride nervously along the Boulevard in search of a suitable tart.

He found one in a bar not far away – a big-framed and heavy-fleshed brunette. He picked her because he thought she looked a little like Carole, but the resemblance was only in his mind.

In her room he rolled her on her back and overlaid her as if he wanted to crush her flat, thrusting like an express-train piston till he crashed into the buffers and exploded.

'You were in a hurry for that,' the tart commented when he got off her. He lay with a hand over his eyes to shield them while he tried to collect his scattered thoughts.

Tarts never remarked on his proportions, which Blaise thought was insulting. Though other women usually found it oppressive, and his own feelings about it were mixed, at least a tart ought to boost his pride a little by congratulating him on it. Or so was his opinion. After all, money had changed hands, and surely he was entitled to something more than the straightforward use of her facilities!

But they never did comment, they said nothing, neither comic nor admiring. He presumed they saw all shapes and sizes in the course of their work – and accommodated them! Was it possible these women of the streets saw nothing extraordinary about his equipment? The thought was mortifying, after all he'd suffered because of it!

Even so, his exposure at the window had an unexpected result. Next day was Saturday and Blaise was at home in the afternoon, talking on the telephone when the doorbell rang at about three. He said *au revoir* and hung up before he went to see who was there. It was Carole — and she was in a tremendous rage. She poked her finger into his chest repeatedly, while she drove him back into the apartment with a tirade of harsh and insulting words.

The least offensive things she called him were *degenerate* and *pervert*. Blaise retreated with his mouth opening and closing in silence, like a goldfish in a glass bowl. Through the abuse he slowly came to grasp the reason for Carole's fury, his standing at the window last evening with his trousers open. Carole chose to describe the sad act of a deserted and despairing lover as a 'crude and disgusting bid to debauch her maid Jeanne!'

The poor girl had been shocked and horrified by what was thrust at her, she had run to her employer almost in tears! At least, that was what Carole said. Before taking further steps to bring this nuisance to an end, she was here to deliver a warning to Blaise that the strongest action would be taken against him, she would insist on it!

When Blaise got a word in, he stammered that his display was for *her*, not for the maid. He loved her, Carole, he adored her, he missed her dreadfully, he couldn't live without her.

'Liar, liar, liar!' she retorted. 'You used me and then cast me aside for another woman. And now you've tired of her and are looking for someone else to use — and my poor maid is close at hand so you go for her! This is disgraceful, Blaise, it is not worthy of you, why are you doing this? To torture me?'

Even Blaise, unskilled though he was with women,

even he knew better than to frame sensible answers to nonsense questions. He repeated that he loved and adored Carole and no one else. Since they had parted he was desperately unhappy, he begged her with all his heart to forgive him.

Blaise had little natural eloquence, but he had learned these useful phrases at the cinema, as an *aficionado* of movies about romantic love, torment, jealousy, heart-break and that sort of misery. To a large extent he identified his own situation with these kiss-and-suffer tales and he had a particular devotion to Arletty and her portrayal of sophisticated world-weariness.

Carole met his declaration with another exclamation of 'liar', but without the sharp edge to her voice this time. Blaise heard the change and stepped quickly forward, throwing his arms about her to hug her to himself.

'Carole, Carole, *je t'aime*,' he murmured, his cheek on hers, his lips at her ear, or where her ear would be if her long hair didn't cover it.

Her arms were round his waist, her body close to his, but she had not yet completely yielded.

'Can I believe you, after what you have done?' she said in a tragic voice. 'Can I trust you ever again?'

He assured her she could, he swore she could, he gave her his solemn and binding word, he vowed eternal faithfulness, undying devotion. Meanwhile he had his hands on the full cheeks of her bottom and he was squeezing them happily. Naturally, the cause of all his difficulties in life stood stiff as an iron bar in his trousers and was pressing against Carole's belly.

That was something she couldn't resist. She kissed Blaise and ripped his trousers open to renew her close acquaintance with a part of him that revived delicious memories for her.

'Swear to me it's mine!' she gasped. 'Mine alone — swear it, Blaise!'

Nothing was easier. A moment later they were in his bedroom, locked in each other's arms, kissing and laughing in sheer joy and sighing words of endearment, all at the same time. It was a reconciliation of quality and style, as one might say.

Blaise's emotions had been in such a turmoil that until this moment he hadn't noticed what Carole was wearing — a pale pink blouse, a checked grey skirt and a white summer coat loosely about her shoulders, as if she were going out. That, of course, was to make the maid believe she had gone out of the building for an hour, perhaps to a café.

The coat slipped from her shoulders during their embrace and lay on the floor. Blaise undid her blouse and brassiere, with fingers trembling to the strength of his emotions. She wore no slip, her luxurious breasts spilled out into his eager hands — the skin was cool to his touch, the flesh full and pliant, the buds a rich red-brown.

He lowered his head to kiss them and suck at them, making her throw back her head and give long sighs of pleasure. She held his monster with both hands, in the firm grip of ownership, and he was thrilled by the thought.

He threw off his clothes and pulled her to the bed. They were both on fire with emotion, their bodies throbbing with passion. Carole slithered down at his side to rub her cheek against his huge virility, and then kissed it.

'*Chéri, chéri*, I have missed you so much too,' she sighed and Blaise wasn't clear whether she was addressing him or that part of him she was playing with and cosseting. But what of that? He was so delighted to have her lying across his bed once again that he felt he was near spurting his raging desire in her hand and over her face.

She knew him too well to let him do that. She was up on her knees, her pale-skinned breasts hanging over him, arousing him to a frenzy. She turned and positioned herself on her hands and knees, showing him the round and moonlike cheeks of her bottom. Blaise was up off his back and behind her, on his knees, his thick length pointed at her.

'My brave bull!' she said. 'Mount me, mount me!'

He slipped his hands around her waist and put his palms flat on her soft belly. He held her while he slid into her, pushing in strongly and deeply, until his belly was up against the hot cheeks and he was fully sheathed.

'Ah, ah, ah,' Carole murmured, 'that feels so good! Give me all of it, *chéri* — push right in hard. Destroy me!'

He slid in and out forcefully, his fingers digging into the delicious flesh of her belly. He was mastering her, using her in the way she wanted to be used.

Carole braced herself on stiff arms, delirious with pleasure to feel him slamming against her and his mightiness sliding so magisterially within her. In a moment she was going to succumb to a ravening orgasm — she felt it on the way, felt it coming close, and knew it would tear screams of delight from her throat.

She had the best of it again, now Blaise was hers once more. Victor the lawyer husband who provided so well for his family, who arranged vacations to far-away and exotic places, who gave presents to her on every possible anniversary. And she had the children she adored, little Victor, Marc and Chantal.

To crown her happiness, she had Blaise, this wonderful lover, this Minotaur, half-man and half-bull! Not kilometres away across Paris, but here in the same building and available every evening her husband was out! Blaise thrilled her as no other man ever had, he fulfilled her as she never believed possible. She loved him, she was sure of it. Well, she was as sure as was necessary.

And Blaise, crying out in ecstasy as his rapture surged into her, he too was happy in his own strange way.

GABY LETS HERSELF
BE ADORED

Although Lucien never talked about his occupation, early in the course of her love affair with him Gaby found that he was well-known. But whether he was liked or respected, that was a cat of another colour and not for her to trouble herself with.

He had very little use for his apartment, she learned, except to make love in. Otherwise he was out and about, from breakfast in a big café where the Boulevard de Magenta met the Boulevard de Strasbourg, to late-night drinks in fancy bars. All of Paris was his living-room, so to speak.

He took Gaby with him everywhere during the day and often she was present when doubtful-looking men slithered up to him for a few muttered words. Only very occasionally did he introduce one of them − an Emile or a Jules, never a surname. All of them had the same sort of flashy clothes as Lucien, though not worn with the same style.

They're all gangsters, Gaby told herself, although she never heard any discussion of criminal events between them. What they talked about in undertones was incomprehensible. Nor did Lucien disappear mysteriously to help rob banks, or whatever gangsters did together. He didn't go to the horse-racing at Longchamp or Auteuil. The only conclusion was that he made his living during the hours she made hers, the evenings.

While she and the troupe were high-kicking through the bogus Latin-American dances at the

Cabaret-Mouchard, Lucien was up to whatever illegal activities supported him in style. They didn't take much of his time, these mysterious activities, because on most evenings he was waiting for her as soon as she had changed into her own clothes.

Lucien was a rogue, without doubt, but he had panache. At the Café de la Paix in the afternoon, on the terrace, he would order a bottle of champagne and have three waiters in long aprons and a bus-boy serving it. At the Brasserie Lipp, when he took Gaby to lunch, there was no question of waiting for a table – he was bowed to one immediately.

On Gaby's evening off he took her to grand restaurants to eat and to the theatre, though only to see comedy – he had no taste for drama on the stage. He was known in the restaurants he went to and particularly well-known in the night-clubs. His manner never changed, whether he was speaking to a restaurant manager, a waiter or one of his mysterious friends he was quick, clear and imperturbable.

His hands were moving all the time, when he was talking and when he was silent. At first Gaby found it strange and perhaps a little unnerving, but she rapidly became accustomed to being touched lightly on the arm, on the back of the hand or on the shoulder. He never touched her intimately in public, on her knee or her breast, not even in taxis. She thought this odd, but he was an odd sort of man altogether and she liked him.

She tried several times to explain this to Suzette but they never agreed about him. Suzette shrugged and agreed Lucien was the best of company, good-hearted, considerate, and generous to those he liked. But . . .

But what? Gaby asked. Suzette said it was good of Lucien to come with Gaby to the cafés she sang in.

She was grateful for his applause, even if he sometimes overdid it. Clapping hands was enough, stamping his feet was *de trop*.

'He likes you,' said Gaby. 'Why can't you like him? He says you're going to be a top singer one day, a real star, and he'll tell his friends he knew you when you were nobody and he always believed in you.'

The surest way to Suzette's heart these days was to say nice things about her singing. Not for Lucien, though, even when his praises were passed on hopefully by Gaby. The fact was Suzette disapproved of the little man and she didn't herself know why.

On the other hand, Gaby was not in love with Lucien, much as she liked him. She made Suzette laugh by relating Lucien's ways in the bedroom. *My dear little fetishist*, she called him with a giggle when she talked about him. Naturally, she in turn was told about Blaise's unusual proportions for she and Suzette had been friends for years, they kept no secrets from each other.

'Is that how it feels?' asked Gaby, slightly awestruck by an account of Blaise in the act of love. 'As if you're being split open up the middle?'

'The sensations are unbelievable,' Suzette agreed with a grin and a slight shudder. 'You feel yourself being stretched apart, wider than you can bear. It's as if you're being turned inside out, it makes you climax instantly.'

'But you're not going on with him?'

'A little of that goes a long way, *chérie*!'

'It's a pity I've been too tied up with Lucien, I'd like to try just once with Blaise to see what it feels like. I know you wouldn't mind. Now I've lost the chance. How big do you think he is?'

'At least twenty centimetres, maybe more, and nearly as thick as my wrist.'

'*Bon Dieu*!' Gaby sighed. 'To think what I've missed!'

'He wears loose undershorts and it hangs down in his trouser leg. In a shop or walking along in the street, if I rub myself against him just casually for a moment, he gets excited and it begins to stand up.'

'Enormous!' said Gaby dreamily.

'Too big to hide,' Suzette agreed with a grin. 'It bulges out through the cloth, he gets embarrassed and he turns red in the face. He starts looking round for a taxi and if there isn't one he drags me into the nearest café so he can sit down and cross his legs to cover it. It's very funny – you can't help laughing at him, he gets more embarrassed and goes even harder!'

'Men!' Gaby said with a shake of her blonde head. 'They are all comedians but they don't know it. Speaking of which – did I tell you Lucien's taken the picture off his bedroom wall?'

Gaby had offered no comment on the Modigliani nude hanging in Lucien's bedroom. She had taken it for a reproduction but with pride he pointed out it was a copy, a hand-painted copy even an expert would have trouble telling from the original. It was by a first-class artist, he said, but the name meant nothing to Gaby.

There must have been something in her rare glances at it that made Lucien understand her opinion of it. And the picture went, it simply wasn't there one afternoon when they went to bed. He never mentioned it again and she let the matter pass.

Perhaps it was her unspoken verdict that led to the removal, but perhaps it was something else – a contrast that had been so obvious, even to Lucien. Up on the wall, was a model lying on her back, an Italian-looking woman, with big round breasts and plump thighs. She was dark-haired, on her head and below.

And down on Lucien's bed lay Gaby, breasts small and pert as a dancer's should be, and palest blonde on her head and between her legs. Although she left only a pretty tuft and shaved the rest, Lucien adored her for it. Some afternoons he made her lie flat on her back with her hands under her head and her legs apart while he admired it at close quarters.

Sometimes he adored every centimetre of her skin with fingers and tongue. He paid devoted attention to her breasts, as might be expected. He also kissed her delicately in her smooth-shaven armpits. The little gold cross round his neck hung on its chain and trailed over her skin, its touch cool and not very holy.

His wet tongue probed into her round dimple of a belly button and explored her groins, his fingertips following closely with a fluttering caress. He rolled her over on her face to reach in the crease between the taut cheeks of her bottom, fingers and tongue together.

All of this was carried out with thoroughness and without the least sign of hurry. In time he permitted himself to reach her blonde tuft, by then Gaby was in a barely controlled frenzy of sensation, her eyes closed, her fists clenched. He did this to her deliberately, whether for her pleasure or for his own as an exercise of power she could never decide. Perhaps it was both together.

An hour would have passed since he began, his tongue licking in her ears, before this moment when she felt it slither inside her. By then she was very wet and slippery, her legs straining apart, the petals of her flower pulled open. The tongue invaded her, vibrated on her swollen bud, the ecstasy that took her was so tremendous her body was flung upward, like a tempered steel spring uncoiling. She screamed shrilly, delighted by the sound of her scream.

After that she needed a little rest and a cold drink. But her body retained the impression, the memory of the pleasure it had just enjoyed and it was soon ready to feel it again. She put down the empty glass on the bedside table, smiled at Lucien and made silent kisses at him. The fleshy part standing fiercely up from the bush of dark hair between his thighs was of moderate size but very sturdy.

And it was achingly ready, that was evident, from being stiff for the long time he played with her, using tongue and fingers.

He spread himself on Gaby's flat belly and plunged in — there were no preliminaries necessary after what had been done to her already. She liked the feel of him inside her and his weight upon her. Most times she reached the crisis before he did and it was the convulsion in her belly that made him spurt.

Gaby always told Suzette that she adored being dominated by a man. Perhaps she even believed it herself. But how true it was, that would not be easy to decide. Often men and women prefer to mask their true personality, from themselves if not from their lovers. Suzette usually smiled and shrugged when she heard Gaby claim to be happiest when a man controlled her body and used it for his own pleasure.

'But it's true,' Gaby insisted. She proved it by mentioning an afternoon when Lucien handed her a package. They had been out to lunch and were in his nondescript sitting-room. This package had an expensive look about it and was wrapped in very elegant paper on which was printed the name of an incredibly chic boutique in the rue Cambon. Gaby kissed his cheek warmly and undid the big bow in the ribbon holding the package together.

Inside it she found, enswathed in palest blue tissue-paper, a tiny pair of knickers, nothing more. This wisp of a garment was made of finest black lace, as light as the down from a raven's breast. So beautiful, so sensual, so impractical! Surely only a screen goddess wore knickers like these, fervent imagination insisted, and only for very important occasions! At her fifth marriage, say, to a devastatingly handsome actor with flashing blue eyes and curly black hair. In the honeymoon suite of an ocean liner, the new husband would rip these flimsy knickers off her with his strong white teeth!

Or when the star's film contract was due for renewal and she arranged to discuss it in person with the studio supremo. If she wore knickers like that it would be easy to negotiate a seven-year contract at twice the salary — and all this inside an hour!

'Take your clothes off, *chérie*, and put them on,' said Lucien in a voice that vibrated with emotion.

'Aha, my little pervert, that's what you want, is it?' Gaby murmured, looking at him from under lowered eyelashes.

She had come to know his caprice in these matters well and to take pleasure in playing a part in the scenarios he devised.

'I won't touch you, I promise,' he whispered, sitting down in an armchair. 'Put them on, I want to sit here and look at you.'

'You won't touch me? We'll see about that,' she said, with a pout of her scarlet-painted mouth.

Off came her little costume, a close-cut jacket of linen in a pretty apricot colour, the pleated skirt, her own knickers and her silk stockings. Lucien in shirt-sleeves sat on a beige arm chair, his legs apart and his desire bulging.

'Walk about a little, that's all I ask,' he said softly.

When she was completely naked, Gaby stood within arm's-length of Lucien to put on the black lace knickers. She turned it into a drama, a ballet, a fantasy, bending over towards him, breasts swaying free. She raised one foot and very slowly slid it into the delicate little garment, hearing Lucien's breath sighing in his mouth. Then the other foot. It was easy for her to balance on one leg after all her dance training and experience.

She stood up gracefully, sliding the lace knickers slowly up her slim legs, past her knees and slower still up her thighs. She wiggled her bottom a little when the knickers were fully on, to settle them into place and then she put her hands behind her back, her elbows out, posing for Lucien.

His eyes were round with wonder, his face pink, his breathing rapid. Before starting to pace up and down before the armchair, Gaby put on her shoes for she knew how that aroused him.

'*Je t'aime*, Gaby, *je t'aime*,' he sighed, hardly able to speak now his wish was coming true.

She was a superb sight as she walked to and fro unhurriedly, showing off her long sleek body and her lean muscular dancer's thighs. Her breasts were taut and did not swing to her step, but they were a delight to see, so round and perfectly shaped, not a man born could see them without becoming frantic to kiss them.

By rolling her hips as she walked she could cause the cheeks of her bottom to slide up and down against each other and even with her back to Lucien she could hear his soft gasping.

'He's a pervert, he uses me,' she told Suzette. 'He makes me walk up and down the sitting-room in fancy knickers and nothing else. And to be truthful, I love it, to be mastered and used in this way. He does not think of me as a person when he forces me into these scenes — I am only a thing to be ordered about. For him I am no more than a piece of furniture for his fantasy. He does not regard me as a woman, only a moving mannequin to wear black lace knickers, the real object of his desire!'

'Is that so?' said Suzette. 'Which of you controls the other in these games? Are you truly his victim, doing what he says, acting a part in his fantasy? Or is it you who dominate him at these moments? He is the passive one, surely, he waits for you to arouse him. You are the active one in this scene, using your body to control him.'

'What nonsense!' Gaby scoffed.

The underwear game usually lasted twenty minutes, never less, sometimes longer. Gaby moved slowly about the room, Lucien got redder in the face, his legs strained wide apart, his breathing grew ragged. He panted and twitched, he babbled he loved Gaby, his fingernails clawed into the chair seat.

In short, he had a marvellously enjoyable time of it, and all it took was Gaby strolling about in flimsy knickers.

When she thought he'd had enough, or when she was starting to become bored, Gaby brought matters to a proper conclusion. The first time they played this game together he had to explain, after that she understood completely what to do to achieve the maximum effect.

The moment had come. She ended her walk in front of Lucien in his armchair and turned to face him. She stood as provocatively as she knew how, her feet apart and hands on her naked hips. He stared up at her face with eyes clouded by desire, knowing what was going to happen to him, wanting it deliriously but also in a panic that it was about to end, this pleasure he wished might go on forever.

'Gaby,' he whispered. 'Oh Gaby, Gaby . . .'

His glance fell from her face to her breasts, the tip of his tongue showed between his red lips. He stared wide-eyed at her lean belly, then lower still at her slender thighs, at the black lace knickers so chic against her creamy skin.

His face was suffused dark-red, almost purple. At times Gaby asked herself what was in his mind at this moment — what was it that drove him to this frenzied lust? The luxurious knickers he bought for her to prance about in or the blonde-haired delight they concealed?

She raised her leg, stretching it out as if for a slow-motion high-kick at the Cabaret-Mouchard. Aimed in her mind at the club owner's pompoms, he was notorious for underpaying his entertainers, and he was always pinching their bottoms.

But there was no thought of inflicting pain on Lucien in her head. Nor any anxiety in his. On the contrary, his legs parted wider, he pushed his loins forward on the beige cushion of the armchair. With care, Gaby placed her foot against the bulge in his trousers and pressed the toe of her shoe on it, the toe of the white glacé leather shoes she was wearing that day.

Through the thin leather she could feel his hardness and how it throbbed, his strength, his desire, tantalised by her foot.

This was the moment when balancing on one leg was vital. Gaby flexed the muscles of her calf and bent her knee a little — the knee of the leg she was standing on — to keep her equilibrium. She put the sole of her shoe flat against Lucien's bulge, that throbbing length inside his trousers, and she pressed hard.

His mouth opened wide in a silent scream of ecstasy, his eyes rolled up in his head. The jerking of his body announced he had achieved the peak of delight after his long climb up the slope. He was spurting uncontrollably in his underwear, his belly was jerking in frantic spasms.

When his heart-beat returned to normal and he was again able to comprehend what was said to him, Gaby was still standing in front of him, hands on her hips, but with both her feet on the floor.

'*Chérie, comme je t'adore,*' he murmured.

'That's good to hear,' said she with a smile. 'You can prove it by taking me into the bedroom and pulling off these knickers you like so much.'

He was up off the chair at once and his arm was around her bare waist to lead her to the bed.

When he took off all his clothes, Gaby saw what she from past experience guessed to be so − he was wearing fine silk knickers with lace and embroidery under his trousers. These had received the sticky tribute of his passion and were soaked through, from the waistband down to the seam between the legs.

'But think of it, the hours that man must spend lurking round underwear counters in department stores!' Suzette exclaimed at hearing of this whim of Lucien's.

'Why not?' said Gaby with a shrug. 'It is his pleasure, and he has every right to indulge it. Some may think it strange, or even slightly perverted. But what of it? It does no harm.'

'But it is too extraordinary, Gaby!'

'For me it is comic and endearing,' she said, and she raised one shoulder in a *don't-care-what-you-say* gesture. 'I am very fond of my little fetishist. He's not one of the men who kiss you twice and jump on top of you − for him making love requires ingenuity and restraint, right up till the climax comes. He has no words to explain himself, but I feel I understand him.'

Knickers and shoes, those were Lucien's two great obsessions. He spent as much time prowling around women's shoe shops as in lingerie departments. High-heeled shoes fascinated him and the higher and thinner the heel, the better. The assistants in shoe shops, expensive shoe shops that is, recognised him as soon as he set foot across the threshold.

If another man had appeared so often and displayed so keen an interest, some action might have been taken to warn him off. It was impossible, after all, for him to hide the bulging stiffness under his clothes while he handled the gleaming new shoes on display. But Lucien had so charming a manner, and spent money so freely, he was welcome in every shop he visited.

For his games he bought new pairs of very expensive shoes at least once a week. By chance Gaby had found the wardrobe in his bedroom was stacked with them and it made her laugh to see his collection. The game began when he took twenty pairs out of the wardrobe and lined them up on the floor, his brown eyes bright with excitement as he touched them.

This game was always played in the bedroom, not the sitting-room, the shoes arranged in a long row between bed and door. All types of shoe were to be seen there, open-fronted gold evening-shoes, bright scarlet shoes with narrow ankle-straps, black-and-white patent leather shoes with sharp-pointed toes, shoes made of gold and green brocade, shoes made of finest wild silk, hand-embroidered, stage shoes set with glittering crystal diamonds − every type of shoe imaginable, all with high heels, some almost as thin as spikes.

For this curious expression of Lucien's imagination Gaby kept her clothes on. Her make-up had to be perfect — that was of the greatest importance to him. In the bathroom she washed her face clean, in the bedroom she sat before the mirrored dressing-table to paint her face and lips, to darken her neatly plucked eyebrows, to comb through her long blonde hair.

All this time Lucien sat silent, which for him was unknown in other circumstances. He couldn't quite keep his hands still, he had to be fast asleep for that and even then, as Gaby knew, he twitched about almost continually. This made him so restless a person to share a bed with that she preferred to take a taxi at four in the morning to her own apartment, rather than stay all night with him.

But while he watched her beautifying herself for his game he was as still as he ever could be. His head craned from side to side to catch her reflection in the dressing-table mirror while she applied her bright red lipstick. His feet shuffled a little on the carpet when she shook out her hair. From a corner of her eye Gaby could see him in the mirror too, she smiled to see how his hands fluttered, touching his mouth, tugging at an earlobe, stroking briefly between his thighs. He was entirely unaware of his own nervous little movements.

When the make-up was at last perfect Gaby slipped off her own shoes and stood in silk-stockinged feet before the long line of expensive footwear Lucien had arranged. He had taken his jacket and tie off, to be comfortable. He turned his chair around and waited in a silence that seemed to throb with heavy emotion.

'I wonder which shoes to wear today?' Gaby said, looking down at the luxurious choice before her, this being how the game was played, 'I'm very fond of the black patent leathers – they make my ankles look slim and elegant.'

'Adorable,' Lucien breathed, finding his voice now, 'superb.'

'But let me see, I wore them yesterday. The crimson pair with the gold trim and the spike heels, perhaps? Very exotic – have you noticed that every man in the street turns his head to look at me when I go out wearing those?'

Needless to say, she had never been out of Lucien's apartment in any of the shoes he bought for his games. They were special, new and shiny, the leather uncreased, the soles clean and pale from never having touched a pavement.

It aroused Lucien furiously, to imagine her walking along the street, her beautiful body naked, with a chic little hat on her blonde head, a pair of his play-shoes on her feet. His bulging trousers testified to his comic arousal, his hands fluttered at the immensity, wanting to touch it, to rub it, but restraining his own desire, letting it intensify for the unheard-of pleasure to come.

But it was only in his mind, this scene of Gaby naked except for shoes. For the actual wearing of the shoes, in his bedroom, he wanted her to be fully dressed. Though Gaby told Suzette she understood Lucien, that she found his games highly comical, the truth was she had only the very haziest notion of what went on inside his head.

He *explained* it to her, of course. He wanted her to share his pleasure. He described how she would look when she sauntered naked along the Avenue de l'Opera in his fancy footwear, her bottom pink and delicious in the sunlight, her silver-blonde tuft down between her legs gleaming. But for all his explanations, Gaby was no wiser. Not that it troubled her in the least, if Lucien found pleasure in his unusual games, there was nothing more to be said.

Sometimes for these imaginary outings he allowed her to wear silk stockings, depending on the shoes she chose. Always black, of course, black silk stockings so fine they were transparent. This he insisted on in his running commentary. A suspender-belt kept them up, he always wanted that in the picture.

Usually it was a black lace suspender-belt, depending on what he had seen lately in the stores where he went to look around the ladies' underwear department in search of little nothings for Gaby to wear. And to fuel his imagination.

In Lucien's mind's-eye the picture was perfect. The narrowest black lace suspender-belt across Gaby's satin-skinned belly, a little above her hips, positioned so as not to hide her dimpled belly button. Elegant black silk stockings from thighs to toes, shiny black patent leather shoes with high heels . . .

Up where her slender thighs met, up above the stocking-tops, ah! Lucien kissed his fingertips at the mention of the silver blonde tuft she left as a little adornment there.

'We've arrived at the Café de la Paix, *chérie,*' Lucien said, in his description of the fantasy outing. 'We take a table on the terrace, everyone there is goggling at your naked body – so young and beautiful. The men's tongues hang out like dogs, even the women want to make love to you! You cross your legs, I can hear the *frou-frou* of silk rubbing on silk, your thighs touching! I tell the waiter to bring a bottle of champagne, and the poor chap is doubled over trying to hide his excitement.'

But that came later, first the choice of shoes had to

be made. Gaby spun it out as long as she could to ensure he experienced the delicious torment he longed for. *This pair, perhaps? No, I think the red might be better today. Or the ankle-straps? What do you think of those*? She kept it going until he was writhing in his chair, his trousers open and his excitement sticking out as hard quivering flesh.

— Now it was on show he didn't touch it, even if his hands were flitting about everywhere. He gripped the chair, his knees, his thighs, he put his hands in his trouser pockets and pulled them out again. They landed everywhere but on the fleshy bar between his thighs, for touching it would put a quick and regrettable end to his pleasure.

'Shall I wear these today?' Gaby asked, speaking to herself, not to Lucien. 'I think I will. They're very chic, everyone is going to look at me and think how beautiful I am when I stroll along the rue de Rivoli and the Place des Vosges, to sit in the café there.'

'*Je t'adore*, Gaby . . .' Lucien sighed, his gleaming brown eyes starting from his head.

'And they're perfect for treading on men,' she continued, not indicating that she had heard him. 'That's all men are good for when you think about it seriously, to lie down and be trampled on by a beautiful woman in shoes like these blue ones.'

The choice was made, Lucien knew what he must do. He slipped from his chair and crawled on his hands and knees to her across the thin carpet. His hands trembled as he fitted the shoes she had chosen on to her stockinged feet.

She called them blue for the sake of simplicity. They were of shiny glacé leather, a rich dark cobalt-blue, their heels thin and high. She raised each foot in turn for Lucien to slip them on, it took him some little time to do it, so intense were the emotions that racked him.

When the elegant cobalt-blue shoes were on, Gaby felt she was at least ten centimetres taller. To Lucien crouching down at her feet she must have seemed five metres tall! With gasps of delight he flung himself flat on his belly and he held her ankles with a light and almost reverent touch while he kissed the soft shiny blue leather.

'Ah, you like that, my little pervert,' she murmured, smiling to see his excitement.

She pulled her skirt up her thighs to show her elegant legs. 'In a moment I expect you to turn on your back so I can walk on your body with these shoes.'

The game never progressed that far, there was no need for it. Lucien looked up from her feet, his gaze travelling very slowly up her silk-stockinged legs, from slim ankles to rounded knees. He slid his fingertips along the silk, sighing continuously as if the purple head of his straining stiffness was experiencing the same delicious friction.

He looked up her raised skirt, he shook from head to foot to see the thin silk and lace knickers stretched lightly over the blonde-tufted delight between her thighs.

Ah, those exquisite confections of lace and satin, embroidery and silk, he bought for her all the time! These trophies of his lurking in the boutiques of the rue Cambon! His forays into the lingerie departments of stores along the Boulevard Haussman!

An instant later Lucien was up on his knees, panting out his feverish excitement, as he pressed furious kisses on the thin silk covering the soft flesh

213

between Gaby's thighs and she felt his hot breath through the silk, exciting her.

His arms were wound so tight about her legs she thought he'd never let her go again. In two more moments he would spurt his rapture over the shiny blue patent leather of her shoes.

FRANCINE DISCOVERS HUNGARIAN JUGGLING

The row backstage at the Folies Bergère started well before the curtain was due to rise, it began during the time the performers were getting into their brilliant costumes and putting on their make-up. At first there was a distant shouting, soon it grew into the most horrific screaming.

'Where have you been all day, you bitch? Tell me!'

It was Gilles Cavillier shrieking at poor Francine. Normally she made no attempt to reply to his bullying, she just suffered it, and his threatened beatings, in silence. But something had made this evening different, her voice could be heard above Gilles' shrilly proclaiming he didn't own her.

The show-girls were arranged in the usual line before the long mirror, leaning forward on their chairs to examine minutely the reflections of their beautiful faces and bodies. They would be on show in half an hour to the paying audience.

Suzette was powdering her breasts peach-blossom, Angelique at her side was presenting her bare bottom to the mirror, craning her neck to look at a bite-mark on the left cheek. She rubbed a little flesh-coloured greasepaint over it, before dabbing with a powder-puff.

'Hear that?' said Angelique. 'Francine's answering him back. I never thought she would, did you?'

'Something important must have happened,' Suzette said. 'It's not just making love with the Hungarian, Gilles knows all about that. In fact, everyone knows about it. They've been doing it ever since Armand Regence's party.'

Angelique's dark-haired head was cocked to one side to listen to the appalling row going on not far away, the love-bite upon her bottom was forgotten and the image in the mirror as beautiful as a full moon. 'Perhaps he thinks it's time she stopped?'

'He's been telling her to stop since the very first time she went to the Hungarian's hotel with him. There must be more to it than that.'

'*Mon Dieu*! he's hitting her!' exclaimed Angelique. 'What a pig!'

And indeed they all heard the sound — a heart-quailing sound of hand striking flesh. They heard Francine's scream following the blow.

'That's enough!' declared Suzette, jumping up, 'We can stop him if we all go to their dressing-room and shame him. Come on, who's with me?'

'Not me,' said Jasmin, shaking her head. 'It's a big mistake to interfere when lovers fall out.'

'They're not lovers,' said Suzette. 'He's left-handed.'

'Then it's up to the Hungarian to go and rescue her.'

'I'm with you, Suzette' said Yvette Sorel. 'Let's go and rip his *couillons* off, if he's got any!'

'Me too,' said Angelique with surprising enthusiasm. Perhaps Jean-Pierre, her boyfriend, had annoyed her lately.

'And me!' other voices chimed in.

Jasmin was shamed into getting up and joining in the rush for the dressing-room door. This reluctance to be involved, as they all knew well, was not a moral objection to interfering between couples. It was because she herself had a ludicrous passion for Gilles, she was in love with his body.

It was futile, of course, farcical almost. Nothing would ever come of her passion, unless she knew how to change herself into an eighteen-year-old boy. But she didn't want to antagonise Gilles, just in case.

As an embattled army of Amazons, the show-girls were perhaps a little less than impressive. Like Suzette, some of them were in costume for their appearance on stage in the opening number – a *cache-sexe* with sequins and rhinestones. And body make-up. The superbly proportioned women almost stark naked were unlikely to strike terror into a bully's heart.

Suzette snatched up the old kimono she wore in the dressing-room to put round her shoulders. It came only to her knees, and she was barefoot.

Two of the others were still in their underwear – brassieres and knickers of assorted colours. Jasmin was completely naked, she had been occupied with toning down the dark-red of the buds on her magnificent breasts. She picked up a towel and wrapped it round her loins as she joined on the end of the crowd making for the door. Perhaps it was in her mind to let the towel fall when she confronted Gilles, to let him see what he was missing.

The avenging army of beauties had hardly begun its march when the dressing-room door was flung open and in ran Francine. Her pretty face was streaked with tears. She at least was fully dressed in blouse and skirt, for Gilles had started his shouting at her the moment she arrived backstage.

Suzette was leading the advance, it was to her Francine ran for help. Gilles was close behind, his face dark with fury. He was half-clothed, that is to say, he had his trousers on and his shoes.

'Save me, save me,' Francine was sobbing, her face pressed in between Suzette's breasts, her tears making long streaks in the powder. She had her arms round Suzette's waist and was clinging on as if desperate.

'Bitch!' Gilles was howling.

Face to face not with one defenceless girl but a phalanx of militant showgirls, he came to a standstill and fell silent.

'Leave her alone,' Suzette said sharply, 'or you'll have us to deal with.'

Gilles began to back away toward the open door. It may have been that the sight of so many bare *nichons* dismayed his fastidious taste in these matters. It was not only shapely breasts confronting him, but lush bellies and thighs. And even one red-gold curly-haired delight, Jasmin's towel had slipped to the floor, she was stark naked and open-mouthed, adoring Gilles in silence.

'Without me she'd be nothing,' he said sullenly, retreating a step at a time. 'I dragged her out of the gutter. By now she'd be a ten-franc whore under a railway arch, but for me.'

'She has a right to her own life,' Suzette answered him. 'You didn't buy her.'

'This is all the thanks I get,' he muttered. 'As soon as I make something of her life she goes off with somebody else just because he rams her, the silly little bitch! What about me? What am I supposed to do without a partner for the act, tell me me that!'

'If you treated her decently she wouldn't want to leave you,' Suzette pointed out.

'Pig!' Angelique accused him.

'Pig!' the others joined in shrilly.

Angelique threw the powder-puff she was holding at Gilles and scored a hit on his dimpled chin. A little cloud of powder – a delicate peach colour, burst

218

over his startled face, making him blink and then sneeze.

He stood for a second biting his lips while the show-girls' abusive chant rose higher. Then Gilles turned and fled.

By now the stage-manager was there, demanding to be told what was going on. Then Sandor came dashing into the dressing-room, cursing in Hungarian, intent on maiming any person causing pain or grief to his beloved Francine. Close behind him to back him up in any fight were his partners in the juggling act, two sturdy-looking Hungarians like himself.

The shouting, weeping, swearing, to say nothing of the blood-curdling threats made by Yvette and some of the other show-girls against various portions of Gilles' anatomy, went on for a long time. But eventually the furore died down and everyone returned to the proper business of the evening, getting ready for the performance.

For safety's sake Francine remained with the show-girls, and the stage-manager went to inform Gilles that as his partner was too unwell to go on, the act was cancelled that evening. And also no doubt to deliver solemn warnings and menaces about discontinuing the act forever if Gilles' provoked further scenes of this type.

As Suzette guessed, something of importance had happened to start off the angry row. Francine explained it in detail, very proudly, to the eagerly listening show-girls applying powder and paint.

Sandor and the two other Hungarians – they were all cousins – called themselves The Magnificent Magyars and had a complicated juggling act. They grew their glossy blue-black hair long and they wore tiger-skin loin-cloths – in other words, they resembled a trio of Tarzans, right down to the daggers in their belts.

They arranged themselves at the points of a triangle on stage and each juggled independently to begin with. One with daggers, one with African war-clubs, the third with white skulls. Not of bone, not real human skulls, but replicas carved from wood.

Then they turned to face inwards, they hurled these savage implements at each other, caught them and hurled them back so fast the audience received the impression of an unbroken stream of clubs, skulls and flashing knives.

It was very skilful, of course. It became more so when other items were picked up and added to the stream – gourds, bananas, short spears – until the air above the stage seemed filled with flying objects.

But now, said Francine, an even more death-defying finale was to be added to The Magnificent Magyars' popular act. Sandor had talked to his cousins, they had discussed the matter – in Hungarian – and a decision had been reached. Hands were shaken on it, backs were slapped, rehearsals had already begun. In their new finale they were going to juggle Francine.

As soon as present contracts expired it was *Adieu Gilles* and *Bonjour les Magyars*.

'*Merde alors*!' said Angelique, astonished by what she heard. 'How can anyone juggle a girl? You'll be covered in bruises!'

Francine said it was not so very different from the acrobatic dance she did with Gilles. The Magyars would lift her up above their heads and pass her from one to the other, whirl her about and throw her up and catch her. And they did all this so fast it looked as if they were truly juggling with her body.

Francine was only eighteen and she looked even younger because she was slender and baby-faced. Her hair was a glossy brunette, she kept it short and she had pointed little breasts and a narrow belly.

Sandor the Hungarian juggler had been her first man. She took to love-making like a baby swan to the river. All that pent-up passion thwarted by Gilles had been poured out for Sandor, her first lover, day after day, hour after hour, night after night. Strong man though he was, even he flinched at the impact of her youthful desire.

He found a way to keep Francine content and in good spirits. One astonishing afternoon, in his room in the miserable hotel the Magnificent Magyars stayed in, the plan went into effect.

The curtains were drawn and the room was half-dark. Francine was lying on her back with her knees up, looking fragile in her youthful charm, her body flowerlike and innocent, though Sandor had been making love to her for almost an hour and had twice raised her to moaning climax.

At this moment the other two cousins came into Sandor's room, Janos and Lazlo. They wore shabby woollen dressing-gowns which they threw off to reveal themselves stark naked. They had broad shoulders and thick dark curly hair on their chests, just like Sandor and narrow hips and muscular thighs. Two stiff lengths of flesh were pointing upwards at Francine.

She sat up quickly and glanced at Sandor lying beside her on the bed. His smile was encouraging as he nodded approval, his broad face sleepy and his eyes hardly open.

Francine crossed her legs, for modesty maybe, but not for long. Lazlo knelt on the end of the bed, and put his big hands between her knees, murmuring something in his own language she could not possibly understand.

Perhaps it was *excuse me* or *open your legs, girlie* or *let me see what you've got there*. His tone was polite, whatever he was trying to convey. Francine did not struggle overmuch, modesty or not, she was convinced no harm would come to her with Sandor at her side.

As her legs parted to display the neat little patch of curls between them and the wet lips where Sandor had twice taken his pleasure, Lazlo became so aroused his stiffness swayed up and down. He stroked the inside of Francine's thighs, his hand huge and surprisingly gentle. Meanwhile, Janos had seated himself on the bed sideways behind her and he pulled her back to lean against his hairy chest.

Francine's eyes were half-closed, she had surrendered herself to the sensations of her body. Lazlo was kneeling between her legs, fingers the size of sausages stroking her wet treasure so fondly. Janos had his strong arms round her and he dallied with her pointed little breasts. Beside her lay Sandor, half asleep, a smile on his face, his limp part lying wetly on his belly.

They were traditionalists, the Hungarians. They had a sense of order and rightness. Lazlo took her first, he was the leader of the juggling troupe. Janos supported her from behind and she let him take her weight gratefully. Lazlo put his arms beneath her bent knees and lifted her off the bed bodily.

She felt the smooth round head of his twitching length touch between her thighs, he was positioning it at the moist entrance to her delight.

In another moment he lowered her and skewered her on it. This was the curiously acrobatic posture for her initiation in the art of love-making for three. She was held suspended, as if she lay in a swaying hammock in a summer garden. Janos' hands were under her armpits, Lazlo's hands were under her knees. Together they held her securely, the two Hungarians, giving her a sense of well-being as Lazlo thrust strongly into her slipperiness.

Francine felt so supremely happy she opened her eyes to look at the man sliding in and out of her. She saw Lazlo staring at her narrow belly, his eyes hooded, his wide mouth open and his breath sighing through it.

He gasped and jerked hard, his loins pushed forward suddenly in nervous spasms, and as she felt the hot spurt of his passion inside her, she cried out in her orgasm.

It was Janos' turn as soon as Lazlo pulled out. Between the two of them, they handled her as if she weighed no more than a doll. They turned her around, head to foot, and over, face down and bottom up, and she never once touched the bed. She let them do whatever they liked with her, she trusted them.

Her head was on Lazlo's strong shoulder, her arms around his neck, his capable hands were under her belly, supporting her on his upturned palms. Janos was kneeling between her open thighs, his hands also a firm support for her trembling body. He pushed deep into her and his stiffness felt exactly the same as Lazlo's a minute ago.

Not even his strokes were faster, he thrust with an identical rhythm and force, until his rapture spurted. Francine uttered a wailing gasp and reached her climax again.

'Yes, yes, yes!' she sighed as the ecstatic sensations faded slowly in her eager belly.

When Janos was done, he and Lazlo gently turned

her face up, and lowered her to the bed. Their broad faces, so alike, showed their warm regard for her now she had satisfied them both. They kissed her belly, between her slender thighs and the pink buds of her pointed little breasts.

Her first love, Sandor, had recovered his enthusiasm and he was hard again. There seemed to be no difference Francine could discern in her pleasure-bemused mind between the hard length standing up between Sandor's thighs and the two that had just penetrated her so deftly. Except those two were soft and slack now, their strength spent for the moment.

She turned her brown-haired head to let Sandor kiss her mouth while his hand slid over her breasts. Ah, such hands, such huge hands all three of them had! Hands that could cover a breast and contain it completely, hands trained by years of juggling, hands that were sure and skilful!

She was on her back and her legs were wide apart. Sandor slid on to her perspiring little belly and with a single strong push sheathed himself in her. He rode her affectionately, pleased he was her first and most important lover, content that Lazlo and Janos should share his good fortune.

When the climax came this time she thought it would never end — it was ecstasy beyond all imagining. She had three strong and good-looking men to love her, three friends to enjoy her young body, three masterful lovers to take her to the peak of delight again and again. And she had three well-trained partners for a sensational new act. If it couldn't be the Folies Bergère after the row with Gilles, there was always the Moulin Rouge.

The friendship of Blaise and Suzette had cooled. He no longer waited for her after the performance and she often went for a drink and a chat to a nearby bar, popular with members of the cast. Angelique also met her boyfriend there, the unsympathetic but well-off Jean-Pierre.

On the night of the row, the three Hungarians were at a table of their own, seated in a protective group around Francine. And poor Jasmin was in a sad mood after baring all to Gilles and he had never noticed.

'I kept my eyes on his face when my towel slipped,' she said mournfully to Suzette, 'and there was not even a flicker.'

'Perhaps you should have looked lower down.'

'I did and there wasn't a flicker there either.'

One of the men interested in Suzette made himself pleasant to her. He was nothing to do with the Folies Bergère but he was in the bar most nights. He was forty or so, heavily built and slow of movement, but acceptably good-looking and well dressed.

Suzette had let him get as far as chatting with her and even let him buy her a glass of Pernod. He said he was a businessman − but everyone said that. His conversation was boring, his only topic himself. To get rid of him she smiled her dazzling smile at one of Miss Hetty's boys sitting alone and looking forlorn.

Jasmin was very happy to take over the businessman's interest and Hetty's boy was very happy indeed to bring his drink across and sit down beside Suzette. It was Anatole, the one who'd been dancing with Hetty when she made cruel fun of Armand Regence at his own party.

His surname was Bord and he told Suzette he was from Amiens. Anatole gave her the impression of being good-natured, with a certain charm though not too intelligent. But what of that? His fortune was his physique. Hetty picked her troupe entirely on their size and bulk. Like the others, Anatole stood almost head and shoulders taller than the average man, his shoulders looked as wide as a taxi, his chest was as big as a wine-barrel.

Seen in a bar wearing a smart blue jacket, a striped tie, and well-pressed grey trousers, he was altogether a different man – not the same person Suzette was accustomed to seeing on stage. Hetty's boys posed in black top-hats and fake leopard-skin briefs, showing off their enormous smooth-shaven chests and their massive muscular thighs. And eye-catching bulges in their leopard-skin.

Wearing ordinary clothes, Anatole had turned into an ordinary, if big, man of twenty-five or twenty-six, eager to please, yet slightly confused. Suzette had not been talking to him for long before it emerged that he loathed Miss Hetty with a deep and abiding hatred.

'Why stay with her then?' Suzette asked.

'What else can I do?' he said. 'All I know is being a garage mechanic in Amiens, before I took up weight-lifting. Miss Hetty pays better than being a mechanic.'

Naturally, the question hanging on the very tip of Suzette's tongue was not whether the boys were required to make love to Hetty, everyone took that for granted. The interesting point was – did they make love to her in a group or one at a time?

Suzette's own view, as expressed to Angelique, was that Hetty took them all on at the same time in a mass orgy with mind-shattering multiple orgasms that went on for hours. But that was only her guess, she was realist enough to know the truth was likely to be less amusing.

It was not a question to be asked casually, this business of Hetty's orgies. At least, not in a bar and of a man she hardly knew to whom she had chatted for barely twenty minutes. But as things turned out, she had no need to ask it. Anatole so detested his employer that he spoke freely about her, without any prompting. Suzette listened, trying to remain straightfaced, to a recital of the grievances of the boys against Hetty.

It seemed Suzette was mistaken, there were no mass orgies on the floor. The American woman did not have all six of her Greek gods at the same time. If any such thought ever came into her head she would have regarded it as French and degenerate.

It was strictly one a night for Hetty, or two if she'd drunk more champagne than usual. Even then it was one at a time, one after the other, the first leaving her bedroom before she sent for the second to join her.

'Hetty looks like a woman,' said Anatole, sounding resentful, 'she has a pair of *nichons* and a slit between her legs, but she is really a man.'

When Suzette asked what he meant, he explained how Hetty made love. The burly boy summoned to her bed would find Hetty naked, fully made-up, her blonde-bleached hair perfect. Without a word of tenderness, he was told to strip and lie on his back. Truth to tell, Hetty's men − it was ridiculously sentimental to call them boys − were healthy animals, not overburdened with brains. By the time the chosen one had gawped at her naked body and got his own clothes off, he was stiff and ready.

Hetty had made her own way in the world, from bottom-of-the-bill club performer in the backstreets of a third-rate American city to international star touring the capitals of Europe, especially Paris − her favourite. She never for a moment forgot to whom she owed her success − herself. Men were there to be made use of, never given a centimetre for fear they would try to take a kilometre. Even Hetty's booking agent was a woman.

In bed it was the same, but more so. No man was ever going to get on top of her and use her for his pleasure. She threw a leg over the strapping weight-lifter on her bed, she straddled him, steered his stiff length into her and she slid down it. From then on it was merely a question of whether she wanted her climax to come fast or slow, she decided how fast and how hard, and moved up and down the plaything inside her as her mood suggested.

Sometimes she wore a fur coat while she ravished the boy, an opulent black sable coat, or a full-length blonde mink, undone to display her body while she rode the gasping victim for her pleasure. These fur coats were the fruits of her work, symbols of what she had achieved. The muscular man between her legs, he too was a trophy of her success.

She was Miss Hetty, international singing star, and she liked to remind herself of that fact every day.

If she was feeling especially triumphant and exhilarated, say the applause that evening at the end of her act had been louder and longer than usual, maybe even with cries of approval and calls for *encores* – well, on an evening like that she bestrode a boy as soon as she got back to her hotel and rode him in a furious gallop. She rampaged upon his stiffness until she shrieked and collapsed in a wet and sticky orgasm.

Even when she felt tired, there was no question of not having her ride before she slept. On these occasions she moved slowly, not bouncing up and down but undulating her hips, like a belly-dancer. This way she could arouse herself and make it last for twenty minutes or half an hour, sometimes longer.

The men dreaded those nights. To succumb before Hetty reached her crisis, to spurt into her before she was ready for it, this threw her into a tremendous rage. Her dreamy up-and-down came to a stop, she screamed and shouted, smacked his face viciously with both hands from her superior position and called him no-good, a weakling. And various other choice French gutter epithets she had learned.

The disgraced one was told to go away and send someone else in quick. But on the very next night the one who failed her was used again, to see if he'd learned a lesson in self-control. If he disappointed Hetty twice, that was the end of his career on stage, he was out of the act.

There was no difficulty in replacing anyone not up to Hetty's personal standard, the sports clubs and cheap gymnasiums around the Paris suburbs were full of burly young men who could easily be lured away from their dreary homes and boring jobs. The promise of a career in show-business worked miracles.

Indeed, sometimes the troupe believed Hetty had deliberately tipped one of them over the edge by spinning out her climax far beyond male endurance. Then she sacked him in disgrace, to give herself the pleasure of auditions with three or four promising candidates.

Needless to say, it was all Suzette could do to keep herself from laughing at this farcical account. It was more ridiculous than she ever could imagine! But Anatole sounded so miserable, he looked so much like a lost puppy, she stifled her laughter though the effort made her ribs ache.

Perhaps it was this lost puppy look, a puppy with sorrowful brown eyes and weighing at least 100 kilos, all of it muscle or bone, that persuaded Suzette to invite Anatole to her apartment that night. 'If he was available,' she said with a straight face. He assured her eagerly that it was not his duty night, that was two nights ago, tonight was Theo's turn.

When they arrived at the rue de Rome and climbed the stairs, the apartment was dark and silent. Gaby was out with Lucien. In Suzette's bedroom Anatole became *distrait* and Suzette guessed what was going through his mind. He was asking himself if tonight he was allowed to be the man, or was he expected to undress and lie on his back, as for Miss Hetty?

He took off his blue jacket and sat on the bed, his sad brown eyes following Suzette, waiting for his cue.

She stood near him and stroked his face, fingers through his hair. He put a hand on her leg, unsurely at first, then as he grew in confidence he slid it up her thigh under her skirt. She had noticed while they talked in the bar he bit his fingernails – a result of frustration, perhaps, and the nervousness created by the American woman's demands.

Poor Anatole – his nails were bitten right down to the quick. When he grew bold enough to slip his hand into her knickers and touch the bareness between her thighs, Suzette thought it felt not so much like a hand caressing her but more like four lovers rubbing their stiff parts against her, all at the same time.

The thought made her smile, though by then Anatole's face was pressed against her and he couldn't see her expression. And now he knew he was the man and it was his right to decide what was to be done, he lost his nervousness altogether.

He held Suzette to him, to sit on his knee, his hand firm now between her legs. He kissed her mouth while he felt her so very thoroughly it was as if he'd never touched a woman before. He stretched her out on the bed, his huge body alongside her.

Suzette lay smiling at him while he peeled off her clothes. She was wearing nothing special, expecting to go home after the show alone, just a pretty cross-over blouse in vermilion with two rows of gold buttons down the front and a perfectly ordinary black skirt.

Anatole took his time to strip her naked, layer by layer. His hands moved over her without the smallest pause, around her breasts and under them, into the hollows of her waist, beneath her to stroke her bottom, then across her belly. She could feel her flesh responding to his touch, trembling as he aroused her.

She thought she understood. Miss Hetty never allowed her boys to touch her body. Anatole and the others had to lie with their hands at their sides. Hetty was the one to do the touching and feeling, before she mounted and took her pleasure. Anatole was making up for that, feeling a woman and exploring every part of her body.

He was so enthusiastic in this that he brought her to a first climax without even realising what he had done. He stared down at her in perplexity as she moaned and squirmed, loins jerking up, her belly quaking in delight. When he understood, he became unstoppable – he threw his clothes off at once.

Suzette looked up in wonder at the heroic body looming above her. Anatole's shoulders were broad and strong enough to lift a large automobile, his biceps swelled out like footballs, his chest was as big as a wardrobe. And all this mightiness was set on a narrow waist and a flat belly ribbed with hard muscle.

His massive thighs were like tree-trunks. Where they joined, in a patch of dark hair, there jutted upward boldly the part of him most important at that

moment. It was of ordinary size, no more, the mighty
development of the rest of his frame here did not
continue in this particular.

Whatever his weight-lifting exercises had achieved
with arms and legs and chest, two significant areas
were passed by in the development, the part between
his ears and the part between his legs. Not that it was
of any great importance, Suzette thought in relief,
high intelligence was of little value in bed, and fifteen
centimetres was as effective as twenty.

Indeed, after her acquaintance with Blaise, it
would perhaps be reasonable to say that too big was
as unsatisfactory as too small. But to be crushed
beneath Anatole's huge and heavy body, that was
marvellously exciting! She was pinned to the bed by
his weight, unable to move, completely at his
disposal – and it was so arousing she was close to a
second orgasm at once.

He slid his average-size deep into her, the
sensations were delicious. She spread her legs wider,
gasping in unbearable joy at the feel of him inside.
He was invading her beautiful body, ravaging her
belly, thrusting and straining to reach his crisis and
fill her to the brim . . . *ah yes, yes*, she murmured.

How good it was to be filled, to lie under a man
and feel his strong thrusts! The delight of having that
firm flesh inside, sliding and pushing! She felt her
orgasm growing in her belly, like an explosion of
golden-yellow light.

She tried to raise her belly and loins to take
Anatole inside her to the limit, but his weight held
her tight to the bed. She could only thrash with her
heels at the mattress as he panted and jabbed into her
flesh. When the crisis took her suddenly, she opened
her mouth wide to scream but the ecstasy became so
dazzling she sobbed instead.

Anatole's own pleasure was short but noisy. He moaned and he groaned, he beat the bed with fists the size of cantaloupes, a brutal tattoo that set the bedsprings twanging in protest. When he was finished, he rolled off Suzette and said in a satisfied tone 'That's more like it.'

Suzette took a deep breath now his immense weight was lifted. She cupped her breasts in her hands to make sure they weren't completely flattened.

When Anatole had recovered his strength, in fifteen minutes or so, she intended to squat over him while he lay on his back – to do it to him the way the American woman did. He'd complain about it, no doubt. But what of that? He was accustomed to being used by a woman.

Miss Hetty was an international star but Suzette was determined to be an even bigger star herself. It would be interesting to find out how it felt to be Hetty, to get inside the skin of a star. How better than by doing it Hetty's way? By riding her overdeveloped weightlifter till his eyes rolled up in his head and he spurted his virility for her?

LUCIEN'S SISTER
EXPLAINS

After two evenings with no sign of Lucien, Gaby telephoned him after the show at the Cabaret-Mouchard. That is, she dialled the number of his apartment — but no one answered. She tried again after lunch, then a third time that evening. The telephone rang and rang. No one picked it up.

She knew Lucien was hardly ever there during the day but he wasn't there at midnight either. She discussed the absence with Suzette and asked what she thought of this sudden silence from a man who had shown himself to be utterly devoted.

Suzette shrugged and said perhaps he had been arrested. Gaby should telephone the police, she suggested, and see if they had him locked in a cell.

Then, seeing she had upset Gaby, she put her arms round her to hug her and press cheeks together. 'He'll send you a message,' she said, 'he's gone off for a day or two on his business.'

'Suppose he's lying injured or ill, alone in the apartment,' Gaby said. 'I shan't rest until I've been there to see.'

This conversation took place at one in the morning, when the two friends arrived home from their work and Gaby had once more tried and failed to get Lucien on the telephone.

'In the morning,' Suzette said in a soothing manner. 'I'll go with you, if you like.'

'No, I can't wait that long. I'm going now.'

'*Chérie* — there's no one there, you've just proved

that. Why chase across Paris at this time of night? It's pointless.'

Pointless or not, nothing could dissuade Gaby. She pulled on a light raincoat and checked she had money for a taxi in her pocket. Suzette sighed and slipped her shoes back on, to accompany her friend on a journey she regarded as idiotic. Gaby kissed her cheek and insisted she go to bed. If Lucien was back when Gaby reached the Boulevard de Magenta she would stay with him and Suzette would have to return alone.

They argued for a while over this but eventually Suzette let herself be persuaded to stay at home while Gaby went off to see if Lucien had returned. or left any message with the concierge. Or was lying in bed with broken bones from a beating by rival gangsters. Or was healthy and had another woman there to assist in his curious games with silk knickers and shiny shoes.

This last possibility was uppermost in Suzette's mind, as her opinion of Lucien was not particularly flattering. It was also in Gaby's mind, though neither she nor Suzette had even hinted at it out loud. Men were like that, they wanted you every day for a month or two, they arrived with gifts of flowers and perfume, they took you to lunch, dinner, dancing . . .

They said they adored you, they had you on your back morning, noon and night. They had their hand down your knickers in taxis and cinemas, they kissed your feet, they licked your backside − then one day they weren't there any more. No telephone calls or flowers or outings. They'd met someone else, simple as that.

Naturally, it was heart-break the first time it happened, the second time was painful but less so. From then on, men were no longer mysterious in their motives or held any surprise, unless they really fell in love. Which could turn out to be very inconvenient at times.

Suzette was twenty-two and Gaby the same age. They had gained a firm understanding of men and their ways. But now it seemed Gaby was heading for a sad and sorry time over a criminal she called her little fetishist. The signs were he'd found another playmate. That, at least, was Suzette's thinking, as she slipped into bed and turned off the light.

Gaby did not have good luck with men, not once since she and Suzette had begun to share the apartment. There had been the lawyer, Claude Ronsard, a handsome man with a thin black moustache like an old-fashioned film star. He loved Gaby to desperation, according to him. He showered presents on her, he took her away at week-ends to stay in luxury hotels on the Côte d'Azur.

He also made tremendous scenes outside the apartment door, if he arrived to find Gaby was not at home.

He was vain and jealous and he behaved like an idiot. More than once, after raging and bellowing for ten minutes, he broke down and wept on Suzette's shoulder. He pleaded with her to tell him why he was being tormented by Gaby in this cruel and heartless way — why was he tortured by a woman he adored to distraction?

He would leave his wife if Gaby agreed to live with him, that he swore. If she refused him, he would throw himself into the Seine and drown. And so on and so on, these dramatic declarations of his were as gripping as any play at the Comédie-Française. When his misery eventually abated, after fifteen or twenty minutes of tragic declamation, he tried to feel Suzette's breasts.

In Suzette's opinion it was a stroke of good luck when Claude made his young wife pregnant by mistake and disappeared out of Gaby's life — good luck for Gaby and good luck for herself. Not that Claude was the worst Gaby had known. Before him there had been a lunatic named Raymond who wanted to move into the apartment with them, a redheaded man with an incomprehensible manner of talking.

Raymond was a five-times-a-day-man, he boasted to every woman he talked to, even complete strangers in bars.

'Something loose in the attic?' Suzette asked Gaby, tapping her forehead and raising an eyebrow.

'He's from Lyon, it's just his way,' Gaby said with a shrug. 'There's nothing loose down below, it's always stiff.'

'Five times a day?'

'Not every day,' Gaby confessed.

And before mad Raymond there was . . . but while Suzette went on with her review of the long catalogue of Gaby's unsatisfactory boyfriends, she fell asleep.

Gaby meanwhile walked briskly from the apartment down towards the Gare St Lazare to the nearest taxi-rank and was soon on her way to Lucien's apartment.

There was no answer at first, but just in case he was asleep or in bed for some other reason, she knocked loudly and waited. After a while she heard footsteps inside the apartment and she rapped her knuckles impatiently against the door-panel again.

The door opened slowly and Gaby's fears were realised when she saw who stood there — not Lucien but a frizzy-haired woman. She was about thirty and she was wearing Lucien's red silk dressing-gown. The dressing-gown was untied and open; a pale pink gleam of flesh showed she had nothing on underneath.

'Who are you, banging on the door at this time of night, what do you want?' she complained sleepily.

'Ah, this is too much!' Gaby exclaimed.

She visualised Lucien in bed, too lazy to get up, sending his new woman to answer the door! With her eyes blazing, Gaby put a hand on the door and flung it wide open, almost knocking over the astonished woman in the dressing-gown. She pushed past her and dashed through the apartment to the bedroom, furious enough to scratch Lucien's eyes out.

The bedroom door stood open, Gaby hurled it back to the wall, her mouth open to denounce the little criminal. But the bed was empty though it was turned down on one side, where the frizzy-haired woman got out to answer the door. Otherwise it was neat and tidy, no one could have imagined love-making had recently taken place on it.

Lucien made use of his bed only occasionally for that. It was not his way to take his pleasures horizontally. But there was no line of high-heeled shoes across the carpet. None of his clothes were in sight − only a white brassiere and plain white knickers, flung down on a chair, with a lemon-striped frock.

The woman in Lucien's dressing-gown followed her through the apartment and was standing just behind her.

'Where is Lucien?' Gaby demanded, her pretty face flushed.

'You must be his girlfriend,' said the other. 'Gaby, yes?'

'And who are you?'

'I'm his sister, my name's Marcelle.'

Gaby stared at her closely and with suspicion, her thoughts in confusion. Lucien had never said he had a sister but then he'd never mentioned any family at all, neither mother, father, nor even where he was born. From his accent Gaby had assumed he was a Parisian, born and bred. But he'd never said so. And for all she knew, he could have ten brothers and sisters.

On the other hand, such acquaintances of his she had met were not exactly law-abiding citizens who paid taxes and told the truth. Just because this woman claimed to be Lucien's sister it did not make it necessarily so. There was no family resemblance Gaby could discern.

Lucien's hair was dark-brown and wavy, Marcelle's light-brown and frizzy. His eyes were dark brown — hers dark blue! His jaw was prominent and his face long, her face was round and broad. He was shorter than average, she was as tall as Gaby herself.

'If you're his sister, you don't look like him.'

'That's what Papa always says,' Marcelle commented, shrugging one thin shoulder inside the silk dressing-gown, 'but then he's a suspicious man and Mama was flighty when she was young. Make what you like of it. Neither of us look the least like the old man. Come and sit down, we'll have a drink while we talk.'

Nothing was to be gained standing like a fool by an empty bed and so Gaby followed Marcelle into the sitting-room. She draped her raincoat over one armchair and sat down in another, letting Marcelle see she was here by right, as the girlfriend of the owner, not on Marcelle's sufferance.

'Where is Lucien?' she asked again. 'Do you know?'

Marcelle was pouring fine cognac into two glasses.

'You haven't said who you are yet,' she observed.

'Gabrielle Demaine, and I'm a close friend of Lucien. Is that good enough for you, Mademoiselle Cluny, if that's your name?'

'It's not,' said Marcelle mildly, handing her a glass. 'It's Marcelle Legrand. And Cluny isn't Lucien's name, any more than it's mine – it's just one he uses for business. I suppose you'd guessed that.'

'Is Legrand the name you and he were born with?'

'No.'

Beyond the simple negative Marcelle offered no information on what her original name might have been, or Lucien's either.

'And what about Marcelle?' Gaby asked. 'Is that authentic or did you change it?'

'I picked it myself. I like it a lot better than the name I was given.'

'This entire thing is absurd,' said Gaby. 'Nobody is who they say they are.'

She took a sip of Lucien's excellent cognac and waited. This sister, if she truly was that, was not to be rushed, so much was clear. She was going to take her own time over telling what she thought a mere girlfriend ought to know.

'You're a dancer, he told me about you,' said Marcelle. 'I thought you might call round.'

'I telephoned a dozen times – there was no answer.'

'Was that you ringing half an hour ago? I was in the bath. I haven't been here until tonight, I wouldn't be here now except Lucien wanted me to drop in and dispose of some . . . well, never mind what. Anyway, I'm here now.'

So saying, Marcelle flopped down upon the beige sofa opposite Gaby and kicked off her slippers. The red dressing-gown drifted open, the belt untied. Her legs were spread, exposing her belly and a curly bush, light brown in colour. Below the curls thin lips pouted prominently. Gaby was used to naked women round her every day in the dressing-room, she hardly noticed the display and paid no attention to it.

'Where is Lucien?' she repeated patiently.

'He had to go away, Gaby, I'm sure you understand. They were looking for him, but he got the word in time.'

'Who is looking for him?'

'The police, who else? He's gone on holiday till things calm down again. Six months and he'll be back, you'll see. A year if he's unlucky and his contacts are not as good as he thinks.'

'This holiday, is it abroad?'

'He didn't tell me. He left something for you.'

Marcelle got up, the dressing-gown hanging loosely about her, hiding nothing. Her breasts were small, soft rather than firm. She went toward the bedroom on bare feet and came back a minute later with a thick envelope in her hand.

'Lucien has a nice line in chat but he's not very good with a pen,' said she with an amiable smile. 'He asked me to give this to you and tell you he adores you and he'll miss you.'

She perched lightly on the arm of Gaby's chair and handed her the big envelope. Gaby weighed it in her hand, guessing what it contained.

'Go on, open it,' Marcelle prompted.

Inside was a bundle of banknotes held in a rubber band. Gaby riffled through and realised it was a great deal of money.

'I hardly know what to say – I don't want this,' she said.

'Keep it or spend it,' Marcelle advised. 'Lucien meant well.'

'Just what sort of business does Lucien make this money in?'

'It's not for me to tell you about his business if he hasn't, is it? The money's yours to do what you like with – put it in the poor box at church if you like. And, by the way, he asked me to give you a kiss for him.'

Gaby smiled and turned her face up to be kissed on the cheek. But Marcelle leaned over and covered her mouth with her own in a long hot kiss which surprised Gaby. As the kiss continued and the tip of Marcelle's wet tongue slipped gently between Gaby's lips, it stirred disturbing emotions within her.

They were also agreeable, these emotions, disturbing in a way that was exciting, and she did not break away from the embrace. Then Marcelle's lips were on her throat, her hand had crept up under Gaby's pretty blue pullover, to stroke her breasts with a gentle affection through her thin satin brassiere.

'Ah no,' Gaby murmured, freeing her mouth from the enveloping kiss that seemed to go on for ever.

But if the truth were told, this *no* of hers had an ambiguity about it which was apparent even to herself. Marcelle was not a threat, she was calmly seductive. Gaby's *no* didn't really mean *this is intolerable – stop it immediately*!

The significance was something more like *what you are doing is unfamiliar and surprising – but perhaps it may be agreeable*.

In effect, without consciously reaching a decision, Gaby had already decided to let this very strange encounter continue for the moment, though only for as long as it remained pleasurable. The instant it started to offend her, she would push Marcelle away and tell her to stop it. And Marcelle would get a telling-off for her insulting and perverse behaviour.

Marcelle had the brassiere undone, she pushed it up to Gaby's neck, out of the way. She turned the pullover up to bare Gaby's enchanting breasts, she leaned lower to kiss them and flutter her tongue over their tips. It felt so very delicious, the way she did that, Gaby was overcome. She lay back in the armchair and let it happen.

It was unbelievable, she had come here to find Lucien because she was worried about him. If he were here, and on his own, she would have screamed at him for his inconsiderate conduct in vanishing for three days without a word. Then she would have forgiven him and played one of his little fetish games with him.

In fact, she was sitting in the same armchair as Lucien the last time they played the game with frilly knickers — she naked and strolling up and down the room, he gripping the cushion and getting redder and redder in the face, staring at her beautiful slender body in motion, at the sway of her breasts and the bounce of her bottom.

It was the delicious contrast of shiny black satin seen against the perfect flesh of her thighs that roused him almost to climax just by looking at her. A strange thought came into Gaby's mind — was it possible the same sight might arouse Lucien's sister to an equal frenzy of desire? Lucien could be made to spurt in his trousers by the pressure of a foot in a high-heeled shoe — what could Marcelle be made to do?

But these were only the whirling images of an intense sexual arousal. Marcelle's hand was under

Gaby's skirt, feeling up her thighs above the stockings, slipping into her knickers. The way her long thin fingers touched Gaby was thrilling beyond words.

'Gaby, Gaby, Gaby,' she murmured, kissing her ear through her long silver-blonde hair, 'you are so beautiful, *chérie*, you are so beautiful.'

In another moment she knelt before Gaby and flung off the red silk dressing-gown to show herself completely naked. She spread Gaby's long dancer's legs apart and put her hand on the little tuft of blonde hair between the bare thighs. She stroked it and sighed in delight. She opened the pink lips beneath the blonde tuft, she pressed a fingertip to the tiny bud she had exposed.

She bent down to kiss it, her hands on Gaby's open thighs and her tongue lapping deftly. It felt to Gaby exactly as if Lucien was pleasuring her. She opened her legs wider, offering herself to Marcelle in an act of surprised surrender.

This is absurd, she was saying in her mind, *I came here to feel a man's tongue between my legs, not a woman's! What sort of comedy is this*?

Marcelle slid her hands under Gaby's bottom to clasp the taut cheeks. She squeezed them, her fingers sinking into the flesh.

Gaby's thighs were impossibly wide apart, she was sighing and thrust her belly upwards to receive the ardent ministrations of the tongue flickering in her. She could feel the climax coming on fast, she sighed again, her head back on the upholstery, her mouth open in anticipation.

Only a few days ago it had been Lucien sitting in this chair and it was Lucien's legs straining apart. Gaby was balancing on one leg, to put her foot against the bulge in his trousers, smiling down into his flushed face. He was unaware of her smile, he was staring as if mesmerised at the shiny black satin knickers she wore. He stretched out a shaking arm, trying to touch them, to feel the satin under his fingers in his moments of ecstasy.

Her leg was longer than his arm, he couldn't reach far enough. She grinned and pressed her foot hard, she felt a sudden hard jerk against the sole and saw Lucien's eyes roll up in his head as he spurted. That too made her grin, he was spurting into the expensive silk knickers he put on under his trousers when they played this game together.

Poor little Lucien, she thought feverishly, he's run away and doesn't have me to play with.

Marcelle's tongue was ravaging her senses away, the brunette's head down there between her parted thighs. Gaby shrieked and bucked in the beige chair as an intolerable pleasure gripped her belly and flung her headlong into ecstasy. It was too much, too much! It went on and on and she was sobbing with delight, unable to bear it, wanting it to stop, wanting it to continue.

At last the tongue was still and the spasms of ecstasy racking Gaby were subsiding. Her belly still trembled and her legs shook as she stretched them out and drew in deep shuddering breaths.

Marcelle straightened her back, smiled at Gaby and then lay forward on her, belly on belly and breasts against her breasts, their cheeks pressed together. Her long fingers were twined in Gaby's hair, lifting it away from her face.

'I saw all the shoes in the wardrobe,' she said. 'They're for Lucien's little games, I suppose?'

Gaby nodded, shrugged, and said she would like another drink. Marcelle suggested they take the cognac bottle into the bedroom and make themselves comfortable. *Why not*? thought Gaby, there must be a lot more to it, this lovemaking between women. So far nothing had happened she'd not enjoyed a thousand times with Lucien and other boyfriends. It was very nice, the way Marcelle did it, but a tongue was a tongue and surely there was more to learn than that.

They got into Lucien's bed naked together, that bed with the badly chosen headboard of pink velvet and big gold studs. They propped themselves comfortably with their backs to it, on soft pillows. Gaby held the glasses, Marcelle poured the cognac. They raised their glasses to each other and laughed.

'*Mon Dieu*! If Lucien could see me now!' said Gaby. 'In bed with his own sister, stark naked! And with a head full of the strangest thoughts of things to do with her!'

'Well, he likes to do strange things himself,' said Marcelle. 'Tell me about the shoes, Gaby, I'm dying to hear. He's always had odd ideas about women's underwear, ever since he was a boy. He used to go into shops and stare till they threw him out with a smack round the ear.'

'He still goes into the big shops and stares but these days they don't smack his head because he's got plenty of money and buys whatever takes his fancy. It's the same with shoes.'

'He wears them himself?' Marcelle asked, snuggling herself closer to Gaby, their shoulders touching. The hand that lay on Gaby's thigh had nails varnished bright pink. There was a ring set with a row of diamonds, Gaby hadn't noticed it before.

'Engaged? Married?' Gaby asked.

She took the hand and raised it for a closer look at the ring. The hand curled tightly round hers in an affectionate gesture, and Marcelle said, 'Neither, not now, only a souvenir. So tell me about Lucien's shoes.'

So Gaby told her how the shoe game was played, in the bedroom with Lucien lying full length on the floor to kiss her feet in shiny new shoes, then up her legs to her silk knickers.

'He's a weird one, my brother,' Marcelle said, and shook her head, 'but you can't help liking him.'

'I like him,' said Gaby.

'And he absolutely adores you, he told me so.'

The hand on Gaby's long thigh was moving now. It crept up to her belly and lingered there, stroking and feeling the smoothly perfect skin. Then with a feathery lightness of touch the short pink-varnished nails began to rake over the flesh. Gaby gasped at the sensation, her body quivering pleasurably. The hand was crawling up from her belly to her breasts, over pink buds that were standing firm as berries.

The nails edged their way down to Gaby's belly again, to the insides of her thighs, and every part of her seemed to come alive under the teasing scrape of Marcelle's pink fingernails. Marcelle had a sideways smile on her face, she knew the effect she was having on Gaby. She felt Gaby's pleasure mounting, she meant to hold back the orgasm, prevent it from arriving, keep Gaby gasping and writhing until the moment Marcelle decided was right for her.

'You have a beautiful body, Gaby,' she murmured. 'Lucien must have tremendous luck to find someone as beautiful as you who is willing to play his curious games with him. I wonder what he'd think of this game, if he could see us in his bed now.'

'He might be very angry,' Gaby sighed, her legs trembling to the slow stimulation of Marcelle's nails in her smooth groins.

'I'm certain he'd be furious, *chérie*. That's what

makes it so interesting, for me at least.'

'But . . . you said that as if you resent him . . .' said Gaby, her breasts rising and falling deliciously, 'I don't understand.'

'Lucien is two years younger than me,' said his sister. 'I am older, yes? That should give some standing. But all my life he has been the important one. He makes the decisions, we are only there to do as he says and share a little in his success.'

Gaby had passed into a delirium of pleasure. The fingernails no longer teased and tormented, deft fingertips pried into her, smoothing, touching, rubbing, flicking, compelling.

'Marcelle . . .' she breathed, squirming in the throes of near-ecstasy, 'please. . . finish it!'

'When I am ready, *chérie*. Now I have this opportunity to take just a little revenge on Lucien, why should I rush it? Besides that, you are so gorgeous with your long blonde hair, your tuft of pale gold down here, I want you with me a long time.'

'All night,' Gaby gasped, her loins lifting, 'I'll stay with you all night, Marcelle!'

She meant it too! Her belly rose and fell to the beat of the blood racing through her veins, her legs strained apart and her heels drummed on the bed as she came closer and closer still to the ecstasy that waited to annihilate her.

'All night, *chérie*,' Marcelle sighed. 'Yes, all night.'

Her fingers moved decisively in the slippery warmth between outstretched legs. Gaby reached her climax, her belly clenched to the powerful throbs of delight there.

'That's it,' said Marcelle, her own excitement evident in her voice. 'Yes, Gaby, do it for me!'

And while Gaby writhed in ecstatic sensation, Marcelle rubbed quickly between her own thighs with her other hand, and brought on her own orgasm. She gasped and sighed and shook, bent double above Gaby, slowly subsiding as her quick pleasure faded, until she lay half over her, her soft breasts pressed down on Gaby's firm ones.

After a while Marcelle raised her head.

'Why are you smiling like that?' she demanded.

'Because it felt so marvellous,' said Gaby.

But that wasn't the truth and Marcelle wasn't deceived. She nipped with her teeth at Gaby's bare breasts and demanded to be told the real reason.

'I was thinking how comical Lucien's face would be if he could see us now.'

'Ah, yes,' Marcelle agreed with a chuckle.

That wasn't the truth either, though it satisfied Marcelle's curiosity. Gaby was smiling because the thought had entered her head of how astonished Suzette would be next day when Gaby told her she had spent the night with Lucien's sister.

Not that Suzette would blame her for making love with a woman — Suzette had no hard-and-fast views on lovemaking, she thought people should do whatever pleased them most just so long as no one was harmed. But she would be amazed by Gaby's story, having known so many of her boyfriends — and disapproved of them. They were not good enough for Gaby, she usually said. With that view Gaby found herself in complete agreement, she seemed destined to meet only rats!

But Lucien's sister! Marcelle Legrand! Except that her name wasn't Legrand and she wasn't baptised Marcelle. Yet another mystery, just like Lucien Cluny, whatever his real name was! A woman with frizzy brunette hair and a sympathetic face, slack little breasts, dark blue eyes and clever fingers!

Ah yes, extraordinarily clever fingers — and an agile tongue that conferred tremors of delight when it touched and licked. A woman of mystery, a mystery that seemed worthwhile to unravel. Now Gaby had tasted a little of the fierce pleasure to be found with Marcelle, she intended to continue.

All night, that was her promise.

Lying on Lucien's bed, contented for a moment, with Marcelle sprawling loosely across her belly, Gaby made another promise — a silent promise to herself — *not just tonight* — *all day tomorrow as well*.

Wherever it was Marcelle lived and whoever she lived with, if there was someone, Gaby meant to persuade her to stay for a few days in Lucien's apartment. It might not be all that difficult to persuade her, she was kissing Gaby's belly again, her breath was hot on her thighs. She was trailing her fingertips over the smooth lips below the silvery-blonde tuft that fascinated her.

Gaby rolled over and pushed Marcelle on to her back, tickling her shaven armpits, making her giggle and squirm, reducing her to helplessness. She threw herself over Marcelle, she pressed her legs apart so she could lie between them, she squeezed her wet plum against Marcelle's. She slipped her hand between their bodies to fondle Marcelle's pliant breasts.

Marcelle let her continue for a while, enjoying Gaby's weight lying on her belly. When she became more aroused she showed her new friend what to do to please her. Marcelle adored having her nipples sucked, the soft little buds became elongated under the touch of Gaby's tongue and hard when she drew one between her lips and into her mouth.

Now it was Marcelle's turn to squirm and sob, to thrash with her legs and clench her fists until her short fingernails cut into her palms. Gaby's blonde head was at her breasts, suckling them like a baby, not taking but giving, giving pleasure beyond Marcelle's capacity to bear it. Her dark blue eyes were blurred by the intensity of her emotions, she stroked Gaby's hair with a trembling hand and sighed her name.

What games did girls play with each other? Gaby was wondering as she teased Marcelle. What games did Marcelle enjoy? If any. Surely not high-heeled shoes, like her brother, that was a game for men to play. Then what? When Gaby found out, and that was not going to take her long, it would be intriguing to play them with her.

Gaby's mouth was at Marcelle's breast, her fingers were down between Marcelle's thighs, sliding in the wetness and warmth of her extreme arousal. Tiny droplets of perspiration trickled on Marcelle's skin, on her forehead, under her chin, between her breasts, down her shaking belly. She arched her back and spread her legs wider, screaming 'Oh Gaby!'

The signs were unmistakable — it had taken less than an hour for Marcelle to become as infatuated with Gaby as her brother.

ENTER A POET

Suzette and Gaby were having lunch together in the rue St Marc after a stroll in bright sunshine from their apartment, window-shopping on the Boulevard Haussman and along the Boulevard des Italiens. Close to the Stock Exchange, the little restaurants here in the rue St Marc were favoured by stockbrokers, and as Gaby was now in the market for a new boyfriend, it seemed a promising place to put herself on show.

Or so Gaby said. Her plan to marry a count or even a duke was now in abeyance. The popular literature she favoured had given her an unsettling impression that aristocrats were fickle above other men in their affections and decadent in their desires to an unnerving degree. Knowing how unreliable ordinary men were, she decided a titled lover might be too much to put up with.

A stockbroker, youngish and stable, but not too dullish – it sounded a better proposition. As a lover and provider of luxury items such as furs and jewels, that is, nothing more permanent.

'What about Marcelle Legrand?' Suzette asked, her impeccable black eyebrows rising slowly. 'After only a few days you've had enough of her loving – is that what you're saying?'

They had settled on trout with almonds for their main course. Both were diet-conscious, being in professions where to gain a kilo was devastating. It was accompanied by a carafe of good white wine, to

help the digestion, and a salad of thinly sliced
tomatoes and chicory.

'No, no,' Gaby protested, 'I adore Marcelle, she
has become a very dear friend. it is very exciting to go
to bed with her.'

'And after the comic antics of her brother with the
underwear, I suppose that lovemaking with another
woman must seem normal by comparison?'

Gaby laughed at that.

'Lucien's version of lovemaking is really very
exciting,' she said. 'If he hadn't disappeared
suddenly I was going to suggest you joined in a
threesome. You'd find it amusing, this business with
shoe-licking and lace knickers.'

'Perhaps,' said Suzette, sounding not very
convinced.

'Anyway, that's off until he comes back to Paris,
which might not be for eight or nine months, if
Marcelle is right. She says bribes are being arranged
and witnesses are being persuaded not to give
evidence, but to me it sounds very doubtful.'

Suzette was too fond of Gaby to declare it was for
the best, this sudden absence of Lucien, but the
thought was not very far from her mind. A
stockbroker would surely be a better bet than a crook
as a boyfriend. Assuming the stockbroker wasn't a
crook in his own way.

'But about Marcelle?' she persisted. 'What are you
going to do? Have you given it any thought at all?'

The well-dressed stockbrokers in the restaurant
were talking deals and big numbers as they gobbled
their huge meals and sank bottle after bottle of
expensive wine. But for all that, their attention was
drawn towards the table by the window.

Some threw furtive glances sideways, some stared
openly, all admired, fascinated by the two beautiful

women, one with raven-black hair and a pretty fringe, the other with silvery blonde hair down to her shoulders. One in a silk frock of lavender and black zebra-stripes, the other in a cherry-red linen suit.

'To tell you the truth,' said Gaby, 'the situation is turning difficult with Marcelle. Naturally we adore each other, just as I said. But in the few days we've been together, it seems she's fallen for me. In fact, she's become infatuated.'

'Seriously?'

'Much too seriously. She has a place of her own out at Ivry – a house, I think, from when she was married, or nearly married. It's hard to be certain of anything with people who turn out to be someone else all the time. I think she owns property, a shop or maybe two, she's nearly as secretive as her brother. Anyway, she's independent and not badly off. Since we met, she's moved into Lucien's apartment. She says she wants to be near me but in fact she wants me to move in with her.'

'*Zut alors*!' said Suzette.

As a response it was wholly inadequate, but nothing else came to mind. At least, nothing she could say without offending Gaby and that she did not want to do.

'She wants us to go everywhere together,' Gaby went on, 'and when I see her she asks what I've been doing since last time we met, it's like having a jealous boyfriend.'

'Like Claude used to be, you mean?'

'Just like that. She even turns up at the Cabaret-Mouchard to see me dancing. Well, so she says, but I think she really wants to make sure I'm not getting friendly with any men.'

'*Oh la la!*' said Suzette, shaking her head in dismay.

'We sit in a bar at two in the morning, just talking, and she has her arm round my waist and is breathing in my ear. We take a taxi back to Lucien's apartment and she wants to kiss me and put her hand up my skirt.'

'In her own way, this Marcelle sounds as if she's as obsessed as her brother,' Suzette observed.

'You'd think it would be irritating, wouldn't you, but so far I find it exciting. I've never had so many climaxes a day in my life! She's determined to meet you — she's jealous we've been friends so long. She's coming to hear you sing next week.'

Not entirely an unmixed blessing, Suzette thought ruefully.

Another acquaintance in the audience to applaud was good, but jealousy was an emotion she would rather not have to observe at close quarters. It was so wearing, and so unnecessary! Strange though the idea was, love brought out the worst in people!

'In bed she is outrageous,' Gaby said, a smile on her pretty face. 'She makes me feel sensations I never even dreamed about. And the little games she likes to play, well! I thought Lucien was obsessed until I met Marcelle.'

'Tell me,' said Suzette, 'make me understand.'

'Until you've tried it, you can't begin to understand. When Marcelle touches you, it's somehow different from the way a man would do it. And she does things with her tongue that drive you insane. She goes on for hours, she's not exhausted after two or three times like a man would be. Naturally, she's doing this to make me fall for her, so I'll move in with her.'

Suzette shrugged and said nothing to that.

'But it's a slave she wants for her desires,' Gaby continued, 'not really a lover. And though I adore

her, I don't even want to be her lover much longer.
It's starting to become fatiguing, being given so
much pleasure night after night. To say nothing of
every morning when we wake up. And sitting at the
table when we have our coffee and brioches. Just
look at the shadows under my eyes – I need a week's
rest without any lovemaking.'

It was Suzette's turn to laugh, she said she never
expected to hear either of them, Gaby or herself, say
she'd had enough.

Evidently, a stockbroker would be a welcome
change. A strong and intelligent man with moderate
appetites, two or three times a week. One who'd
shower expensive presents on Gaby and buy her chic
clothes and take her to the best restaurants and clubs.

But, as in all things human, there was an
imperfection in the plan. The well-fed men admiring
the two friends at their lunch most certainly looked
as if they wouldn't be too demanding, and not
exhausting at all. They also looked dull enough to
make you scream. And there was hardly a broker
among them below the age of fifty.

In the nature of things, Suzette's and Gaby's
boyfriends were older than themselves, there being
few men of twenty-two with time and money enough
to qualify. The overblessed Blaise Fulbert was thirty-
six, Claude Ronsard the moody lawyer thirty-two,
Robert Dorville twenty-nine but he was a special
case, with a father who financed him.

Boyfriends as old as forty were not unknown, but
both women set a limit there, it would be very
exceptional to go beyond it. A man of fifty was a
grandfather, not to be considered.

This they agreed upon, after a careful survey of the
lunchers around them. Gaby said she might perhaps
make an exception for one in a dark blue suit with a

flower in his buttonhole, he had a look of authority
that could be interesting. And he winked at her, when
he thought his table companions were not looking.

'Authority, what does that mean?' Suzette
demanded. 'Will he pull your knickers down and
smack your bottom? Is that what it means to you?
This restaurant is useless for what you think you're
looking for. Let's pay the bill and find a café terrace
in the sunshine somewhere.'

When the bill arrived, the waiter mentioned to
Gaby that the Monsieur across the other side of the
restaurant, over there by the wall with the other two
gentlemen — had instructed him to convey his
respects to the two ladies and in particular to the
blonde-haired lady.

'There are times when I think that American
woman was right,' said Suzette, 'most men prefer
blondes. I used to think it was only American men
she meant but now I'm not so sure.'

Gaby borrowed the waiter's pen to scribble their
phone number on the back of the bill.

'Show that to the gentleman,' she said with a
charming smile, 'and ask if his respects extend as far
as paying our bill.'

They watched in great amusement as the waiter
went to whisper in the ear of the gentleman in the
dark blue suit with the tiny white flower in his button
hole.

'I suppose you could say he's well-preserved,'
Suzette said, 'that silver hair is quite dashing in its
way. Like one of the old-time film stars. But he's
putting spectacles on to read the bill, that's not a
good sign. You can't see if he has a paunch while he's
sitting down but he must have.'

The waiter came back to tell them the bill was
taken care of, at which both women shrieked with

laughter. They left a decent tip for the obliging waiter and he bowed them to the door. Gaby paused for just an instant to wave prettily to the stockbroker in the dark blue suit.

'Did you really give him our number, or a wrong one, Gaby?'

'Our proper number, why not? I have expectations of him when he rings. He's a man with money to spend, he needs a girlfriend to bring a little joy into his dreary life with the stocks and shares and boring wife and grown-up children.'

'You mean to rub his pink little paunch for him?'

'Whenever he likes. And I mean to bring him to hear you sing, so Marcelle can get a good look at him and start to understand she doesn't own me.'

'Ah, I begin to see now. You're going to hide behind Monsieur Stockbroker from Marcelle's enticements. Why not? He's proved himself to be a generous man.'

They strolled along the rue du 4 Septembre in the sun as far as the Avenue de l'Opera, and crossed it to reach the Café de la Paix. The terrace was crowded but an appreciative waiter found a table for the two beauties, a service they were used to receiving wherever they went.

While they waited for coffee and drinks to arrive, Gaby was grinning like a lunatic.

'My poor Lucien!' she said, trying not to laugh too much. 'I told you he has these mad fantasies of taking me stark naked to public places – one of his little fetish dreams has me arriving here in black silk stockings and high heels. He described it in detail to me, how I sit down and cross my legs while he orders a bottle of champagne.'

'What goes on in that man's mind!' Suzette exclaimed. 'He's wasted as a crook, he ought to be an artist! He'd be famous in no time. Remember the painting we saw in the Louvre when Robert decided we needed culture? A picnic in the woods with the men dressed and the girls naked?'

'You're right!' said Gaby. 'If my little pervert ever turns up again I'll tell him. He could call it *Champagne at the Café de la Paix* and it would be a sensation!'

'Mademoiselle, excuse me,' said a nervous voice at Suzette's side.

As she turned, a piece of paper was pushed into her hand. She stared up at the young man standing beside her.

'For you, because you are so beautiful,' he said quickly.

Then he was gone, darting between the tables to the pavement and quickly lost from sight among the pedestrians on the Avenue de l'Opera.

'They're everywhere,' said Gaby, tapping her forehead with a scarlet-nailed finger. 'What did he give you?'

'I know who he is,' Suzette said. 'At least, I know his first name. You remember the night I sang for the first time, at that atrocious bar Jacques-Charles plays at?'

'Chez Bobo – I shall never forget it!'

'He was the one I talked to outside. I told you about him.'

'Ah!' said Gaby with a grin. 'The one who pushed you into a doorway and ran off with your knickers in his pocket! So that's him, is it?'

'That's Michel,' Suzette agreed, reading what was written on the sheet of paper he'd given her.

'What's he written?' Gaby asked. 'Obscene suggestions, or is he begging for money. He looks as if he needs it. Or is it just a boring love letter?'

'It's a sort of poem, I think. Look!'

Gaby took the paper.

'His handwriting's not the easiest to read, but it's a poem,' she agreed. 'At least, I think so, though it doesn't rhyme.'

She read the first few lines aloud:

In the Place Vendôme, a jewellery shop,
A bracelet of ice and fire,
Diamonds cut square, heart's-blood rubies,
The tall man at her side
Clasps it on her wrist,
His love, he says, will last as long

'He said he was a student,' said Suzette, 'though I took him for a sailor. There are fashions in verses, just as in clothes. And anyway, modern poetry doesn't have to rhyme.'

'His heart's in the right place,' said Gaby. 'He wants to buy you a diamond bracelet at Cartier. Pity he hasn't got two *sous* to rub together.'

She handed the poem back with a little shrug.

'Do you think he's been following you about?' she asked. 'Or did he see us by chance when we sat down here?'

'I don't know, but he's had this paper in his pocket for ages — see how creased it is. That's very romantic!'

'He didn't stay long enough to get a good look at,' said Gaby 'but his jacket was frayed and ready for the dustbin. If he's a student he's hard-up. Be as romantic as you like, nothing says you can't be as passionate with a stockbroker as with a poet, and my new admirer's sure to have a friend who'd like to meet you.'

'No grandfathers for me,' Suzette said firmly.

The more she thought about it, the stranger it seemed — Michel Whoever-he-was looming out of nowhere like that then vanishing again. But there was nothing to be done about him, except wait and see if he appeared again.

More than seven weeks had passed since the fearful evening of Suzette's debut as a singer Chez Bobo. If this Michel was of a mind to renew an acquaintance that had lasted about twenty minutes, in which time neither of them had said more than five words, being otherwise preoccupied, evidently he was in no great hurry.

The truth was that he was cripplingly shy. After the briefest encounter with Suzette at the cheap bar he dreamed of her night and day, his studies forgotten and neglected. After a week he screwed up his courage to the point of returning to Montmartre, to ask Bobo where to find the beautiful lady who sang there.

Bobo threw him out on his ear. Bobo was still fuming because Suzette had not accepted his ardent invitation to step into the kitchen with him for a quick thrash on the table.

For almost a week Michel lurked outside the bar, waiting for the pianist to arrive. He asked him where Mademoiselle Suzette could be found. Jacques-Charles knew the young man's passion at once, it was the same as his own, and he detested him for it. A more aggressive man would have imitated Bobo and knocked Michel down, Jacques-Charles took the easier path of lying. He said he never saw the singer before that night, hadn't seen her since, didn't know her last name or where she lived.

But in seven weeks Michel's longing had grown imperious, until it overcame his shyness. He discovered Suzette's family name was Bernard in a roundabout way — he recognised her in a poster for the Folies Bergère. She was in the background, of course, along with the other show-girls, almost lost to sight behind the stars in the foreground. But it was her, he was certain of it! From then it became possible to find out her name.

All he had to do next was to check the telephone directory to decide which of scores of Bernards was likely to be her. A day came when he stood in the rue de Rome, on the pavement outside her apartment. He watched her leave with a woman who had blonde hair to her shoulders, but neither of them saw him.

He followed them, he waited outside the restaurant while they ate and talked, he trailed their steps to the café terrace. And summoning all his courage, he stepped up close, pushed his poem into Suzette's hand — and fled, aghast at his own temerity.

A train of events had been started. On the very next day, in the morning about twelve, Suzette heard a very gentle knock at the apartment door. She was alone, Gaby had gone to have lunch in an expensive restaurant with her stockbroker, who had phoned repeatedly until he found her in.

'If he takes you to a hotel afterwards,' Suzette advised, 'be careful — you don't want the poor old thing to get over-excited and drop dead of apoplexy while you stand there without your knickers on. The police can be very sarcastic, I've been told.'

She went to the door and there stood Michel in his frayed old jacket and trousers — and the same roll-neck pullover he'd worn when they first met. His large dark eyes never wavered from her face, his expression was shy, embarrassed, but at the same time determined. Suzette smiled and stood aside for him to come in.

He slid into the apartment almost furtively, as if

feeling he ought not to be there. In the sitting-room he didn't look round at all, he kept his eyes on Suzette, almost as if he was seeing a vision of the Blessed Saint Mary Virgin herself in a sky-blue robe and a golden halo.

'Mademoiselle . . .' he said faintly.

Though no virgin, Suzette was a veritable vision of delight. She had not been long out of bed, her face was fresh and clean, without a trace even of lipstick, her hair sleek and combed, as glossy-black as a raven's wing. She was planning to go shopping for food and had put on grey slacks and a white shirt which was close-fitting to show off her superb breasts.

'Thank you for your poem, Michel, I like it very much.'

His long eyelashes dipped and for a moment she thought he would blush like a girl.

'You were bolder when we met before,' she said.

'Can you ever forgive me?' he breathed, really blushing now, 'I'd drunk a lot, I didn't know what I was doing.'

'What nonsense! You knew very well what you were doing and I liked it. I hadn't been in a doorway with a man since I was fifteen. Standing with my legs apart and my back to a wall revived some ridiculous old memories.'

'You find me ridiculous!' he sighed, and his face was a mask of misery. 'I suppose I must seem so to you, mademoiselle.'

'You are impossible, Michel!' she said, trying not to smile.

Something had to be done, or he would stand there like a fool blushing and blinking and lost for words! She guessed his age at nineteen or twenty, but he seemed without self-esteem. If he was ever to be of use sober to any woman, he had to learn quickly.

His worn-out brown jacket was undone, perhaps it had lost all its buttons. Suzette reached out to him and slipped the jacket off his shoulders, it fell to the carpet. She took his arm and pulled him down on to the sofa.

In a moment she had his ragged trousers open, his male part in her hand — limp and small, as dejected as the rest of him.

There was one sure way to restore a man's self-esteem, it was so simple Suzette was always surprised by the *obviousness*, the *obtuseness*, of male emotions. She rolled his slackness between her perfectly manicured fingers, teasing it to rise and thicken into passionate awareness. It grew taut and strong in her hand very quickly, Michel stared down at his lap with eyes that seemed stupefied.

'Mademoiselle Suzette,' he whispered, '*je t'aime. je t'aime.*'

'Of course you do,' she said in an encouraging voice.

His stiffness strained upwards in her moving hand, it was at full stretch now, thick and hard, the head purple and shiny.

'*Voilà!*' said Suzette. 'You are a man, Michel. You know what men do with women.'

'Do you mean it?' he sighed, unable to believe his luck.

'Have you forgotten what you did to me when we first met? You pushed me up against somebody's door and took my knickers down. Come into the bedroom.'

He sighed to hear her words, his stiffness bounding, the very violence of his desire made him shake. His eyes aglow, he threw himself on Suzette and there on the striped sofa he slid his body over her

and pressed her down on her back. Clearly there was
no time to transfer the action to the bedroom — his
mouth was on hers, his eager tongue between her
lips.

Suzette let him have his way, willing him to lose his
shyness and become an adult human-being. She felt
his hand fumbling for the way to open her slacks,
first at the front, over her belly, then at the side, by
her hip, until he found the zipper at last and slid it
down. His hardness was against her thigh, trembling
a little in its impatience.

She sighed in pleasure when his hand forced its
way down into her knickers and she parted her thighs
for him to feel between.

'Ah yes!' he gasped as he caressed the soft lips.
'Bare and smooth! That memory has haunted me
ever since, it was driving me half-mad! I didn't know
if I'd been dreaming, was it the wine I'd drunk that
night? But I remembered you smooth and bare. I
couldn't be certain, I thought it was only my
imagination. But it's true and real and marvellous . . . let me see! I must see it!'

In an instant he was on his knees by the sofa,
dragging down her slacks and flimsy knickers, to
bare what so excited him.

'Like a flower,' he murmured, 'like a pretty pink
orchid.'

'For you, Michel,' she said softly, to spur him on.

Without another word he bowed his head and
kissed between her thighs. She felt his hot tongue
licking up and down the smooth lips. His stiffness in
her hand was leaping and she expected it to spurt any
second. She gripped it hard, shocking him out of his
delirium by the rake of her fingernails.

He raised his head to gaze, uncomprehending, into
her eyes. She dragged him over her, using what she

held as a hand grip. It was impossible to open her legs fully because of her slacks round her knees, but Michel's belly lay on hers and his hard flesh at last touched her 'pretty pink orchid'.

How strong he felt against the inside of her thigh, hard and ready!

'Push,' she whispered and felt him slide into her a little.

Above her, Michel's golden-brown eyes were staring wide but seeing nothing. His mouth strained open, as if in a long cry. A fierce shuddering racked his body. Suzette realised that he had slipped into orgasm, a suspended orgasm of the mind, making its unstoppable way down through his nerves and muscles, the length of his body, down from his brain to his twitching loins.

'Push!' she said again. 'Deeper, Michel!'

She too was trembling with desire and she started to moan while he forced himself into her belly, struggling to penetrate her. For a moment she stopped breathing, then a wild delight seized her entire body as the hardness inside her gave a frantic jerk and spurted hotly . . .

At about five o'clock that afternoon Gaby returned from lunch with her stockbroker. The bathroom door stood half-open and she heard splashing – she went in to bring Suzette up to date with the comedy of her latest and unlikeliest conquest.

Her stockbroker's name was Jean-François Delacroix, he was fifty-two years old, married and with children as old as Gaby herself. He lived grandly in the Avenue Kléber, which impressed her.

After a magnificent lunch in a restaurant that was secluded and expensive, he conveyed her by taxi to a private hotel she had never heard of.

It proved to be a very discreet little rendezvous in a quiet street off the Place de la Madeleine. Monsieur Delacroix seemed to be expected for he and his companion were shown at once up to a charming suite, without question or fuss. A bottle of champagne stood in a silver ice-bucket. And fresh flowers in the bedroom.

Jean-François took great pleasure in undressing Gaby. In fact he made a theatrical performance of it, she sitting in a chair and he kneeling to take off her silk stockings. For a moment an uncomfortable thought crossed her mind that he might be another fetishist like poor Lucien but as matters progressed she found it was simply a demonstration of the more formal manners of an earlier age.

He wanted to see her naked and kiss various parts of her – not her shoes or knickers, she was quite relieved to discover. But he took much preliminary pleasure in removing her clothes, item by item. He kissed her behind her knees, in her smooth groins, marvelling at her neat little silvery-blonde tuft, kissed under her breasts, and in the hollows of her throat.

When his own well-cut suit and silk shirt came off, Gaby saw with a private grin that he did have a little pink paunch, just as Suzette predicted. And why not? He was a man of importance and settled habits, a broker who dealt in large sums of money, an eater of gourmet lunches and gourmet dinners each day of his life.

She stroked his little pink paunch fondly, she giggled to see how the touch made his stiff part nod as if in approval. So it should, she decided, and tickled along the length of it with a scarlet-painted fingernail. When at last Jean-François laid her on her back and mounted, he did so with a certain authority and style, as she had half-expected he would.

She closed her eyes, the better to enjoy the sensation of his sliding in and out of her. His thrusting was forceful, not fast — and determined, his hands caressing her face, his fingertips fluttering at her red-painted mouth. He aroused her so much she wound her long legs round his waist and jerked her loins upward to meet him as she helped herself into a long delicious orgasm.

Back home again in the apartment on the rue de Rome, she went into the bathroom to tell Suzette of her afternoon. And there, to her surprise, facing each other in the bathtub filled with hot scented water, sat Suzette and the mystery man from the Café de la Paix.

At a glance Gaby could tell from Suzette's expression of calm radiance the young stranger had made love to her well and often that afternoon. And he, this vanishing poet, now Gaby could see him close at hand and sitting still, was not a bad-looking man. He was very slender without his clothes, perhaps he didn't get enough to eat. But he had thick dark hair and a sensitive face, with large expressive eyes.

His dark eyelashes were as long as a girl's, though evidently there was nothing in the least girlish about his ability in bed — Suzette's expression made that clear. His head was turned to look at the newcomer standing just inside the bathroom door — Gaby in her prettiest frock.

In the past few hours, alone with Suzette, Michel had learned to stop being so absurdly shy in the presence of women, however beautiful. He was not allowed to reach the ordinary masculine conclusion, that women were toys for him to play with, that the fifteen centimetres of flesh between his legs gave him dominion and absolute privilege.

He would probably never come to hold the usual male view, his nature was too gentle. But he had learned that women like love making as much as men do. He smiled slowly at Gaby, who thought him charming.

'This is my dear friend, Michel,' said Suzette. 'He is a poet, a remarkable poet. You read what he wrote about the diamond and ruby bracelet in the Place Vendôme. He's been writing poems for me ever since we met outside Chez Bobo.'

Gaby nodded and smiled.

'He's been reciting some of his other poems,' Suzette went on with a dreamy look in her jet-black eyes. 'Altogether there are nearly fifty of them — what do you think of that?'

'I think he adores you,' said Gaby.

'They're all in his head, can you imagine? But he's going to write them down on paper for me. I'm going to persuade Jacques-Charles to set them to music and make them into songs for me to sing. He can put the rhymes in where they're needed.'

'That's nice,' said Gaby, bending down to kiss Suzette's cheek and offer her hand to Michel, sitting there up to his middle in scented water.

'There's a most marvellous one — it's about stepping out of a limousine at the opera in a ball-gown of black velvet, backless right down to the cleft between the cheeks and festooned with diamonds.'

'I like his style,' said Gaby. 'What else is he planning?'

'There's another where a doorman in uniform bows and says *bonjour, madame* as I leave my luxury apartment in the Avenue Foch to walk a fluffy little white dog.'

'He is a connoisseur of high life, your poet,' said

Gaby with an ironic grin. 'He has great ambitions for
you. I like him for that.'

'Gaby is my dearest friend,' Suzette informed
Michel, who was staring at the newcomer with a
puzzled look, not at all certain if she was friend or
foe, supporter or derider.

'We share the apartment, she and I,' said Suzette.

'And pretty well everything else,' said Gaby.

She slipped off her shoes and started to undress. In
moments she was naked, her long lean body fully
displayed, the silvery-blonde tuft between her thighs
catching Michel's attention. His expression testified
to his bemusement – and to his pleasure.

Suzette laughed to see his face as Gaby stepped
gracefully into the bath behind him. She sat down
with her legs out straight on either side of him. Her
hands rested on his thin shoulders and she kneaded
them gently.

'But . . . but . . .' he stammered, the situation
beyond him.

'Hush, *chéri*,' said Suzette, touching a finger to his
lips.

Then her hands were down in the sweet-scented
water, feeling between his parted thighs for his
limpness, to bring it back to life. Gaby's wet hands
slipped under his arms and round to his hairless
chest, to tickle his flat buds with her scarlet nails,
making him gasp with sudden pleasure.

'Dear Michel, put your hands behind your back
and feel what I've got for you,' Gaby murmured in
his ear.

THE CONSOLATIONS
OF ILLUSION

The inhabitants of Montmartre seem hardly ever to leave it. The true inhabitants, that is to say, the locals, not the pimps and tarts, souvenir-shop owners, striptease artists and others who move in for the sake of their trade. Like cuckoos they come and go, this sort. But as for the natives, born there and brought up there, living their lives in tumble-down old buildings along crooked little streets of cobblestones, they regard themselves as citizens of a free commune and stay put.

For them there is a frontier that divides their little world from Paris – the Boulevard de Clichy that skirts the bottom of their hill. Certainly they hardly see themselves as inhabitants of Paris, that for them is a foreign place, *over there*.

They walk up and down their twisting streets, sell each other chickens and carrots for the pot. They drink a glass or two of cheap wine at a long wooden bench in a cellar or sit in the sun on a rickety chair and gossip.

They believe they are villagers still, as their grandparents may have been. And this belief they cling on to in spite of the evidence of their own eyes – the tour buses unloading hundreds of foreigners each day in the Place du Tertre and the thousands of tourists with cameras on the steps of the white-domed Sacré Coeur.

But then, we all select the illusion which pleases us best.

Jacques-Charles Delise was a native of Montmartre, but he was one who ranged further afield. Perhaps it was his early musical education that had given him an awareness of the importance of Paris, not merely his own little street but an appreciation of the high culture and elegance of the city.

He was strolling in the Tuileries gardens in the sunshine, it was the end of summer but a pleasing day. He strolled among the crowd, taking the air, and between the flower-beds surrounded by their neat little boxwood hedges. He ignored the statues of important persons of the past and he paused under the shade of the trees. It was not long now until autumn when the greenery would turn to orange and red.

Near the fountain he found a vacant folding chair and sat to watch a boy launch his toy boat with red sails on the basin of the fountain. Close by stood the shirt-sleeved father, calling out well-meant but unnecessary advice.

Jacques-Charles turned the chair round to face the Place de la Concorde. In the distance, beyond the tall thin stone needle of the obelisk there, he could see the Arc de Triomphe, a good two kilometres away, at the far end of the Champs Elysées.

He half-closed his eyes and turned his face upwards, enjoying the feel of the sun on the bald front portion of his head, that extended forehead where a slowly receding hairline produced an intellectual appearance. He was drawn back from his reverie of the beautiful Suzette by a man's voice greeting him by name.

He looked, it was that fellow Dorville, with a pretty girl on his arm. Jacques-Charles had met him only once before, and that was months ago, but he recognised him. And for the best of all reasons — at the time of their introduction Robert Dorville was Suzette's lover. For that reason he was an object of dark envy, grudging respect, seething hatred, baffled esteem and murderous intention to Jacques-Charles.

What a gamut of emotions to feel all at the same time by one person, yet such is the illogicality of men and women in love!

Suzette never discussed her boyfriends, except with Gaby, but it was not difficult for Jacques-Charles to pick up hints when she came for lessons. It was a surprise to him to learn she had dropped Dorville, he was the type Jacques-Charles believed most likely to appeal to her.

The type with good looks, smart clothes, plenty of money and no need to work for a living. The witty and chatty type, always at ease with women. Everything Jacques-Charles himself was not.

Dorville's new girl was pretty, it must be conceded, but not a patch on Suzette. But then, no other woman in the world could match Suzette, in the frank view of the lovelorn pianist.

'*Bonjour, monsieur*,' said Jacques-Charles, rising to his feet to take the hand Dorville extended to him.

'Mademoiselle Odette Charron,' Robert Dorville introduced his girlfriend, 'Jacques-Charles Delise, who is a most accomplished musician.'

Jacques-Charles threw him a baleful look for that, certain it had been said in mockery. To Mademoiselle Charron he presented a pleasant smile, he didn't go so far as to kiss her hand but he pressed it respectfully. She was worth more than one quick glance, he conceded. She was long-bodied, long-legged, her hair was dark brunette and beautifully waved, her clothes simple but elegant, suggesting she might be involved in some way with fashion.

It was because Odette's hair was so flawlessly in place that Jacques-Charles knew she hadn't rolled on the bed with Dorville — not yet. But at this time of day perhaps they had just left a restaurant and were strolling to settle their lunch before they went to Dorville's apartment to make love.

Jacques-Charles surveyed her with his lustrous brown eyes and decided she would be very exciting to play with. It was easy to imagine her lithe body naked, her emerald green frock stripped off, her little straw hat discarded, her underwear removed, to reveal her round young breasts and her long thighs.

Those eyes of hers, a fascinating light green in colour, they would surely darken with desire when she was caressed between the legs.

'It must be the sun,' Jacques-Charles thought to himself, 'giving me these pleasant little ideas about her. I'd better put my hat on before I get sun-stroke!'

With a little bow to Odette he put on the wide-brimmed panama hat he used every summer to protect his half-baldness from sun burn. Once it had been white, this venerable hat, alas, like its owner it had seen better days.

He was not silent while these lustful thoughts about Odette were passing in slow motion through his mind, far from it — he was annoying Dorville by telling him how well Suzette's career as a singer was developing.

'What!' Robert exclaimed. 'She is singing professionally? I don't believe it!'

'But yes,' said Jacques-Charles, hardly troubling to conceal his glee at the discomfiture he was causing. 'She is still only at the beginning of what I truly believe will be a momentously important career, but she is being paid to sing at last, though the fees are still modest.'

'She's given up her job at the Folies Bergère? Is that what you're telling me?'

'Ah no, not that yet. But it will not be long before she puts all that behind her, I am sure of it. She is becoming an artist of talent and promise, not a show-girl who stands naked on a stage in ostrich feathers and sequins for tourists to gape at.'

'Well!' said Robert, struck almost breathless.

'I shall convey to her your regards and good wishes for her success,' said Jacques-Charles, his brown eyes flashing and his smile thin, rubbing salt into the wound.

'What? Yes, of course! Look here. It's been some time since I saw Suzette, I'm right out of touch. Can you spare twenty minutes to join me for a drink and bring me up to date?'

A drink, that was an invitation Jacques-Charles had never yet been known to refuse. But he made an elaborate show of thinking whether he had time before his next pressing appointment to spare a few minutes for Robert. Then he accepted graciously.

'You don't mind, do you?' Robert said to Odette, and it was a statement rather than a question. 'We can cut through to the rue St Honoré, to the café there.'

Whether she minded or not, she went along with the suggestion. His eagerness confirmed what she already suspected, that he was still more than half in love with this Suzette. Odette had not met her, and was never likely to, but she knew what a stunner she was, this naked showgirl, from the photograph she'd found hidden in Robert's apartment when he was out.

As for her own chance with Robert, Odette was realist enough to understand she had none. He was a dear friend, a useful and amusing friend, no more than that. It was extremely convenient to live in his comfortable apartment and to be taken to dinner most evenings. This made it possible to save nearly everything she was earning, ready for the day she felt established enough to move into a place of her own. All she needed to do in return was let Robert make love to her. That was no burden — he did it very well and gave her a lot of pleasure.

She had made a good start on her career as a magazine artists' model. It was almost autumn, Paris was about to come back to life after a month when everyone was away on holiday. She expected a serious upturn in her opportunities. Well, to be precise, Laurent Breville had made promises.

Jacques-Charles was quite wrong in his assumption that Odette and Robert were on their way to his apartment to make love. The obvious is very often misleading. But then, Jacques-Charles had not the least suspicion that Odette had been living with Robert for weeks. They had settled into a routine of making love when they went to bed at night, like any married couple.

Of course, if Jacques-Charles had known about this, he would have passed it on to Suzette, hoping to discredit Robert further.

Nevertheless, there was about Odette a certain air, not easy to explain, that had been caught by Jacques-Charles and roused thoughts of making love to her. He felt he was almost able to see through her stylish frock, to gloat over her pretty breasts and her long slender thighs.

Not that it was possible for him to guess, the reason for her sensual radiance was that she had been posing for Laurent Breville that morning, a new commission from *Bon Chic* for night attire.

In his studio she had undressed behind the

fantastic screen with the painted peacocks. She put on the garment, a charming little nightgown so flimsy it was no more than a wisp of silk mousseline, high-waisted, the neckline very low-cut and ruffled. It had short puffed sleeves and a hem-line one centimetre below the knee.

Naturally, so very flimsy a nightgown was transparent. Odette flicked at the russet tips of her breasts with a finger to make them stand firm and pointed through the fragile silk. She stepped out from behind the screen and stood with a hand on the chaise-longue, attempting an appearance of nonchalance.

The neatly clipped heart shape between her thighs was visible to Laurent, sitting behind his drawing-board and fiddling with brush and watercolours. He was wearing a pink silk shirt that morning, with very fine wool black trousers. Odette allowed him time to dash off three sketches of her before she started to tease him. During the weeks of their acquaintance she had been able to formulate a routine which worked very well on him.

The starting point was to tell him he was glaring at her like a rapist in the park at night. He denied it, he was looking at her intently to get the line and colour right, he insisted. She refused to believe him, she demanded to be told whether he was misbehaving himself behind the drawing-board!

Laurent's face went red when he denied it and Odette knew it was impossible for him not to open his trousers now she had put the idea into his head. She changed position a little, letting him see her thighs move under the silk mousseline.

His brush trailed over the paper, his attention was elsewhere now. In another minute Odette went round the drawing-board to his side and she grinned to see the stiff part jutting out of his open trousers.

'Wicked, wicked, wicked!' she said.

She smacked it lightly, making it sway sideways and bringing a gasp of shock and pleasure from him.

'Were you with your fiancée last night, Laurent?'

'I took her to dinner, we went to the Chatelet to hear Jascha Heifetz play,' he said, his voice trembling because Odette was plucking the strings of his own violin.

'And did Mademoiselle Marie-Louise de Beaucourt-Villiers come back to your apartment afterwards?' she asked him. 'I see you look embarrassed, that means she did. What did you do together, Laurent *chéri*? You stripped her naked, didn't you? You threw her down on your bed — you've gone red in the face. Did you lie on top of her and push this long stiff thing up her? You can tell me everything, I understand you.'

The teasing continued until she had Laurent teetering on the brink of ecstasy. Careful judgement was required, a few strokes too many on his bounding Jean Jeudi and he would spurt over the front of his pink silk shirt and he would not be ready for what she intended him to do next.

'But I think you must be lying to me,' she said. 'If you made love to Mademoiselle de Beaucourt-Villiers all last night, then why is Jean Jeudi standing up so hard now? His strength should be exhausted by pleasing her but it is not. Why is that?'

'Last night was last night,' said Laurent fervently. 'You are so exciting in that nightgown, Odette, I can see every part of your body through it!'

'I am not so vain as to believe I am more exciting than your fiancée.'

'But you are . . .' he sighed, horribly ashamed to admit to this gross disloyalty.

For a man who made a living drawing girls in expensively chic underwear for fashion magazines, he seemed innocent to a degree Odette had not encountered before. Teasing him was so simple it might eventually become boring. Tempting him was no problem at all.

She insinuated herself between him and his drawing-board, her legs apart and the expensive nightgown held up round her waist. Laurent's eyes, then his hand, went to the pretty little heart of curls he had clipped for her. Odette pushed her smooth bare belly forward, smiling as he stroked her, waiting for the right moment to let herself be satisfied.

'The truth now, Laurent,' she said. 'You did not make love to her last night. And we both know why — it is because you can't do it with a woman. Even after you've taken her knickers down and felt her.'

'I did, I made love to her, I did, believe me,' he moaned.

His fingers played feverishly in Odette's moistness, sending little thrills through her.

'No need to try to deceive me,' she said, 'I know you well, I understand you perfectly. You're left-handed, you go searching for handsome young men in bars and bring them back here. To me it's of no concern, I'm not your fiancée, I'm your friend.'

In the time they had known each other she had trained Laurent well. His guilt was the secret and the weakness she worked on, the guilt of his unsatisfactory engagement to a woman who did not excite him. To accuse him of being different devastated his emotions, it also had the curious effect of arousing him.

And to touch her *little heart*, as he was doing now, overcame him completely. He slid off his high stool, he stood very close to Odette, his feet in grey suede shoes between her bare parted feet.

'You know that's not true,' he sighed. 'I've proved it to you every time you've been here!'

To convince her yet again, he pressed his belly against hers, let her guide him to where she wanted him, then pushed up into her. Even before he began to move, in short hard stabs to show off his strength and virility, Odette felt the climax arrive in her belly. The exultation she derived from controlling Laurent was so powerful it brought on her ecstatic crisis every time.

At a table outside the café by the Place Colette, Odette was thinking about Laurent and how she had manipulated his emotions that morning. She half-listened to the scruffy-looking Jacques-Charles tell Robert about his former girlfriend and her stupid singing. Odette watched people walk by along the pavement, she was occupied with her own thoughts.

The café was at the intersection where the Avenue de l'Opéra met the rue St Honoré, the traffic was slow and noisy . . . But the café was a most useful place for window-shoppers drawn by the high-fashion boutiques of the area. And being so close to the Louvre and the Palais Royale it was a very convenient place for tourists of all nationalities to rest their tired feet.

To be truthful, for Odette a sense of boredom soon set in. To moon over an *affaire* now ended, as Robert was doing, was to her quite pointless. But men were sentimental creatures, she knew, and had to be humoured. A thought occurred to her that made her smile secretively − if only she could gain control of Robert as simply as she had Laurent Breville! How useful that would be!

There had been a difficult quarter of an hour the first time Robert saw the neat *little heart* between her legs, after he was accustomed to her lovely wild thatch.

'But why, Odette *chérie*?' he demanded. 'I adored you when you were *sauvage*. Why have you done this?'

It was impossible to explain it was another man who had reduced her wildness to this tame little design. It was necessary to lie elaborately, to say she found there were commercial artists who complained if their underwear models were hairy. So, as this was becoming her new profession, something drastic needed to be done. Didn't he agree?

Naturally, it was a great pity, but what else could she do? In fact, she was considering if it was best to remove her curls entirely, she said. She was testing Robert, to see the reaction she got from him.

'No, don't do that,' he said hastily. 'I much prefer you with curls. They suit you, they are exciting.'

Of course, she knew what he really meant — he didn't want her to look like the former girlfriend, the showgirl who shaved it all off. That told Odette as much as she needed to know about the state of Robert's emotions.

It being understood that Robert was paying for all the drinks Jacques-Charles decided he would have cognac. Robert drank only a single glass, Odette sipped a glass of Vichy water with ice and in the same time, Jacques-Charles finished three. He boasted about his own part in Suzette's budding career, the importance of his teaching, his encouragement when *others* doubted.

It was unnecessary to put names to these *others*, Robert knew who was intended and he groaned inwardly, cursing himself for a fool. Jacques-Charles mentioned his present contribution toward Suzette's eventual triumph, writing very special songs for her.

She had acquired some quite interesting verses, he said, from a casual acquaintance. The words themselves were of no particular value but with the right tunes something could be made of them.

The amount of work involved in this was colossal, as Monsieur Dorville would readily appreciate. Jacques-Charles had taken an hour from his unremitting labour only to refresh his spirit in the pleasant surroundings of the Tuileries gardens. All must be finished and ready and rehearsed in time for Suzette's premiere performance in three week's time.

As long as the waiter continued to bring glasses of cognac to the table for him, Jacques-Charles was content to go on talking of Suzette. And Robert displayed a melancholy resignation about listening to him. It was left to Odette to bring this miserable state of affairs to an end. She asked Robert the time, she made other inconsequential interruptions, she tapped her fingers on the table top. Finally he realised she was bored.

He called for the bill, shook hands with Jacques-Charles, and departed with Odette in the direction of Place de la Concorde and the Champs-Elysées. Jacques-Charles made for the Metro and home. He was in a very good humour, the result of the cognac to some extent, but even more to the chance of crowing over Robert Dorville.

It was too elevated a mood for him to sit at his broken-down piano and compose songs, even for the beautiful woman he adored heart and soul. He left the underground at Place de Clichy and went straight into the first bar he came to. Naturally, now he had to pay for the drinks himself it was not cognac he ordered.

A pleasant hour passed, Jacques-Charles' mood became jauntier still. He tried to remember if he was supposed to play anywhere that evening, but couldn't – such trifling matters had receded into a blur. The only sensible thing was to ignore the question and order another drink. So the time went by, until eventually he ran out of money.

It was after ten that evening when at last he reached the rue Lepic and turned into the alley where he lived. He whistled a little tune, perhaps one of his own, he wasn't sure, as he came to the tenement. It ought to have fallen down in a heap of rubble and dead rats years ago. It leaned over to one side and had done so since 1932.

He halted on the stairs before he got to his room at the top, chuckled again at his triumph over that damned fellow Dorville, and knocked at the door of the neighbour who lived in the room beneath his own. This was Madame Boujot, a widow with whom he was on good terms, when he remembered her.

Her husband had been killed in the war, she said, but it was not generally believed that the soldier she referred to was her husband in any legal sense. But what of that? The intention is often superior to the deed. Besides, it was fifteen years ago and of no particular relevance now.

Madame Boujot was a tall thin woman of indeterminate age, her hair dark brown and thick, her face long, her expression one of permanent surprise. What possible surprises were left for life to offer her, that was not easy to say, but she was cheerful by disposition.

She was home and she was pleased to see Jacques-Charles when she opened the door to his knock. She alone of all his acquaintances called him *Professor*, being impressed by his ability at the piano. She thought him a cut above other men she knew and it was a pity he drank too much. Anyone could see what he needed was a woman to take care of him and make sure he ate proper meals.

And so on and so on, the usual rigmarole women make up about unmarried men. In short, Madame Boujot would happily take upon herself this role in Jacques-Charles' life, if he asked her. Not that the idea had ever crossed his mind.

Her day had been a long one, her feet ached and in another ten minutes she would have been in bed and asleep. Her preparations had advanced to slippers and an old grey dressing-gown, but she was always pleased to see a man of culture at her door. One of the reasons Jacques-Charles was pleased to see her was that she always had a bottle of red wine open.

'*Bonsoir, Professeur*,' she greeted him, standing back to let him in.

Her room was larger than his, not having the restriction of a sloping roof. It had an alcove for cooking and one for washing oneself in. It was also cleaner and tidier than his room, it is needless to say. She put a bottle on the scrubbed wooden table, at which Jacques-Charles seated himself, and two glasses.

They drank a glass to each other's health and they chatted a while, as neighbours do. Both knew why he had dropped in to see her on his way up the stairs. Between friends who have known each other for years there is no need to hurry these matters. They sat side by side at the table, talking of this and that and, in particular, if the landlord could ever be persuaded to repair the street door, which scraped and stuck when it was opened or closed.

When the moment arrived at last, it was with a casual gesture Jacques-Charles slipped his hand into the top of Marie Boujot's old grey dressing-gown. He stroked her breasts through her thin cotton nightdress, and squeezed the warm flesh fondly.

'You're an impatient man, Jacques-Charles,' she said with her curious half-smile.

Inside the dressing-gown her breasts were large and loose, but still pleasing to the touch. Jacques-Charles used the ball of a thumb to find the long bud, he rubbed over it gently and heard her sigh. He tickled it to firmness.

'Those fingers,' she said, 'you touch me with them as if I am the keyboard of your piano. What tune will you play?'

'One you know well, Marie. The most interesting tune in the world.'

Her hand lay on his thigh, and she too squeezed affectionately. A moment later she was undoing his trousers.

'Go on, have a good feel,' she urged, and she parted her legs to encourage his further attentions.

'Let's lie on the bed,' he suggested.

'Yes, you are impatient for it tonight, I see,' she said.

They moved across the room to the divan, which was her bed at night, and lay on it. Jacques-Charles fumbled with the belt of her dressing-gown, he got a hand up underneath her nightdress. He stroked up her lean thighs, he pressed his palm against her thin belly, feeling the warmth of her body.

'Go on, then,' she said, her hand sliding briskly up and down his stiff length.

He felt downward until he touched her sparse patch of curls.

'What beasts you men are,' she said. 'Thank God for it.'

She moved her legs apart in a gesture of welcome, he fingered the long lips between her thighs until she was wet and slippery to the touch. His eyes were closed, he was creating a vision in his mind of Suzette, naked and lying on the broken old divan in his room upstairs, her beautiful legs apart.

But it was impossible to make himself believe Suzette's bare-shaven and smooth-petalled flower was under his fingertips now. Not with this curly hair to draw him back into reality from his dreaming. Suzette he never touched with his hand, simply by staring at her nakedness he was able to bring her to a climax, no finger was needed.

He touched Suzette with his tongue, of course, to please her, to renew her ecstasies, that was special and different. She lay on her back, her legs spread, for the worship of his tongue, an adoration as profound as a religious experience for him, an act of devotion more intense than could be imagined. He never dared to ask if she felt anything of the same. He hoped with all his heart she did, he feared with all his intelligence she did not.

But this was not Suzette, the woman he loved so fervently, so desperately, so hopelessly, so futilely. This was Marie Boujot, his friendly and obliging neighbour, and the difference was so great Jacques-Charles felt he would burst into hot tears.

At this same time, only two kilometres away across Paris, but much closer than that in an emotional sense, Robert was making love with Odette in his fine apartment off the Boulevard de la Madeleine. After they had left Jacques-Charles at the café near the Louvre their outing went sadly awry.

Both knew the reason and neither dared mention it. It was hearing about Suzette that did it. Robert became depressed listening to Jacques-Charles praise her as if he were her lover, shabby old piano-thumper that he was! Robert realised how much he missed Suzette.

He and Odette were heading for the Pont d'Alma when they had come across the pianist sitting in the Tuileries gardens. They were planning to enjoy a little excursion that sunny afternoon, an hour's cruise on the Seine, aboard a *bateau-mouche*.

In the event, the river cruise proved to be a failure, Robert sat with arms folded and stared morosely at the river, thinking dark thoughts and saying nothing.

They went to a cinema to see the new Japanese movie everyone was talking about. Robert decided it was boring, much too long, too far-fetched, in brief, too Japanese. He didn't even put his arm round Odette, much less attempt any more intimate caress in the dark. Over dinner in one of his favourite small restaurants they almost quarrelled. He was behaving ungraciously, in other circumstances Odette would have thrown her soup at his head and stormed out.

She was not yet ready for that. True, she had savings now he didn't know about, and important prospects if she continued to manipulate the emotions of Laurent, as she fully intended. But she had been on the edge of poverty, and worse, when by chance she met Robert that day on the terrace at Fouquet's. He rescued her, but the experience of near-destitution was too agonising to be quickly forgotten. She was determined to stay with Robert for as long as possible.

Therefore it was impossible to pour her delicious crab soup over his silly head. She cajoled him into a better temper by an exertion of almost superhuman charm. And when dinner was ended she suggested, with a coquettish batting of her long eyelashes, that they went straight to his apartment . . .

Now here they were in the bedroom, clothes off, Odette lying on her back with her legs open. Robert was kissing her belly. Despite her anger at his unreasonable behaviour all day, she started to feel little surges of pleasure. It was possible, she hoped, to establish friendly and affectionate relations with him when he stopped moping over the show-girl.

She felt his wet tongue on her belly, felt it move downward. His fingers touched between her parted thighs, she knew he was staring at her neat *little heart* of brunette curls.

One day, if he annoyed her beyond endurance, she would tell him her *little heart* was Laurent's artistic creation. Even now she regretted the loss of her original thick and curly mat, and she would like to let it grow again. However in the interest of her career, it could not be so. Laurent must be encouraged to have his way with her curls, to keep him feeling guilty and under control.

Robert stared at this curious symbol of love between Odette's slender thighs. He remembered all too well Suzette's perfectly smooth flesh, the long bare lips he had so often kissed before sliding his stiff length between them and into her.

His middle finger gently explored Odette's moistness and he made her sigh and squirm in pleasure, though he felt little himself. It was Denis Diderot, the eighteenth century encyclopedist, who made a comic observation as true now as then: *Every day men sleep with women they do not love and do not sleep with women they do love*.

In Montmartre Jacques-Charles had removed his shabby clothes and thrown them on the floor. He was lying on top of Marie, her long thin legs spread wide to welcome him in. He could feel by the way her belly jerked under him that her pleasure had become intense. He moved faster to bring on her orgasm and she hit at him with her fists in her excitement, beating his shoulders.

He panted and shook, his belly clenched hard, his back rigid as steel, as he spurted furiously into Marie. In his mind he was moaning, *Suzette, je t'aime* and Marie was thrashing beneath him and sobbing in her delight.

Robert had Odette on her back, her knees up on either side of him as he lay upon her, belly to belly. His hands were beneath her, grasping the small taut cheeks of her bottom to steady her while he pushed in. He was warmly embedded, he held her tighter and beat his belly against hers in rhythmic smacks.

'*Robert, chéri,*' Odette murmured, her body twitching to waves of pleasure rolling through her, '*ah oui, oui*!'

Suppose anyone had asked either Robert or Jacques-Charles their opinion of Diderot's words, both would have agreed with him it was a melancholy truth, a strand of the tragedy of life. But Odette, if asked, would have shrugged her shoulders and asked why love should be a necessary part of lovemaking.

More important to her was to find the string and pull it, the string on which Robert would dance like a marionette, with his Jean Jeudi sticking out, permanently stiff. To pleasure her of course, that was understood, but, more importantly, to provide a way of controlling his affections to her advantage! If only she could find the key to Robert's sensuality as she had found the key to Laurent's!

'*Ah chéri*!' she gasped, as the sweet torment of ecstasy took her and shook her like a rag doll.

'Odette!' Robert moaned.

He lunged frantically to the sudden spurt of his delight. But in his heart he sighed, *Suzette, je t'adore, je t'adore* . . .

SUZETTE IN
BLACK VELVET

The day when Odette moved her clothes and other belongings into Robert's apartment without any formal invitation, he was filled with gloomy misgiving. Though he wished her well and would help her, he had not bargained for this invasion. Yet on the day she moved out again, he was plunged back into despondency and this shows how far removed from reason are men's emotions.

Naturally, she wished to remain on the best of terms with him and therefore saw no reason to tell him the rent of the small but pleasant apartment on the Left Bank she was moving into was to be paid for by Laurent Breville.

He was employing her as a model on a regular basis, naturally at top rates. Besides that, he was making her known to fashion editors and she was forming a useful circle of contacts.

To encourage Laurent to yet greater endeavour in her interest Odette decided to install herself closer at hand. She intended to bemuse him daily with fantasy rewarded. And to press harder on his sense of guilt. Dear Laurent was due for the pleasure of seeing her in flimsy underwear day after day, of being handled by her to guilty pleasure. And her *little heart* to pierce — day after day.

Odette was well aware plans more often went wrong than right. If the career under Laurent's patronage ran into problems, then it would be useful to have the option of moving back to Robert. This in her opinion

presented no insurmountable difficulty, he was unable
to say *No* to her, dear Robert.

All she need do was turn up twice a week at his
apartment and let him have a turn at playing with her
little heart.

She kissed him warmly, Robert that is, and he carried
her few boxes and cases out to the waiting taxi. An
affectionate little wave of her hand through the window
and she was gone, the taxi accelerating away down the
Boulevard as if competing at Le Mans — but then,
everyone knows taxi drivers are demented.

It was a little after eleven in the morning, Robert
stood on the pavement feeling foolish and wondering
what to do next. After a period of sombre reflection he
decided he might as well call on Madame Sassine to pay
his respects and wish her a good journey. She and her
husband had been in Paris for the last three days — she
had telephoned Robert soon after arriving.

He had not gone to visit her and this was the day they
left. It would do no harm to drop in for ten minutes, it
was merely a matter of courtesy. Nothing could
possibly happen, for which he felt grateful, not being in
the mood after Odette's desertion.

In the marble and mahogany magnificence of the
Hotel George Cinq he had his arrival announced by the
concierge to the suite of Monsieur and Madame
Sassine. Knowing something of Sassine's habits,
Robert was reasonably certain he would be out until the
very last moment before departure, leaving Ariane
alone to pack and prepare.

So it proved. He was requested to go up, the door
opened the instant he knocked and Ariane welcomed
him with open arms. She dragged him into the sitting-
room. He was holding a bouquet he had bought from a
flower-seller in the street, only a small bouquet and
certainly not roses. That would give her a mistaken

view of his emotions toward her. It was white and pink
carnations, just a few of each, as a polite gesture.

Ariane took the flowers with a hasty word of thanks
and she dumped them on a marble-topped side-table in
the Louis XV style. She embraced him furiously, her
mouth hot and wet and thrust her tongue deep between
his lips.

In the circumstances, Robert was encouraged to see
she wore a navy-blue costume and a pearl necklace,
evidently she was ready to leave as soon as Sassine
returned.

'Oh Robert, where have you been?' she gasped,
when the kiss came to an end at last. 'Three days I have
waited for you!'

Robert embarked on a long and complicated lie,
there had been illness in the family, worry and disorder,
he had been summoned urgently out of town.

None of this was necessary, Ariane wasn't even
listening. She dragged open his trousers to plunge her
hand inside and capture his dangling part.

'If only we had time!' he said, to sound gallant. 'But
alas, I fear Monsieur Sassine will be here soon and I
must go before he sees me.'

Saying is one thing, events are not necessarily true to
words — and the fact was that Robert's male part was
already stiff in Ariane's hand. And she? She expected
nothing less, she rubbed up and down with an
authoritative grasp.

'There is time,' she murmured, 'I must have you,
chéri.'

'But the danger,' he sighed.

Even as he spoke, he put his hand up her elegant
pleated dark skirt and felt between her thighs, above
her silk stockings.

'We must be quick,' she said with an eager gasp.

She let go of him while she took down her knickers.

They were small, elegant, of matt black satin and she flicked them on to the side-table with his flowers. Her flesh was warm and soft to his fingers, the curls thick and strong.

Robert looked at the door to the bedroom, he had forgotten he was not in the mood. But Ariane shook her head and said 'no time for that, *chéri*.' She hitched her skirt up round her ample waist and sank to her chubby knees before a Versailles-style armchair of gilded wood and tapestry upholstery.

Robert threw himself to his knees behind her, inspired by her spontaneity. He handled the plump bare cheeks she was offering, his dejection gone, swept away by the feel of her flesh.

'He will be back soon,' she said quickly. 'Do it, *chéri*!'

Robert steered his hard flesh to the dark-haired lips between her thighs and pushed. He could not penetrate far, the abundant roundness of her bottom kept him at a distance, even though he pressed close. But he managed to get enough in to excite him by the slide of flesh on slippery flesh.

His hands were under Ariane's plump belly and he held her thighs high up, his fingertips deep in her groins. He gripped hard and made her pant and the sound spurred him on. He thrust harder and faster, a flurry of movement sending nervous tremors of delight through his belly.

'Be quick, be quick,' she babbled, twitching and shaking.

A moment later he spurted violently, forcing himself as deep into her as he could go. Ariane wailed and shook, not in climax but in frustration. Almost before he was done, she scrambled up and turned to sit on the chair, her legs spread wide.

'I want to feel you deep,' she said, red-faced with

emotion. 'Put it in again, quick! Do it, *chéri*, do it!'

From this daunting trial of strength Robert was rescued for they heard a sound at the door. Panic seized him, he was sure it was Monsieur Sassine. He jumped up from Ariane, his heart pounding in fear, while he stuffed his sticky length into his trousers.

Ariane sat with her mouth open, her broad bare belly heaving in outrage. Then her meaty thighs closed and she was up on her feet, smoothing down her skirt.

Robert looked about wildly for a way of escape. The farcical nature of the situation was lost to him, only a blind desire to get away possessed his mind. Ariane put a hand on his arm and shook her head angrily.

'It's not my husband, you fool,' she said, a note of contempt in her voice. 'Do you think he knocks at his own door. Sit down and be quiet.'

It was a bellboy in hotel uniform, come to deliver a bouquet. Not a modest one like Robert's but an immense and flaunting armful of bright red roses, as big as lettuces. Ariane glanced round for her handbag to tip the bellboy, didn't see it anywhere, and asked Robert attend to the matter.

Robert was sitting in one of the gilt and tapestry armchairs, pretending nonchalance. In his trousers there was a bulge, his arousal not yet diminished. The bellboy almost grinned – he had seen the satin knickers flung casually on the side-table and he reached his own conclusion about what he had interrupted.

Robert was embarrassed. To gain the goodwill and silence this witness, he handed over ten times the expected tip. The bellboy bowed and was grinning openly as he thanked him and departed.

'My husband is so romantic,' said Ariane, her smile strained. 'He sends me flowers very often, he pretends it is gallantry.'

'A charming gesture from a husband,' said Robert.

He wondered why she seemed to be complaining.

'After he makes love to me, he always sends flowers, the next day,' Ariane informed him. 'But it is not charming, it's because he's uneasy. It is a sure sign he has also made love to another woman. I know him, the beast, and his deceitful habits! He was with a young girl yesterday before dinner when he said he was at a business meeting.'

'Then after dinner he made love to you?'

She nodded and laid the flowers on a side-table alongside the small gift of carnations Robert had brought.

'Does this happen often?' Robert enquired.

He was puzzled about the condition of the Sassine's marital relations. His impression was Ariane's husband neglected her in bed and that was why she paid gigolos – before Robert met her, that is. Not since, that would be unacceptable.

'Every night,' she said, her shrug indicating her surprise at the question. 'I am his wife, naturally I insist on it. But he deceives me, in the day he goes with French girls.'

She sighed and picked up her knickers but did not put them back on. Robert's ardour had cooled, he said he must go, he wished her *bon voyage*, and so on.

'But you can't leave me like this,' she begged 'Only another minute, *chéri*, that's all it will take.'

Robert made his apologies and headed for the door with Ariane close behind him. After the shock to his nervous system caused by the bellboy's interruption, to say nothing of the embarrassment of being grinned at knowingly, he was determined to make a getaway before Monsieur Sassine arrived to find him on top of his wife.

But Ariane's determination was equal to Robert's. She gave him no time to open the door. She trapped him up against the wall, the weight of her bountiful body holding him in place. She told him she wouldn't let him go until he gave her what she wanted, what she must have, what she would die without!

Down between their bodies, her eager hand was groping for his limp part.

Robert told her to raise her skirt and in an instant she had it up round her waist. By now it was looking creased and rumpled, she couldn't go out like that, she would have to change before Sassine came back. Robert put his hand between her thighs and she smiled and sighed.

With impatient fingers he opened the wet lips. He stroked her with a slightly desperate haste, wishing he was anywhere but in the Hotel George Cinq — held captive by a woman aroused almost to a frenzy. How slippery she was, how hot! She trembled, she panted, but nothing more!

Robert reached behind her with his free hand, reached round her big bare cheeks, warm and wobbly. Between them, down in the crease, his fingertip found the muscular knot it sought, hot to the touch. He tickled it, then pressed inside.

'Ah ah!' Ariane gasped, to feel herself stimulated fore and aft at once.

She rocked her heavy loins back and forth in a quick, nervous little motion. She moaned in pleasure. She gripped Robert in a cruelly tight clenched hand. His nature being what it was, his sticky flesh was losing its limpness, but it was nowhere near strong enough yet to penetrate her.

Robert was tempted to let her complete the process, to bring him up to full stretch so he could penetrate her once more. But his commonsense warned him, he reined in his sensuality. He was determined not to let Ariane have her way, he intended to bring on her climax fast by stroking her, and then go.

'Now!' he said. 'Now, Ariane, do it for me!'

'*Chéri, chéri,*' she panted, her face scarlet.

Her belly was jerking back and forth in a double-quick tempo. He would not have thought any woman could hold out for so long, surely she must be getting close now!

'Do it!' he said, struggling to control his own hysteria.

Her head was back, her eyes wide and staring. By brute force of willpower and ravaging fingers he compelled her to reach the crisis. Her long cry of ecstasy was so piercing he was sure it must be heard throughout the hotel.

He continued to caress her as long as her shudders and cries continued. Only when she was quiet again did he kiss her cheek briefly as he slid out from between the wall and her now-relaxing body. He felt for the door handle, his eyes on her eyes to calm her before her desires rekindled.

'*Au revoir, Ariane,*' he said quickly, and slipped out of the door.

He fled down the hotel corridor, doing up his trousers on the run, expecting at every moment to hear her calling after him to come back. The incident had unnerved him, he felt flustered and shaken. He needed a glass of cognac to restore his equilibrium. The hotel bar was highly thought-of and popular but an absurd worry gnawed at him — suppose Ariane pursued him there?

He dashed out of the hotel and up the busy Avenue George Cinq to the Hotel Prince de Galles, sure he would be safe there. And after a few glasses of excellent cognac he lapsed back into the gloom of earlier that morning, when Odette had packed her clothes and left. The truth was, he told himself, nothing had gone well for him since he and Suzette had parted.

A decision was made, this calamitous state of affairs must be brought to an end. He went home and showered, perfumed himself from head to foot with expensive cologne and put on a clean shirt and underwear. On the way to the Gare St Lazare he stopped for a cheese sandwich and a glass of red wine. It was almost three when he reached Suzette's apartment. A reconciliation was what he had come for and he meant to achieve it before he left.

If he had ever troubled himself to read what Jean-Paul Sartre wrote, he might have hesitated. The apostle of Nothingness and the Meaninglessness of Life, the Universe, etc, also hit upon a more useful truth: *Three o'clock is always too late or too early for anything you want to do.*

It was Gaby who opened the door. Suzette was not at home, she said, surprised he should think she would be. Where was she? Why, rehearsing, of course, tonight was her big night.

Disillusioned, Robert slumped on the sofa and stared at Gaby with sad and shining brown eyes, so like a spaniel, she almost laughed. But she liked Robert and somehow kept a straight face.

Does Suzette hate me? I still adore her, what do you think — is there any chance for me? What shall I do to get her back? He asked these and similar questions, sounding more miserable than any man ought to be. From her knowledge of Suzette Gaby guessed he had no chance of reinstatement but she didn't want to upset him any more and said Suzette was too busy with her singing to have time for a boyfriend.

In this she was not lying precisely, there was no point. She was only indulging in the small insincerities of life that form a barrier against too much unpleasant reality.

Gaby had not expected a visitor. She was dressed casually for her afternoon at home in blue shirt and white slacks, gold sandals and her long blonde hair was tied back in a ribbon. The shirt was silk and belonged to Lucien, it was one of many left behind when he had fled from the police.

Gaby had taken it and one or two others, knowing Lucien would have no objections, if he ever found out. She liked this one in particular because the colour matched her pale blue eyes well.

'My poor Robert,' she said, edging a little closer to him on the sofa, 'stop fretting yourself like this. When Suzette wants to see you again, when she's ready and has time, she'll let you know. Till then you must cheer up and enjoy yourself a little.'

To demonstrate her willingness to assist in this cheering-up, she took his hand and laid it upon her right breast. Robert did nothing, she unbuttoned her silk shirt for his hand to slip in, to clasp her bare breast for she had no brassiere on.

'But this is a betrayal,' said Robert in a sorrowful tone, 'I know we shall regret it, both of us, because of our closeness to Suzette.'

'Perhaps we shall enjoy it,' said Gaby, a tiny shrug making the warm breast move gently in his hand.

Men get the strangest ideas, she was thinking. Robert seemed to imagine he was still close to Suzette. Perhaps he was, in his own mind. It didn't occur to him she'd had other men since.

As for herself, she and Suzette had shared more than one boyfriend in the past. Part of their closeness was that they could do so, compare results afterwards and giggle together.

Robert was fondling her breast pensively but the look on his face was not eager, it was mournful. It amused Gaby. She smiled and this he misunderstood.

302

'The pleasure is sure to make it so much the worse,' he said.

'Do you think so, Robert *chéri*?' and she helped things along by pressing her mouth to his in a tender kiss.

Despite his forebodings, Robert was feeling her breasts in an interested way, his fingertips fluttered over the buds to coax them to firmness. Without breaking off the kiss, Gaby reached down to open his trousers and put her hand in. She touched hard flesh and caught the heady scent of cologne as she caressed him lightly.

She felt Robert's hand flat on her belly, the palm hot to her skin through her silk shirt. He slipped the hand between waist band and shirt and down the front of her slacks. They were cut to fit close, and to ease his way she quickly unzipped the side fastening. 'Robert,' she sighed as his hand insinuated itself into the top of her tiny knickers, fingertips finding her silky tuft and then the soft lips below. His finger pressed slowly inside, then deeper and touched her moist bud.

No words were needed, they rose from the sofa and went to her bedroom. This was the first time he'd seen it properly, before he'd never caught more than a glimpse through a half-open door. Her room was very unlike Suzette's. It was tidier for a start, with no stockings scattered about on the dressing-table and chairs. The colour of the decoration was lighter, the walls pale peach, the furniture blonde.

All of which was of little importance while Robert undressed Gaby. Off came shirt, slacks and tiny silk knickers, and she stood beside the bed for him to admire. She was delighted to have him in her bedroom, that was evident, her pale blue eyes shone, her smooth skin seemed to reflect the afternoon light.

He had seen her dancing at the Cabaret-Mouchard and knew how graceful she was. But naked, as now, he realised how perfectly balanced her body was. The slenderness of her waist gave to her small round breasts a greater prominence and made the curve of her hips seem more desirable.

Her back was long, as a dancer's should be, her bottom small and taut-cheeked, her thighs long and firm. The silvery-blonde tuft between them set Robert murmuring in pleasure. The former coldness that had afflicted him was gone, his blood was on fire and he crushed her in his arms, sliding his hands up and down the length of her back to feel the satin smoothness of her skin.

She smiled at him, her unpainted mouth soft and full, waiting to be kissed. Robert complied, his hands clenched on the bare cheeks of her bottom. The temptation was overpowering to fling her down on the bed on her back and ravage her in an instant. A gleam of sanity held him back. Gaby was too beautiful to be so dismissively treated.

No, his lovemaking was going to be tender and ardent, both at the same time. He would touch her and kiss each delicious part of her a hundred times. He would hear her sobbing with passion before he slid his belly on to hers and brought her to a climax to be remembered!

Poor Robert was confused again, of course. He was not in love with Gaby, nor she with him. She had invited him to her bedroom for a less exalted reason. She liked him and wanted to see how he used to set Suzette squealing in delight when he stayed with her, squeals which Gaby had heard very clearly through the wall between their bedrooms.

When he undressed she was favourably impressed. He was well-made and muscular, broad-shouldered and lean in the flank. His daily routine of exercise had not changed throughout the summer while Odette was

staying with him − even if she had laughed at first to
see him sweating at his chest-expander and performing
his knee-bends. Most important to Gaby though, the
stiff part that stood up strongly from the nest of curls
between his thighs − was at least fifteen centimetres,
she estimated, and pleasantly thick.

He lay beside her, kissing her and touching her, his
tongue on her lips, on her breasts, between her legs.
Once again Gaby blessed the day she first trimmed her
little tuft and bleached it silvery-blonde, to match her
hair.

Men went crazy over it, she thought with
satisfaction, they wanted to touch it and kiss it. And
Robert was no exception, he became fascinated by it.
He stroked it and put his lips to it, he pushed his tongue
into her. He brought her to a climax twice without
letting her pause for breath.

When he started the third time, she twined her
fingers in his hair and pulled his head up, away from
her parted thighs. She stared down the length of her
beautiful body, her eager gaze on his face, willing him
to release her now from this excruciating pleasure.

'Do it properly,' she gasped. 'I can't wait any longer,
do it to me, Robert!'

He grinned fiercely and was on top of her in a
bound. She was astonished by the strength with which
he took her, the profound voluptuousness of his
caressing was now transformed into raging desire. His
knee forced her thighs brutally apart and she groaned
in delight to feel his hands grip her flesh at the hips.

As if she weighed nothing, he lifted her loins up,
spread her open with careless thumbs, and forced his
stiff part into her.

It was inside her! She gasped at the push that slid it
into her belly. Robert lay on her and stabbed between
her thighs in a wild, violent rhythm that brought her to

another climax in moments. He had become so aroused while he was caressing her he forgot he was making love to the wrong woman.

The legs opened for him were Gaby's, not Suzette's, the head rolling from side to side on the pillow was silvery-blonde, not raven-black. But the comedy of his situation passed Robert by.

'*Formidable*!' said Gaby, when she was rational once more and able to speak. 'Do you always make love like that, Robert?'

'You inspire me,' he said and for a moment he meant it.

Later that afternoon, after they had made love again and were content, he asked Gaby to have dinner with him, meaning to take her home with him for the night. She kissed his cheek and slid off the bed, saying it was impossible, she had arrangements and could not change them, and so on.

Only then did he remember about Suzette's big night. He pondered if he should offer to escort Gaby to it.

Eventually he decided it would be insensitive to let Suzette see him with Gaby, after an afternoon in bed with her. For one thing, he was near as maybe in love with Suzette, therefore he owed her respect. As for Gaby, he admired and adored her now he had made love to her, there was something disrespectful to her also in taking her to hear Suzette.

It was fortunate Robert reached this conclusion, from the very highest of motives, and did not make the suggestion. His self-esteem would have been devastated to hear she had an escort already. A tender *au revoir*, a promise to meet the next day, and she eased Robert skilfully out through the door.

From the squalor of Bobo's cellar in Montmartre to the chic of a private club on the plushy Avenue

Montaigne — what a tremendous journey for a singer
to make! But there Suzette was that night, to make her
real debut. What had gone before she saw as merely a
rehearsal for this night.

No riffraff could get in here, the club was for
members only. And the members were celebrities, it
went without saying. These were the beautiful people.
There were international playboys of incredible charm
and means but little purpose, ruggedly handsome male
film-stars, half-naked starlets hot from Cannes and
important politicians of the Right and the Left
snatching a brief hour's respite from guiding the
nation.

There were enormously influential couturiers known
to detest women, African potentates come to Paris to
bribe Ministers, the aristocracy of unheard-of distant
countries, most of which had been Republics since 1918
and French business tycoons of interesting if doubtful
reputation. There were smooth and successful gangsters
still at liberty and Arab sheikhs in France to buy war
planes and bombs for their country.

They were famous, the club members. Or if not
exactly famous, at least they had pots of money. The
men, that is to say.

As for their companions, they were strikingly
beautiful, as was to be expected, and perfectly groomed,
expensively dressed and exceptionally desirable.

For the most part they looked to be about nineteen
years old, these companions, while the men were over
forty — Except those who were older. Only in
America is it possible for adolescents to become
millionaires by amusing other adolescents. In France
it takes ten or twenty years to become truly rich —
not to mention a certain degree of intelligence and a
large measure of cunning.

Suzette stood under a muted spotlight, leaning

casually on a white baby-grand piano. Her raven-black hair was glossy and her fringe elegant, her close-fitting black velvet frock left her shoulders bare and displayed her body to perfection.

She sang her song *'Place Vendôme'*, the words written by Michel Radiguet, adoring young student, the music composed by Jacques-Charles Delise, adoring bar-pianist.

Neither was present at this momentous event, however, as the club did not admit poor persons of no importance. Suzette had that afternoon rehearsed her songs with the three-piece band, distributing to them scores hand-written by Jacques-Charles himself.

At the rehearsal the three players were in shirtsleeves, now they wore dinner jackets and their hair was sleeked down smooth with brilliantine. The music was easy to play, and pleasing. It may have been entirely Jacques-Charles own work or it may have derived from older and more famous composers – who could say what was what inside his Pernod-scrambled head?

All three members of the band, the instant they saw Suzette, were captivated. They put their heart and soul into making sure her first appearance at the club was a resounding success.

In this atmosphere of luxury Suzette blossomed like an exotic flower in the summer sun. She sang as Jacques-Charles taught her, she sang to individuals in the audience, choosing them not quite at random. She addressed the most important of them, naturally, and the ones who looked most susceptible: the oldest with the youngest girlfriend, the one who everyone said would be a Minister after Pierre Mendes-France reshuffled his government and the film star with the craggy chin who was divorcing his third wife.

They responded very satisfactorily, this audience. They liked Suzette and they liked her song. Each one imagined himself the tall man clasping the diamond and ruby bracelet on her wrist.

And being rewarded for it in bed, in ways individual to each, some of them curious in the extreme.

Gaby was there to hear Suzette sing as her stockbroking friend Monsieur Delacroix was a member of any club he chose. His table was up near the tiny dance-floor, a bottle of champagne and two glasses on it. Gaby looked every bit as desirable as any of the pampered ladies present, her blonde hair cascading to her bare shoulders, her lithe body half-in, half-out of an elegant evening frock of white satin that her stockbroker had bought her.

He, Jean-François Delacroix, listened to Suzette singing with a pleasant smile on his distinguished face, his hand under the table on Gaby's thigh. Naturally, he couldn't know her feelings about him were slightly complicated and by no means as adoring as he believed. She loved the expensive presents he gave her, she loved to be taken to restaurants where the food and wine were delicious and to clubs where celebrities danced the night away.

But, there was no point in denying it, Jean-François was not Lucien. The little criminal fetishist and his games amused Gaby at the time, strange as they were. She missed them now. Nothing at all Jean-François dreamed of doing gave her the pleasure of standing with feet apart while Lucien grovelled on the carpet.

She missed the little pervert. She missed Lucien kissing her feet in high-heeled shoes. And licking his way up her legs, his flushed face between her open thighs, his breath fiercely hot through her black lace knickers. And the comic look on his face as she pressed her shoe against his bulge and made him spurt into the women's silk underwear he was wearing under his trousers.

And Robert? The afternoon had been marvellous, but he was not Lucien either. It was thrilling to be taken so fiercely, almost like being a wolf's prey. But if Robert continued like that, it was sure to become boring. Gaby thought she would allow him once or twice more, just to see if he continued as he started, almost as a rapist. Perhaps it was guilt on his part that drove him so frantically, because she was Suzette's friend. If so, it would wear off and something else in bed might be hoped for.

Perhaps he could be taught some of Lucien's games? It seemed worth a try, though of doubtful outcome. Robert was almost thirty – any inclination he had in that direction would surely by now have manifested itself in bedroom games. And if he had no such talent, then it would be 'goodbye, Robert'.

When the applause for '*Place Vendôme*' rippled into silence at last, Suzette sang another of her songs. This was called '*Palais Garnier*' and it was the one about stepping out of a shiny black limousine at the opera, dressed in a Dior ballgown and a kilo of glittering diamonds.

Her songs evoked scenes familiar to her audience, they adored being accorded the respect and recognition they knew themselves to be entitled to. After all, this was not the poverty-stricken Belleville mob, sentimental over women who loved brutal drunks who beat them senseless and stole their money.

No, no, the people Suzette sang for were men who truly bought bracelets of diamonds and rubies, sable furcoats and similar expensive toys for girlfriends. They were men of significance who arrived at important events in limousines with uniformed chauffeurs, or in vast open-topped white sports cars if they were trying to be thought young.

Their natural habitat was the sixteenth arrondissement, these men, along the Avenue Foch and the Boulevard Lannes, in elegant and luxurious apartments of staggering value with floors of Italian marble, silk upholstery and the gold bath-taps. And those who didn't live in such splendour hoped to, one day. They were much in sympathy with what Suzette was singing about.

The men applauded her singing because she was beautiful and they wanted to take her to bed. The women applauded her because they believed her songs were about themselves and their lives. They were flattered, each thought to herself: *Yes, that's me in the limousine wearing the Dior gown and the diamond necklace, I look so sexy the men are drooling as they kiss my hand.*

And when Suzette sang another song, they pictured themselves walking a fluffy little white dog on the pavement of the Avenue Foch, pausing on the grass under a tree for a moment. Waiting for them in a luxurious apartment, on satin bedsheets, was a handsome young lover, rich, elegant, his body golden from the sun, ready to plunge them into ecstasy beyond words.

Suzette knew she was succeeding, she could tell she held her audience in the palm of her hand. The club was going to ask her to sing regularly, she was certain of it, and that was only the beginning. All Paris would hear about her.

She would be a big-name star at the Lido, before long, or the Casino de Paris. And at the Folies Bergère, she thought to herself with an inward grin.

She'd be wearing a ballgown on stage, not five kilos of ostrich plumes on her head and a five metre train dragging behind her bare bottom! To make her point, she'd insist on a row of show-girls posing behind her while she sang, their *nichons* hanging out for the customers to leer at. Hers would be covered — she'd be the star!

In the tiny club dressing-room, at the last moment before she came out to sing, she had hoisted up her black velvet frock to take off her knickers. She was naked above her silk stockings.

This she did for luck, she believed a turning point in her life had come when an unknown young man in a roll-top sweater had taken her knickers down in a doorway in Montmartre. She had gone back into Bobo's squalid cellar to sing with new zest after that.

Having no knickers brought her good luck, she was certain of it. If those listening to her songs in the Avenue Montaigne club did but know it, she was even more naked than most women with no underwear — their tarty little girlfriends, for example.

Suzette's natural little black fur coat was diligently shaven off. The soft flesh between her thighs was sleek and bare — and very kissable.

A selection of Erotica from Headline